lost stars

lost stars

LISA SELIN DAVIS

HOUGHTON MIFFLIN HARCOURT
Boston New York

www.hmhco.com

The text was set in Adobe Garamond Pro.

Library of Congress Cataloging-in-Publication Data
Names: Davis, Lisa Selin, author.
Title: Lost stars / Lisa Selin Davis.
Description: Boston ; New York : Houghton Mifflin Harcourt, [2017] | Summary:
"A teenage girl grapples with her sister's death and her own place in the
universe over the course of one fateful summer in upstate New York. With
an epic '80s soundtrack blasting in the background, Lost Stars is a novel
that encapsulates teenage-life and all its awkward longing, heady passion,
and introspective questioning"— Provided by publisher.
Identifiers: LCCN 2015045412 | ISBN 9780544785069 (hardback)
Subjects: | CYAC: Grief—Fiction. | Love—Fiction. | Popular music—Fiction.
| BISAC: JUVENILE FICTION / Love & Romance. | JUVENILE FICTION /
Social Issues / Emotions & Feelings. | JUVENILE FICTION / Family / General
(see also headings under Social Issues). | JUVENILE FICTION / Performing Arts /
Music. | JUVENILE FICTION / Social Issues / Drugs, Alcohol, Substance Abuse.
Classification: LCC PZ7.1.D38 Lo 2017 | DDC [Fic]—dc23 LC record available at
https://lccn.loc.gov/2015045412

Manufactured in the United States of America
DOC 10 9 8 7 6 5 4 3 2 1
4500615556

To Amy, Julie, Katie, Kristin, and Rachel
My protective shield

Prologue

THAT NIGHT, I WALKED UP THE WOBBLY footbridge-in-progress, rolling my bike next to me until I stood in front of the abandoned observatory, rain leaking from the yellow rain slicker into my slightly-too-small hiking boots. What a shame that this was my night to be solo beneath the stars: I could barely see them.

The observatory door was locked, but years ago Ginny had shown me how to prop open the window, stained glass framed with now-rotting wood. I squeezed inside, scraping my leg on the stone walls as I scaled them. My backpack landed with a thud on the hard stone floor.

It was ghostly, damp and echoey, its round shape, its dark stones looming over the flat green fields of the park. Two benches stood against the walls, each clad in dark red velvet, worn now and threadbare in spots, but good enough for a bed. I took off the wet boots, rolled the rain slicker into a makeshift pillow, and lay down. I was so weirdly calm. Not scared to be alone in the park at night. Not scared to be homeless-ish. Not scared to be in the very spot where, two years earlier, I had had my last glimpse of Ginny.

I looked up to the domed skylight, remembering the night it had opened when I was eight, Orion's belt gleaming and all that hope blinking in the stars. I wanted to go home, but I knew I couldn't. I couldn't face all those things that had swallowed my hope.

I took out my notebook and traced my calculations, the careful pencil drawings, with my finger. That was one relief: it wouldn't be tonight. I wouldn't miss the comet, not yet. Maybe tomorrow, the beginning of the end of the summer, the beginning of the end, would be the night it arrived. Maybe, like the Paiute Indians used to think, the comet signified the collapse of this world and the start of the next.

No, I wasn't scared to be there. But once the tears came, there was no stopping them.

Chapter 1

"THAT'S THE LAST TIME," MY FATHER YELLED, pounding the arm of his flowered dusty-rose armchair. "I mean it—I'm not gonna take this crap anymore. This is no way to start the summer."

"What are you gonna do about it?" I yelled back, stomping up the stairs and slamming my door. The room buzzed with the electricity of our screams, and my hands shook as I placed the record on the turntable: the Replacements singing "Unsatisfied." I let the sweet, sad sound of the guitar calm me down. The joint helped too.

"Carrie, put that out." His voice rode the line between pleading and pissed. "I can smell it from down here."

I flung open the door. "I stole it from *you*," I yelled down the stairs. "You're such a hypocrite."

"Caraway—"

"Don't call me that! It's Carrie!" I knew I was screaming so loud that the neighbors in the giant house next door could probably hear me, but that only made me scream louder, so loud my voice began to crack. "Why did you guys have to name me after a loaf of rye bread?" I stomped down the stairs and threw one of my jelly shoes at him, and he ducked. Then he stopped. He just stood there, stunned and irate, his whole face descended into blankness, as if he had sudden-onset Alzheimer's and didn't know anymore who he was or who I was or how we had gotten there. Which was probably the case.

I was still heaving with all that anger, breathing hard. It welled up in me sometimes, a fiery asteroid of it. It just took over in my bones. But when he froze, I did too. We stared at each other for a minute, and then it was as if he crumbled, his whole six-foot frame collapsing into that armchair, the one that had become his makeshift home since our family fell apart. I could hardly hear him, he was whispering so low. So I had to step closer. And then closer.

"We didn't name you after rye bread," he was saying. "It's a spice."

He looked up at me, and I thought for a second he was going to reach up and hug me, and a terrible pool of feeling, not one particular feeling but just a messy stew of everything, started flooding me, and I felt like I had to throw something or break something or cut something or smoke something, and I let out an enormous grunt, like a white dwarf star, collapsed and out of gas.

He put his head into his hands and started whispering again. He was saying, "I just don't know what to do with you. I don't know how to help you. It's getting worse, and I don't know what to do."

* * *

What he did was ground me. I had arrived home reeking of cigarettes and pot, nearly falling into the house at six p.m. when I was supposed to be at work ringing up fingerless gloves and neon half shirts at Dot's Duds. I'd never shown up, and most likely Dot had called him. Most likely I'd been fired. Again. This was, as he'd said, no way to start the summer.

So he laid down the law: no going out with friends. No walking downtown to buy records. No going to Soo's, where I was supposed to be by nine o'clock. Worst of all: no going up to the roof to monitor the progress of the Vira comet, otherwise known as 11P/Alexandrov, which any day now would blast through the sky, this ball of ice and dust that grew a tail of gas when it neared the sun, as it would this summer for the first time since 1890. It only came around every ninety-seven years.

I was eleven when my parents first took me and my sisters up to the observatory to see Mars at opposition—when the planet is closest to Earth and all lit up by the sun, a beautiful, almost orchestral eruption of light. Even then, before the accident, something about the laws of the universe made so much more sense to me than shop class and school dances and the elusive species known as boys. The story of how Earth hangs there in the sky, tied to the sun but always turning away, day after day, as if trying to escape: that was a story I understood. Unlike my family, which even then seemed to have some green patina of dysfunction—translucent, but always there—that pure, rule-bound vision I saw through my telescope made all the sense in the world.

The telescope, unfortunately, had disappeared about three months ago, just before my mom took off and things went from worse to worst. Punishment for another one of the terrible things I'd done, I assumed, but I still had the roof. Until now. "You have to at least let me up there," I begged my father. "It's a once-in-a-lifetime thing. Maybe twice if I live to be a hundred and thirteen. Or three times if I hit two ten."

I thought I saw a smile creeping to the corners of his lips — the roof had been our spot, once upon a time, the telescope our shared obsession. But he just said, "Add it to the list of life's disappointments."

I stomped back upstairs and blasted X's "Real Child of Hell," collapsing on my bed, pulling the star sheets that my mom had bought me years ago up over my head. My mom wouldn't have punished me. My mom would have defended me, saying, *Paul, sweetie, lay off—she's just a teenager. Let's let her be. Let's choose to trust her.* But maybe she'd learned not to say that kind of thing anymore.

Since there was no talking on the phone, I couldn't even tell Soo of this next level of injustice (she was the only one to whom I revealed my secret nerd-dom) or that I couldn't show up at her house that night. Impossible to sneak it, either, because we were a one-phone household, just our touchtone mounted to the wall in the kitchen, the beige plastic smudged from how often Rosie and I talked on it, and fought over it. My dad had had to replace it twice in the last year, after I ripped it from the wall in one of what he called my "fits."

Now Rosie was standing outside my locked door, yelling, "Turn it down, please—I'm trying to study!" Rosie was the only person I knew who went to summer school voluntarily.

"You should stop studying and have some fun," I called, kind of meaning it. Every once in a while I liked Rosie. Now was not one of those times. "School's out, for crying out loud."

"You should stop having so much fun and start studying," she yelled back.

I put the Pixies EP on the turntable and used all of my concentration to place the needle on the record and pretend I couldn't hear her through the door.

"I wish you would just leave, Carrie!" Her footsteps receded down the hallway.

Why hadn't I thought of that?

"Great idea!" I called out. If my father caught me, I'd just tell him Rosie had told me to go. At some point in our family history, Rosie would have to do *something* wrong. My sneaking suspicion was that Rosie was normal because they had given her a normal name. It was still a spice—Rosemary—but it passed as regular. Ginny, too. Most people hadn't known that her real name was Ginger until they saw it on her gravestone, and even then, it wasn't that strange. But call your kid Caraway and bad shit is bound to happen.

My window screen clicked as I slid it open and did a perfunctory check for parental patrol. My father wasn't outside, and there was just enough cover from the pine trees next door to form a kind of protective canopy.

We lived on a narrow street of humble, and sometimes crumbling, little Victorian houses that hid behind a wide boulevard called Grand Street. Our town had once been a resort for fancy New Yorkers, but now it was mostly run-down except for the pockets of wealth, one of which happened to be right next to us. Grand was full of mansions, thus constantly reminding us of our station in life back here. Our little house—four tiny bedrooms, low ceilings, asbestos siding—was in the shadow of Mrs. Richmond's place, a big white house with huge columns, separated from us by a high picket fence. I almost never saw Mrs. Richmond herself—she reportedly had a multitude of houses —but that was a good thing; it meant she never caught me when I snuck out.

I slithered out the window and onto the roof of the porch, then scaled down the porch column and onto the bricked-over dirt we called a yard. Pretty amazing for someone whose only exercise was adjusting telescope lenses (before they were taken away) and playing guitar.

In the clear, I took out my Camel Lights and puffed all the way to Soo's. It was June and the perfect temperature, that velvety kind of early evening air, that fading golden light. It all made a weird hard ball in the center of my chest and I wished I had my guitar. Or another joint. Or that it was already late at night and I was heading to a bus stop somewhere on the outskirts of town with my guitar slung over my shoulder and it would turn out that my life was actually a movie, some small-town *Breakfast Club* kind of deal where there were happy endings all around. And boyfriends. My kingdom—or really, my crappy house—for a boyfriend.

When I got to Soo's, the partying was in full swing. Soo's dad owned a bar downtown—a skeevy but apparently very lucrative biker bar in which we were never allowed to set foot—and was never home at night. Her mom, well, she was usually too intoxicated herself to even come down to the basement to check on us. "One of the world's few female Korean-American drunks," Soo often noted.

Soo had a finished basement that she'd done up all 1970s: fake wood paneling, red pleather couch, a killer sound system, a mirror ball—the kind of stuff rich kids had, but which I, through the miracle of Soo's generosity and our family tragedy, had access to. It was like having our own discotheque, even though nobody liked disco anymore. Or, well, almost nobody. Secretly I still loved "I Will Survive," my favorite song when I was six.

The boys were all there, including Tommy Patarami and Tiger Alvarez and Justin Banks, and they'd set up a couple of amps and mikes and a drum kit in the back of the room. The guys were standing in front of Soo's dad's enormous wall of records, picking out what to play. "The Ghost in You" by the Psychedelic Furs was on. I did my goofy dance, sort of the-twist-meets-mosh

—I was not that into the Psychedelic Furs—and Tommy yelled, "What's up, Rye Bread?" and I laughed, even though I hated when he called me that. "Not much, Pastrami," I said, and someone else said, "She got you, Patarami." There was nothing better than making people laugh. Well, almost nothing better. I was pretty sure a couple of things were better.

"Carrie!" Soo and Greta left the scrum of half-intoxicated boys to greet me, handing me a beer and huddling around me like the world's prettiest football players. I could smell the sticky sweet scent of Soo's mousse, and I was semi-suffocating inside their group hug and pushing them away, but only lightly. Some part of me just wanted to stay in there forever. "Our little Carrie is here!"

"Yay," I said, my normal deadpan. "Let the rejoicing begin."

I was sixteen, going into eleventh grade, and they had all just graduated, as Ginny would have too. These used to be her friends, and then, in her absence, they were mine; I had been subsumed by her world. The only thing I missed about my old life was astronomy club. At this point, I no longer had any extra-curricular activities other than songwriting and amateur drug taking. And who would do that with me when they were gone at the end of summer, off to their new lives at college? It would be like losing my sister all over again.

"They're not going to play, are they?" I asked Soo, nodding at Justin, who was standing in front of his Flying V guitar, as we sank into the red pleather couch. I'd always thought that was a dumb-looking guitar. "They suck, you know. And they have the worst band name in history."

"Piece of Toast isn't that bad."

"It's always a bad idea to name your band while tripping," I said.

"Well, they might play," Soo said. "Depends on if my mom passes out or not. She's been complaining about the noise. Apparently alcohol does not dull your hearing."

The boys didn't bother coming over. Tommy buried his face in a pile of records. I hadn't seen him since he'd shoved his fingers up me in an attempt at something vaguely sexual, which had happened on the football field when we got wasted the weekend before. It seemed he had decided to pretty much ignore me, which was fine, so I traced the rim of my beer can with my fingertip and tried to look bored so I wouldn't look unmoored, as if I were in danger of drifting off the couch and out of orbit, holding on to the upholstery buttons for dear life. It wasn't like I liked Tommy anyway. We were just the only two perpetually single people in the group.

Soo tossed her hair back, her perfect pearl earrings sparkling. "So what's with the fashionable lateness?" She took an expert sip of her beer. Mine was sweating on the table.

"I was waiting outside for the butler to present me," I said. "Wait—this isn't my coming-out party? The debutante's ball? Huh."

Occasionally Soo was immune to my humor. "I wasn't even

sure if you were going to show." She wasn't looking at me, a sign that she was hurt that I was so late, that I hadn't even called.

"I wasn't allowed to leave my room!" I said, and I was already so raw and tired that the flood started coming, my hands in parted prayer position, reaching into the air. Heading toward a fit. "Not all of us have parents who don't have any rules!"

"Okay, Car—it's okay." She grabbed my hands from the air and brought them back down, spreading my fingers out on the sticky fabric. She always knew how to calm the wave. "What happened?"

I pressed my hands against the pleather until my heartbeat slowed. I gulped my beer. "Eh, just the usual." The beer was warm, but I drank it anyway because Greta and Soo and the rest of them were drinking it, and they were my real family, the collective Daddy Warbucks to my orphan Annie.

"You know, a little parental freak-out and some Spider-Man-style escape."

I wanted to tell Soo about the fight with my dad, but sometimes it seemed like the past couple of years weren't real. That wasn't me screaming and throwing things. That wasn't me in the middle of the sidewalk, face-down, kicking my legs, being dragged off in the ambulance. That was someone who lived inside me. My devilish alter ego. Mr. Hyde. It wasn't me. So I just told her, "I used my Spidey sense."

"You're such a dork," she said, and she was smiling, but I wasn't sure she said it to be funny, because when they had rescued me from the funeral and what would have been a lifetime of depressing days after it, my dorkdom — though softened by my guitar playing and encyclopedic memorization of Public Enemy lyrics — was still firmly intact.

The truth was, I had never been cool, but Ginny had been the quintessential popular girl. Not the cheerleader kind. The beautiful-girl-with-the-short-dyed-black-hair-and-bright-green-eyes-and-cat's-eye-glasses kind, the introduce-your-kid-sister-to-Elvis-Costello-and-Velvet-Underground kind, the skip-school-but-still-get-good-grades kind, the run-with-the-fast-crowd kind. I had been scrambling to keep up with her even before she was gone.

"I'm just glad you're here." Soo lifted up her beer. Oh. Maybe I was wrong. Maybe I had kept up. "Cheers."

Before I had even clinked her can, Justin sidled up to us. The perfect eighteen-year-old human being, Justin was a jock and an art room druggie all at once, Johnny Depp-meets-Scott Baio looks with shaggy, chestnut-colored hair and green eyes. He crouched down next to Soo and picked up her hand and stroked it. I pretended to vomit. Justin got that look, like he didn't know if he should laugh.

"Oh, no — don't take it personally. I've just had too much to drink." I raised my nearly full first beer. He still didn't laugh. "I'm just messing with you," I said, and lightly punched his arm.

"Ow," he said. At least I'd thought it was lightly. "I'm getting another beer."

Soo went with him, and Greta sat with me. In her fuchsia Cyndi Lauper dress, strapless with a fluffy crepe skirt on the bottom, her Converse high-tops and her long, feathered, perfectly curly strawberry blond hair—achieved naturally, no perm necessary—she looked like a movie star: Kim Basinger, but somehow even prettier. Greta. She was good at tennis and still a hippie chick and a cheerleader anyway. She was so good at holding her liquor. So statuesque. How could one person be so many good things? No wonder she always had a boyfriend. Everything about her was pretty. I was wearing one of my mom's old T-shirts with the sleeves cut off and the bottom sliced into fringes, and cutoff Lee jeans.

"Drink up, kid," she told me with that perfect smile. I'd do anything she said. So I drank, even though I much preferred my mom's iced tea, the kind she made from the mint she grew every summer in pots on our porch. Beer no longer tasted like toe fungus (or what I thought toe fungus would taste like), but I would never actually like it. "So what's up?"

"Let's see," I said. "I'm currently locked in my room, as you can see."

"Ah, the father," she said.

"Yeah, it sucks when they pretend that they actually care about you so they can ground you."

"That's what they say. Luckily my dad doesn't even pretend."

"God, you *are* lucky," I said, smiling at her joke. I wondered if she knew how lucky she was. I'd never met her dad, but I figured he must be wealthy and handsome and worldly and kind if he'd sired her.

Justin and Soo stood in the corner now, holding hands,

cocooned in a private world. "Mmm, young love," Greta said, as if they were so naïve, as if she knew something they didn't. What did she know?

Greta had not gone a day without a boyfriend since she was twelve—break up one day, find a new one the next. But Soo hadn't dated much. She'd been more like me: on the sidelines, occasionally pulled into the action but never claimed. And now she was In Love.

What did she know? What did they all know?

In the evening after Ginny's funeral, Greta had retrieved me from the reception and taken me with her and Soo and their friends, driving in some older boy's car with the windows rolled down and the soft spring air on my face, stunned and numb and comfortable in the womblike enclosure of Ginny's friends, with Janis Joplin's "Bye, Bye Baby" blaring through the speaker: *You just got lost somewhere out in the world,* she sang, *and you left me here to face it all alone.*

I'd never heard Janis Joplin before. Her voice was sort of like sandpaper and sort of like an organ played by the goddess Athena.

Ginny's friends smoked and drank—things I had not done until that night—and we ended up at a roller-skating rink called Diamonds, because roller skating had been Ginny's favorite activity, and there was lots of toasting her, drinking from Ginny's own flask—how did they get that?—the flask I was sure my parents never knew she had. The first time I drank that cheap bourbon, I felt my gray matter turning black, felt the stars dim, a feeling I both craved and hated.

And then, suddenly, all fogged in my brain, I was laced up and floating in circles around the place with Greta and her then (and now again) boyfriend, Tiger. I was wearing something I'd taken from Ginny's closet, before my mother cleaned out her room: a pink and gray striped shirt with thin bands of silver between the stripes. Disco-ish, but I hadn't yet learned that we'd declared war on disco.

Greta had gone off to the parking lot with Justin and Tommy to drink some bourbon from the flask, and Tiger and I were still roller skating around the rink by ourselves, and then I felt his hand grab mine, his fingers curl around mine, a feeling it seemed I had waited my whole life to feel. We rolled and glided together across that shiny floor, strobe lights blinking, "Eye of the Tiger" blaring through the speakers, which somehow made it feel like fate, even though that was one of the least romantic songs ever. Dark circles of sweat stained the armpits of my shirt, so I tried to keep my arms plastered to my sides, but that was hard to do and hold Tiger's hand at the same time, and then my palm was so sweaty that my hand slipped out of his and he drifted away and I didn't know how to get him back.

Later, in the bathroom, when I showed Greta the sweat stains, she said, "Don't worry, honey," and took off her white button-down shirt and helped me into it, and then she said, "Hold on a sec," and took out her Love's Baby Soft and sprayed it on my neck and then put some strawberry-scented gloss on my lips, which I immediately got on my front teeth because I had never worn my retainer and my overbite had come right back after my parents spent all that money on braces, as they had reminded me constantly before something far worse happened. "There," she said. And she left the bathroom, looking oh-so-chic in her thin white tank top.

I stood there and looked at myself in the mirror for a few minutes, trying to like what I saw. But it just looked like me with a little lip gloss and Greta's shirt. I wasn't particularly fond of my teeth, the way one of them jutted out, or my hands with their stubby fingers. My head was too small and my brown eyes were too close together and my brown hair was frizzy instead of perfectly curly like Greta's and the space between my nose and my upper lip was too big and I was so, so, so, so, so short and everything about me was off. Worst of all, I was alive.

As I came out, there was Tiger, and he pressed me up against those icy concrete walls and kissed me and it was wrong and bad and it was amazing and I didn't understand. Why had he turned his attention toward me? Did he feel sorry for me because my sister had died? Did Greta know? Tiger was so cute: half Puerto Rican, half Irish, dark skin, dark eyes, a gold chain around his neck, a football jersey, totally out of my league. Or maybe totally out of my league until Ginny had let me step into hers. Ginny, with that little space between her two front teeth, always visible because of her huge smile, and that too-loud laugh, and her perpetually perfect wave of blue eye shadow and her fingerless lace

Madonna gloves—she had walked off, or driven off, leaving a path for me. Was I supposed to be happy about the life she'd left me in her wake?

And then the kiss stopped and Tiger walked back out to the rink. And the evening ended. And we all piled in the back of the car, me and Greta and Tiger, and the two of them made out, but he reached back and held my hand for a minute, gave it a squeeze. A consolation prize. Greta got love and sex. I got a hand squeeze. Ginny would never have anything again.

When I got out of the car, Greta handed me the flask.

Now I picked out records to play: Sam Cooke, Hüsker Dü, R.E.M., the Ramones, and, what the heck, Nina Simone's cover of the Bee Gees: *You don't know what it's like,* she sang, to love somebody like I love you. That feeling of one tune connecting to the other, making a story out of a series of songs, of being hit right in the chest when the music gets it right—it was the best.

"Good mix," Tommy said, nodding his head, hand stroking his stubbly chin like he was appreciating Van Gogh's *The Starry Night* (as if Tommy would know what that was). Apparently Tommy was talking to me again. "Except that Hüsker Dü shit is totally screwed up." The song was "Don't Want to Know If You Are Lonely."

"I'm known all over town for my screwed-up-ness," I said. Which, sadly, was true. I could feel Tommy looking at me, now that he was drunk and swaying. "And, Tommy, Hüsker Dü is rad."

We all drank and drank and drank and then we smoked and smoked and smoked. For a long time, I put my head on the back of the couch and looked at the drop ceiling, all those little pockmarks like some kind of constellation that I couldn't quite figure out, a map I couldn't read. Every time I looked down from the ceiling, people were making out—Soo and Justin, Tiger and Greta. Tommy studied the record covers in faux oblivion. Tommy. So not my type. Short hair, thick wrestler's body, not so smart, too into Rush. I liked them tall and skinny and long-haired and into Big Star. At least in theory I did.

Somebody passed me a joint, and I took a long hit and laid my head back again and listened to the song that was playing now, the Velvet Underground with Nico's smoky voice singing "I'll Be Your Mirror": *Reflect what you are, in case you don't know.* The song ripped open a hole in my chest, and for a minute it was hard to breathe.

When I looked up, my vision blurring, Justin had his hand on Soo's face like they did it in old movies and they both had their eyes open and they kept stopping to look at each other and squeeze hands.

"Get a room, why don't you?" I called, my words all slurry and echoing in my own ears. Soo looked over at me, her eyes fierce. And then she left. She just left me there, *Bye-bye, baby, bye-bye.* She probably went upstairs to her bedroom, and I knew what she was doing there, something I'd never done even though I'd thought about it once last year when that nineteen-year-old boy Anton Oboieski was on top of me and I knew everyone else was doing the same thing in the rooms all around me but then he opened his eyes for a second and narrowed them at me, as if realizing only then that I wasn't Ginny. When he closed his eyes again, I pressed against his chest and said, very softly, "Sorry," and grabbed my plaid shirt and leggings and crept out of the room, waiting with a warm, undrunk beer until the rest of them were finished. Since then, I'd let those boys do so many things to me but that one thing—I was just saving that one thing. I was holding on to it in the hope that someday I'd want somebody and he'd want me, too. The same amount.

Now Tommy grabbed me and shoved his hand down my shirt, and I was enveloped by the whole thing, the music and the drugs and the meaningless touches. I just left my body and let it happen, let him grope and paw and lick and kiss. I let myself get erased.

It was almost five in the morning by the time I got home. Justin had come back to retrieve me, driving Soo's Le Car, and now the two of them were dropping me off as I groaned, prostrate on the back seat.

I forced myself to sit up when we got to my block. "I gotta walk from here," I said, even though I had vertigo. I pushed the door open and hung my head between my knees.

"You drink too much," Justin said. I waited for Soo to object but she didn't. I liked the protective shield my friends provided more than I liked alcohol, but Justin didn't know that. And besides, it was they who had introduced me to all the illegal substances I now regularly consumed. Everything was their idea.

"Yeah, I do everything too much," I said. "This has been pointed out to me before." The therapist had said to me, *I believe you have some kind of impulse disorder and essentially feel all of your emotions too strongly to regulate them.*

To which I had replied, *Have you ever heard of the term fuck off?*

I scooted out of the car and hobbled down the street, past Mrs. Moran's and the Chins' and Missy Tester's house. One pinpoint of light shot across the sky, the beginning of the meteor showers, the preview to Vira, and then it was really quiet in that perfect small-town way, crickets and rustling leaves, and I so did not want to be alone.

I crept up alongside the fence that separated our yard from the big house's grounds, toward the back door of our house. Amid the low sound of the crickets and the occasional thrum of a car driving down Grand Street, I heard something. Someone was playing guitar, somewhere over by Mrs. Richmond's. I recognized it—the lick from the Jam's "English Rose." Whoever it was played all those notes almost perfectly but really quietly, so you wouldn't hear it unless you came right up close. Which I did. I walked up to the fence and stood on a metal pail to get a look, because I wasn't sure if I was making it up or not, what with my head throbbing in that terrible coming-down-from-being-wasted way, and my stomach reeling from all that watery beer.

On the front step of the big house sat a boy—or, not a boy, but maybe a college kid—with a beat-up Guild on his lap, picking out the notes and occasionally stopping to look up at the cornflower blue early dawn sky. He was tall and thin and had long hair, and he had on a worn blue-and-yellow-striped rugby shirt and ripped jean shorts and combat boots with the laces undone, and he was beautiful. He was just beautiful. Then I somehow kicked the pail out from under me and it clanged and the boy looked up and I swore he saw me as the light went on in my father's bedroom. I scampered inside and forgot to shut the screen door slowly and it slammed. The whole house shuddered.

I slinked up to my room. My father was standing outside my door, arms crossed, hair all spiky and bags under his eyes from interrupted sleep.

Rosie called, "You woke me up, you jerk," from inside her room. Rosie could fall asleep almost anywhere instantly, and slept hard, so this was a rare and unwelcome event. She opened the door and threw her hands in the air. "Get yourself some help." Then she went back into her room and collapsed on her bed.

My father didn't say anything. He just watched as I went into my room and shut the door.

I took out my *Saturday Night Fever* record, wiped it clean with the red velvety lint brush that seemed like the most luxurious thing in my life sometimes, and I placed the stylus oh-so-gently on the record and plugged in my headphones, so big and fluffy, giant leather clouds over my ears. I put the needle on track five, "If I Can't Have You." *Don't know why, I'm surviving every lonely day . . .* I lay down on my Snoopy-in-space pillow and cried along with the beat, just cried and cried until I fell asleep.

Somehow I slept the entire day, squirming to life in my bed at four p.m. I woke up with my head throbbing, the sun bright in my window and making me squint. I breathed in and felt that tentacle-ish pain in my chest—I almost liked that sensation, the ache of having smoked far too many cigarettes the night before. It was a kind of trophy.

Outside my room, my father waited. Had he been there all night? All morning? All day? But no. He'd clearly been out somewhere, for he stood there very calmly, holding a sea-foam-green hardhat and a brochure. I could make out the pictures: young people smiling happily in those same hardhats amid a backdrop of tall pines.

"What in god's name is that?" I asked, rubbing my knotted, bed-headed hair and fake-yawning.

He handed it over to me, placed the hard plastic right in my hands and pressed them against it.

He said, "I figured out what to do with you."

Chapter 2

IT STARTED IN THAT STRANGE, ATMOSPHERELESS TIME two years ago, right after Ginny died, when my father took me on what he'd termed a "special time trip." We traveled by train up to his friend Pablo's country house in Vermont, hours of staring out the window as the trees grew thicker and the sky clearer and I thought about when we'd scattered my sister's ashes by the observatory. I kept seeing that moment over and over again: my sister as dust, gone back to nature. Occasionally on that train ride, my father would squeeze my shoulder with one hand and I'd feel my whole body soften. We barely said a word the whole time.

His friend was a nice shaggy hippie fella—a professor of biology at the local college in our town, who studied trees and did his research up there in that dense forest. I occupied myself by sitting in front of the fire in Pablo's living room and leafing through his *Illustrated Encyclopedia of Outer Space*. I got fixated on the idea of absolute zero, the lowest possible temperature: −459.67 degrees. Why, I wondered, wasn't there an infinitely low temperature? It made me feel better, as astronomy always did:

there were constants in the universe, if you knew how to look for them.

Pablo took us into the dense forest and hand-drilled into a sapling and pulled out a straw-shaped cross-section of it to show us all the rings; each ring counted for a year of the tree's life. "It's just a little bit older than your sister was," he said. I think he meant to make me feel better, but nausea rose inside me at his words.

Before Ginny died, that was how it felt when I got upset: like I was about to throw up. Ginny used to be the one to talk me down, to stand at the door of my room and say, softly, "Caraway, take a deep breath, come here, hold my hand," then lead me into her room and put a record on — the Beatles, usually, because they were the ones we listened to the most as kids — and sit with me until the red drained from my face.

It had always been bad, but after Ginny was gone, it turned into something else, something crimson and throbbing and powerful and mean, something I couldn't control. Everything that happened after that trip, the trail of burned bridges, the fights, the tantrums in the middle of the street, my banishment not just from Pablo's house but from every babysitting gig I'd ever had, and the visits to the place my father assured me would be better for me in the end — it was bad. But it wasn't me.

He wouldn't call it boot camp. "It's a work program," my father said as he took me to Kane's, the shoe store downtown, to get the boots I'd need for the job. Clearly this was a directive and I had no choice, but I didn't object because I wanted to be with my friends, and if this was what I had to do, okay, I would do it. Except for one really big problem: the shoes.

"I have to wear shitkickers?" I threw my hands up when I saw the ochre-colored leather work boots he'd picked out for me. "Dad!" I knew the intensity of the whine rivaled a Valley Girl, but I wasn't joking. What could be a stronger boy repellent than a hardhat and shitkickers? The *Flashdance* phase had come and gone; the national obsession with the dancer/welder had faded.

All he said was "Yes." He used to talk to me all the time. Used to take me with him onto the roof and look through the telescope, adjusting the focus until I could see the bright lights of the nebula sparkling in the sky. Used to whistle all the time — an old standard called "How High the Moon." Even gave me an Ella Fitzgerald record with it on there for my collection once. Before. Now it seemed all the sound had leaked out of him; he was too deflated for words. "And you'll need to wear long-sleeved shirts. There are some of your mother's old flannel ones in her closet."

"Great."

For the last couple of years, since Ginny died, my dad had been keeping track of everything I did, everywhere I went. Which was nuts because up until then I'd been so careful, so scared of everything. I'd never drunk or done drugs or kissed a boy or gotten detention. I'd had these mini fits, and whenever I had fights with friends, my old friends, I'd fall onto my bed and sob and sob, but it all seemed sort of normal—or at least a second or third cousin of normal. And then all of a sudden, I had my dad's eyes on me. But not my mom's eyes, because she'd started to check out pretty soon after that, retreating to her room for increasingly long periods of meditation, followed by vociferous crying. She stopped enforcing the few rules she'd agreed to: no sleepovers on school nights, all homework done before we could watch MTV, no dessert until we'd eaten all the vegetables on our plates. It was as if she'd decided that nothing she did could protect us, so why try?

But my dad, he tightened the restrictions and the reins. I'd never needed a curfew before, but now he'd glue his eyes to his watch. He'd sniff my breath—I started keeping packs of Dynamints in my coat pocket. He'd beg me to call him if I was at a party, rather than get a ride home from anyone who might have been drinking. And I'd say, "Dad, Dad—cut it out. I won't get in any car like that, okay?" But I did. Over and over, I did. And he'd ground me more and press harder and tell me not to see Soo or Greta. He'd tell me they were bad influences, that their parents were bad influences. He'd beg me, he'd yell at me, he'd take away my privileges, and finally, as a last resort I guess, my telescope. He'd never told me that he'd done it, but by then he'd pretty much stopped talking to me anyway. He took it away when my mother left for her mountaintop rehabilitation, where she was going to silently meditate for three weeks, even though that was thirteen weeks and four days ago. Her clothes were still hanging like ghosts in the closet, but at least I could bear to see them, to touch them. Ginny's room, at the back of the house, remained closed.

In the beginning, we'd asked my father every day when Mom was coming home. "Three weeks," he'd said. Then, "Eighteen days." "Two weeks." "Twelve more days." "Another ten days." "One week." "Three days from now." "She was supposed to be back yesterday." She was supposed to be back a week, two weeks, three weeks ago. And finally: "I don't know." And then we'd stopped asking. She never called, but a couple of times a week letters appeared, with seeds shaking inside them. I put them all right in the trash.

"You've grown," Mr. Kane said now, smiling at me as if I were a normal kid while he measured my feet. Maybe he was the one person in town who didn't know all the sordid details of my past. I waited for him to say something about the shoes— why would a sixteen-year-old girl want shitkickers?—but he just made small talk with my dad, who became his old chatty self. My father loved strangers. It was much harder for him to talk to people he actually knew.

On Monday morning, my father did me the favor of getting my bike out of the shed and strapping the hardhat to the rear rack himself. "You can keep the bungee cord," he said.

"Wow, Christmas."

He didn't laugh, just patted the bike to send me on my way. Rosie was standing at the screen door, watching the whole thing.

"What are *you* looking at?"

"You," she said.

I heard it again. The music. From the other side of the fence. One of my favorite Elvis Costello songs, "Alison" — *I know this world is killing you.*

I begrudgingly took the bike from my dad.

"You know where it is, right?"

"Yes, Dad, I know where it is. It's in the park. Where I had birthday parties number one through twelve." Where Ginny's ashes had sifted into the wind.

"You have to be there in twenty minutes. You should go."

It was the most normal conversation I'd had with him in weeks, or maybe months. Maybe a year. The first day of junior high, I stood in this same yard with this same bike and had a similar conversation. Except Ginny was alive then and my mother was still around and my father wasn't so mean and Rosie was a benign blur of a kid instead of the embodiment of perfection to which I would never live up. My mother had taken me to the mall to buy the bike, one of the rare moments of alone time with her — that's what happens when you're the middle child. Really, the only thing that remained of that day was my bike, my dear old bike: a twelve-speed Fuji Espree, sparkly gray-blue. Its beauty was marred, I thought, by that hardhat.

"And I expect you to be home right after."

"I know."

"If you're not here by five twenty, you'll be grounded for the rest of the summer."

I pushed the bike away from him, toward the street. "I know."

As I hopped on and pedaled away, I could just make out the outline of the long-haired boy, sitting on the steps with his guitar.

And that's how I came to be pedaling down Avenue of the Pines, the long road lined with white pine trees that formed the entrance to the state park. It always made me feel like I was embarking on an adventure, the narrow road that would open to some magical vista, the arrival in Shangri-La as the vast green fields came into view. But I always had to pass the spot where the small white cross was still affixed to the tree. Or — maybe it still was. I didn't look.

When I pulled up to the park's offices, set in the wide flat parking lot where my mom had taught me to ride my bike, I stood for a minute by the bike rack, wondering how I could get out of this, first-day-of-school anxiety mixed with a muddy dread. But it was 9:07, and I was already late, and the only way to slink along to safety was to walk in. So I did. I followed the handwritten signs to a fluorescent-lit room with kids seated at too-small elementary-school-style desks.

A tall fellow with thick, sculpted arms and a name tag that read *Lynn* stood in the front of the classroom, smiling beatifically.

"How ya doin', ma'am?" I said to him, fake-tipping my hat, but he failed to appreciate my humor. He must have grown those muscles to make up for the feminine name.

I slid into my seat and surveyed some of my companions, many of them from my grade, kids I hadn't talked to for ages. I barely had classes with any of them, since I was a year ahead in math and English and science—history was my shortcoming—and at lunch and gym and any other intergrade activity, I was with my older friends. How had so many of them become ingrates and inmates and screwups and outcasts like me?

We scrawled our identities on HELLO MY NAME IS . . . name tags, but I vaguely remembered some of them: Kelsey and that scrawny boy named Jimmie and, crap, Tonya Sweeny. Great. I wrote *Caraway* on my name tag just to freak them out, to show that I was different. For once in my life, I was glad that I didn't belong.

Lynn handed out black and white composition books and golf pencils with the park's logo on them. Also black fanny packs (blech) and small hammers, all of them branded by the park.

"Thank you so much for coming," he said.

"Did we have the option not to?" I asked, looking around, assuming my compatriots in forced labor would commiserate. But nothing. Staring straight ahead, which seemed strange for kids who were purportedly troublemakers. They were a compliant set of miscreants. Lynn didn't smile either; I wondered if my father had called ahead to warn him of my history of misdeeds.

"We're pleased to welcome you to the inaugural Youth Summer Workforce Camp."

"It's camp?" I said. "Yay. Color wars!"

Only the skinny boy, Jimmie, laughed and then stifled it when Lynn looked at him. The flatter my jokes fell, the greater the itch to tell them.

"Not that kind of camp," Lynn said, his voice laced with so much syrupy understanding that I had to fight to keep from rolling my eyes. "We'll be teaching you some basic construction skills, as well as familiarizing you with the native flora and fauna of the park." He said this as if he were offering us free rein at Sizzler, or an extra week of school vacation. "Each week we'll work on conservation and improvement projects. And by the end of the summer, you'll be able to see the fruits of your labor."

Tonya looked pleased. I wondered what she'd done to land in here.

Lynn told us that he was finishing his masters in psychology and took this job because he loved working with kids and wanted to share the power of nature and how good it felt to do hard work and how much he loved the low grumble of hunger in his belly after he'd been out in a field, reaping or sowing or building or tearing something down. "I'm really excited to work together," he said, his John Lennon glasses reflecting the sun. I stopped listening, instead opening my notebook and doodling —I was very good at drawing flowers, and I could just spy the heads of pink roses unfurling above the windowsill. It reminded me of that song by the Jam. And of that boy. And his guitar.

"Caraway?" Lynn was standing in front of my chair. From the looks of it, he'd been saying my name. "You with us?"

I slumped in my seat. "Yeah, I'm with you," I said. "Do I have a choice?"

Lynn took it easy on us that first day. Just a hike around the park to show us the massive calcium deposit that had formed around a geyser—a streaky white-and-rust-colored mass that looked like a giant's half-rotten tooth—and the spots along the creek where the sweet orange flowers called jewelweed grew.

"Jewelweed has healing properties," Lynn said, picking a few buds and passing them around. Each of the kids did their due diligence, studying the delicate orange petals, but I just passed it on to Tonya, who was sweating in her off-brand JCPenney version of an Izod shirt, with a fox instead of an alligator, dark smudges beneath her armpits. I tried my best to smile at her when I saw the way she was pressing her arms down against her sides, trying to hide the watery stains.

The only other person I knew who was obsessed with Mars, Tonya was the one I had taken with me to the NASA exhibit down at the New York State Museum in Albany when we were thirteen, to see the *Fourth Planet from the Sun* exhibit. I had sort of, kind of, wanted to talk to her about it when the Mars Ares rover disappeared into the ether earlier this year, erasing our chances of knowing the planet better.

Now Tonya was closely examining the petals of jewelweed.

"This is awesome," she said. "Very interesting that it has this translucent stalk." She pressed it between her fingers. "There's gold liquid inside."

"That's the healing salve," Lynn said.

She touched one of the seedpods nestled inside the flower, and it popped out. "Amazing," she said. She looked at me for a minute, the first time we'd made eye contact in weeks or months or years, who knew? She probably assumed I would share her enthusiasm for the biological profile of jewelweed, but I stayed silent.

Lynn had taken us to the path along the creek that ran through the center of the park. Farther up the path, at the crest of the hill, the observatory loomed. Stone steps led up to it, but it had been closed, of course, thanks to the public revelation of the observatory as teenage party spot. Or because of budget cuts, which was what the park gave as the official reason. Between here and there, the walkway was muddy and worn away. It would have been hard to get to even if it were open. Even if I could have handled it.

"What are we actually doing?" I asked Lynn, who had crouched beside a rut in the dirt; the other kids circled around him.

"We're identifying the optimal spots to build the footbridge," he said, as if that should have been obvious to me.

"Um," I said, "shouldn't you leave that footbridge stuff to the professionals? I do not have an impressive history with wood-working projects."

Lynn stood up and smiled at me so earnestly that it was like bright lights shining in my eyes. "Kids, listen up: don't tell me that you can't do something. Tell me that you want to learn to do something—that you don't know yet, but you will. Got it?" He took his own hammer out of the loop on his pants and held up a shiny nail. "Look," he said. "This is a hammer. This is a nail."

"And this is your brain on drugs," I said.

"You may not know how to use them now," he continued, ignoring me, "but by the end of the summer, we'll have built a bridge in the park. And"—he emphasized this last part— "with each other." I fake-gagged, but I couldn't get a laugh out of anyone.

By the end of the afternoon, my boots were caked with mud, I had dirt under my fingernails, and I was exhausted. My summer job at Dot's Duds had mostly involved sitting on a chair, folding accessories (many of which ended up in my pocket), and stepping out to smoke cigarettes that I'd stolen from Dot. But, of course, I had told the therapist about that, too. I was essentially unemployable because of her, even though technically I'm pretty sure her big-mouth-ness was illegal, or at least unethical.

Before we left, Lynn had us sit in a circle beneath the very welcome shade of a beechnut tree and write in our notebooks about our impressions of the program after day one. I had already lost my golf pencil, so I told Lynn, "I'm gonna do mine in invisible ink." But he gave me his own pen, black and green marbled, heavy and cool to the touch.

"This is one of my most prized possessions," he said. "Make sure you give it back. A good pen is hard to find." Around me, my fellow inmates were furiously scribbling. I just wrote, "I hate this job already," and closed the notebook tight. I kept his pen.

My father wasn't home when I pulled my bike into our yard. As I went to lean it against the house, I heard the sound again, the music. Somehow I missed the side of the house and the bike came crashing down, right on my foot. I yelped.

"You okay?"

It was the boy. He was tall enough that he could see over the fence, and he was holding his guitar in his left hand. His hair was messy, hanging in front of one eye. He was too cute to look at.

I was somehow hoping that if I didn't move, he wouldn't see me, wouldn't see the hardhat and the work boots caked with mud and the dirt that had wedged beneath my fingernails and my mother's old flannel shirt and my godforsaken canvas painter's pants with my brand-new shiny hammer hanging from a loop.

I just said, "Ummmm."

And that was it. Then I turned and ran into the house and stood at the screen door, and I could almost discern his movements behind the fence. He stood there for a minute, then returned to the big house's porch and sat down with his guitar.

He sang a little bit off-key, just the tiniest bit flat, a hint of twang in his voice. I loved twang.

For some reason I was out of breath, as if I had one-time adolescent asthma. There were two things that helped me breathe: pot and singing. So I trudged up to my room, taking my filthy clothes off as I went, and got a joint and changed into a tank top and cutoffs and bare feet, and got my guitar — a beat-up old Gibson with a rich, bell-like sound that my mother had played in a band in college. I opened the window and climbed out onto the roof of the porch with my guitar. I didn't look toward Mrs. Richmond's giant fancy house. But I could hear. He was playing a song by Squeeze: "Goodbye Girl."

I went out to my corner of the roof with my guitar. The sun was setting, zodiacal light glinting off the horizon. And very softly, I played along with the simple song: D, then A, then D, then G. Maybe not loud enough for him to hear me. I didn't know.

And then my father was yelling, his voice surely carrying over the fence: "Caraway, get off the roof! And you left your filthy clothes all over the floor. Come down here this instant and pick them up!" My father yelling, my real name, my filthy clothes. The music stopped. On his side too, the music stopped.

Chapter 3

THE POINT OF OUR BEING IN THE PARK, besides to rehabilitate us, was to build a footbridge. Most of our summer-long program, Lynn declared, would be spent designing and constructing a three-hundred-foot bridge that would span the muddy, makeshift walkway from the giant calcium deposit, across the creek, and all the way to the stone steps of the observatory.

"It's possible that they'll be reopening it at some point," he said. He didn't look at me throughout the announcement. Did he know?

"So let me tell you how this is going to work," he continued. "We'll choose a design. We'll do some waymaking, which is what they call making a path in England." He offered no explanation of why we should be learning the British version, but okay. "We'll be learning all the steps and all the tools needed. Got it?"

The kids nodded their heads.

"Got it?" Lynn asked again.

A few said "Yes!" or "Got it!" but that wasn't good enough for our lead Boy Scout, Lynn. "Let me hear you say it!" he shouted. And then the whole group, everyone but me, shouted, "Got it!"

Tonya yelled the loudest, and most enthusiastically, of all. Maybe she was competing for the title of most rehabilitatable. Lynn leaned back, arms crossed, a satisfied smile on his face.

"I'm going to pass this around for inspiration," he said, displaying a book called *Footbridges from Around the World,* waving his hands past the cover like a car-show model.

"This is a thing?" I asked.

"What do you mean?"

"People care about footbridges enough that they published a whole book about them?"

"Yes," Lynn said. "People care about all kinds of things that you have never even heard of."

While I waited—with breathless anticipation, of course—for the book to come around to me, I adjusted the calculations in my notebook. I'd started them earlier in the year, when I knew that Vira was on its way. It had been discovered back in the 1600s by Dmitri Sergeevich Alexandrov, a kind of tragic figure in the history of physics, Newton's shadowy nemesis. It always traveled in an elliptical path around the sun, just as we did. At last count, it was still zooming its way past Mars at 128,000 miles an hour. It was still more than two hundred million miles away.

I couldn't imagine how footbridges would possibly be more fascinating than comets, and I was prepared to just pass the book on, as I had with the jewelweed. But then I saw a couple of them as Jimmie handed it to me. There were ones made out of whole logs; ones with curved side rails, painted red; one with zigzagging planks like Jenga; one made out of arched rock.

"How do they get that to stay that way?" I asked. Apparently I hadn't voiced a rhetorical question, because Tonya answered me.

"It's how an arch works," she said. "Two weaknesses that form a strength when they lean together. Basically just two forces, one downward and one outward." She said this as if she really wanted to say "dumbass" at the end of her sentence. We had not had a real conversation for almost two years.

"Right," I said, as if I'd known the answer all along. Which I should have. "It's defying gravity."

"No, dumbass," she said, quietly enough so that Lynn didn't hear. "It's *using* gravity. 'Every force has an equal and opposite force,' as I'm pretty sure you know." I looked down at my still-newish work boots. "They're pushing against each other, and that holds them in place."

"Right," I said again. There was one in which the handrails and posts were made out of a tangle of vines, storybook style; one with flower boxes all along the sides, long, weeping flowers hanging toward the water, weirdly beautiful and sculptural; and some really boring ones with plain old sticks of wood at the end.

"Ours will be like the ones on the last few pages," Lynn said, and I felt the small descent of disappointment.

I hated it. This was no surprise to me, and probably not to my father, but by week two, after the introduction to weeding and elementary hammering, it seemed to surprise Lynn.

"Caraway?" he said, walking up to me and putting a hand

on my shoulder as I vaguely picked at some weeds that were doing their best to choke the path that wound through a grove of cypress trees. Why had I told him my real name? "Need a hand?"

"No," I said. I crouched down, or at least I tried to, but the boots were still stiff, the leather unforgiving, and it was hard to bend with my ankles held captive inside them. My canvas painter's pants were too scratchy. My mother's gardening shirt, green and blue and black plaid, which I'd somehow grown attached to, was now covered in dirt. I reached for a weed and yanked on it, but it was tenacious and it didn't come with me as I leaned back. I ended up falling on my butt. I looked up to see if any of the other kids had noticed, but they all seemed perfectly focused as they wrested unfriendly vines from the ground.

The morning had started with a brief presentation on the kinds of flora and fauna found in the park, what was good and what was harmful and what to go toward and what to avoid as we began to weed and clear the path.

I had doodled in my journal through the whole thing, making 3D letters of the lyrics to that Jam song—no matter where he roams he returns to his English Rose—so I really had no idea what we were supposed to be doing here. Weeding, apparently, in the spot where we would eventually build the footbridge: a youth chain gang.

A breeze drifted in and the park turned golden and hazy. I leaned back with my park-issued trowel in my hand and watched as a red-winged blackbird landed on a cattail in the swampy stretch a few hundred feet from us. Beyond the field, I could see the curved gray walls of the observatory. I tried not to think about why it was closed. Then I tried not to think about the boy. I thought about the boy.

"I'm hungry," I said, and no one replied. "Ugh, this is hard." Still nothing.

"Just try to enjoy that feeling of hunger, of how hard you're working for it," Lynn said. "It gets easier and easier."

"That's what my mom used to say, and then she left because nothing got easier," I said, and that shut him up. I didn't know why I said that, let that tidbit of information, normally kept locked away, slip. I knew better than to trust professionals in the mental health field.

"Try it like this," Lynn said, and he grabbed a clump of timothy grass by its base, where the stem disappeared into the ground. It slid right out.

"Okay." I shrugged, and did as he said. And, yeah, it slid right out.

"It feels really good to make one small adjustment and have everything align, doesn't it?"

How one person could smile so much, at so many tiny and unimportant observations, was beyond me. Except, okay, yeah: it did feel a little bit good to make one small adjustment and have everything align. But I wasn't going to say so.

We were working in a small group in the field, and it reminded me of my parents' honeymoon photos. They had gone to a city in Sicily, an under-the-radar place called Enna, which was one of the highest elevations on the island (not to be confused with Etna, the giant volcano). It offered the magical combination of clear views of the sky for my father and particularly good growing conditions for herbs, which appealed to my mom. That was where they picked the rosemary and the caraway and saw the occultation of Regulus, when an asteroid passed in front of the Regulus star, blocking its light. They'd found everything near and dear to them in one beautiful place. They had photographs of the old women in black scarves amid the fields of herbs, and if I squinted just right, we looked like that here in the park, except we were wayward teens amid the weeds in hardhats and canvas pants.

It seemed as if hours had gone by, and we'd barely made a dent in those weeds, and I was sweating and stinky and so bored of listening to Kelsey and Tonya compare notes on the members of Duran Duran.

"Simon is totally my boyfriend," Kelsey said. She was very small, even smaller than I was, with coffee-colored skin and a frizz of black hair.

"No, it's Nick—that hair. Totally decent," said Tonya. She'd grown heavier since we'd stopped being friends, and it seemed like it was kind of hard for her to breathe with all the hard work. I thought about offering her some water from the cooler, but then she said, "I am so totally having Nick's babies."

Their happiness, to me, was like some giant balloon expanding in my face. I had no choice but to pop it. Duran Duran was just not acceptable.

"They're all gay," I said. "You know that, right?"

Their faces took on the potent combination of surprise and annoyance, while Lynn's eyes widened in what looked like fear and his mouth shut sharply. This was foreign territory for him. He was great at talking about hard work and the variety of promising construction tools, but homosexual teenage icons? Not so much. Tonya scrunched up her face and shook her head.

That cocktail of shame and satisfaction swirled inside me, and I moved over to another section of the path. I took another cassette out of my old worn backpack and changed Big Star to Hüsker Dü in my Walkman, then put the headphones over my ears and pretended to concentrate on the task at hand, the untamable weeds spilling over the land.

I also pretended that I couldn't see Lynn's crazy muscly calves as they stood before me, weird bulbous hairy calves that ended in olive-colored socks and brown leather hiking boots—he was some kind of cross between a hippie and an army sergeant.

"Caraway, um."

I kept picking at the plants.

"Caraway?"

Finally he reached and carefully took my headphones off my ears. "Caraway, we need to watch our language and make sure that we don't say things that could be construed as"—he paused, collected himself—"or rather, interpreted as insulting. Okay?" He offered me that wan smile. Lynn. I kind of liked him. He was a nice guy. Probably shouldn't be forced to shepherd a bunch of unruly kids like us. "Okay?"

"I know what *construed* means," I said. I kept looking at the weeds, limp in my hands.

He said, "Okay."

Lynn told us to break for lunch and to get our journals, and he passed out Styrofoam cups of water and carrot sticks as we unpacked our lunches and sat on hollow logs and, in theory, reflected on the work we'd been doing and how it made us feel. *I feel hungry,* I wrote with Lynn's pen, and *Carrot sticks just aren't cutting it.* And then: *Lynn is afraid of gay people.*

Then I turned to the back and futzed with my calculations, applying Kepler's Second Law of planetary motion—the closer the object got to the sun, the faster it would go. It was getting closer now, and if I kept charting its movement, kept up with my calculation, I'd know for sure, all on my own, when we would see it. Just thinking about it made my whole body exhale. It released me from my own head and sent me to the stars.

As we were packing up to return to the land of forced labor, Tonya sauntered by. I saw her looking at my notebook, and my equations, and I shut the book sharply.

She didn't even look at me. She just said, "Duran Duran is not gay. That's Boy George."

After lunch, each kid returned to stockpiling the weeds, bales of the unwanted green that we were going to take over to the industrial composter—Lynn's face absolutely bloomed at this announcement. I returned to my task, lazily pulling at what was left of the weeds.

I had the smallest pile, I noticed. Tonya's was the biggest, and she'd not only been dutifully tugging at the weeds all day but had started acting as some kind of coach, or maybe a drill sergeant, to the rest of us. "Soldiers, commence weeding," she'd said when we started. And now, "Troops—pull up those roots." I noticed she had worn-looking dog tags on a ball chain around her neck.

"I lost," I said to her, holding up my pathetic pile.

"It's not a contest," she said. "You only lost to yourself."

Oh, please, I thought, but honestly I was too tired and sweaty to even say it.

Then Tonya looked more closely at my pile. "Carrie, you're not supposed to touch that," she said as I wrested my last batch of weeds from the ground. For some reason, all the kids had left patches of plants untouched.

"Why not?" I said. I had only one work glove on—they were so stiff that I found it hard to get a grip with them on—and I used my bare hands to take hold of the tall stalk with serrated leaves and an eruption of sad-looking small yellow flowers at the top.

"Were you listening this morning?"

"Listening?" I asked as Lynn came over to check on us. I smiled up at him, but he was frowning. "Sure. I was listening."

"I don't think you were," Lynn said. "Come with me."

* * *

He took me back to the park offices and washed my hands with special soap. "I don't know if it's going to work," he said. "That was a lot of wild parsnip."

"It sounds delicious," I said. "If I liked parsnips."

"It causes a terrible rash."

It was quiet in the bathroom, the industrial green paint soothing in the late afternoon sun, the tile cool. Lynn dried my hands with a graying towel and looked up at me. "You're funny, Caraway," he said.

"I know." He didn't seem amused by that.

"But that doesn't mean you can get out of things. That doesn't mean you're excused."

"I know that, too," I said, looking down at my hands that seemed poison-free. For once: poison-free. He was holding the towel, and my hands were in it, nesting in the cloth.

"You can do this," Lynn said. Did he know the sordid tales of my youth? Or was he just saying that I could handle the hot sun and the rigorous demands of weeding and footbridge building? He handed me a bouquet of jewelweed to rub on my hands.

I wanted to answer him, but something was stuck in my throat. It was hard to talk. The only thing that came out was a whisper: "I don't know if I can."

Chapter 4

THE BOY WASN'T THERE THE NEXT FEW afternoons when I rolled my bike into the yard after work. For this, at least, I was grateful. I didn't want him to ever see me with my hardhat and shitkickers and flannel shirt again. Maybe he'd left for good. Maybe he had been visiting Mrs. Richmond and had already gone home. Maybe he was an apparition, a vision of the future. I hoped so. If he wasn't real, I hoped he would be someday.

My father had put a moratorium on leaving the house or having visitors, but the phone, thank god, was now within limits, and when I talked to Soo that night, she spoke of Justin and Justin and Justin. I picked at the calluses on my fingertips, my badges of pride, grown there after years of playing guitar, and I tried to listen, but with every word about their upcoming co-adventure at college in the wilds of western New York, my chest tightened more.

"Do you think they'd ever let us room together?" she asked me. "Does that happen?"

"Hold on, I just happen to have the manual on co-ed collegiate cohabitation right here," I said.

"Ha ha." We fell silent for a minute, something that happened more often it seemed. And in that silence I reached for my default vocabulary; the only way to explain what was occurring here on Earth was to use the stars.

"Accretion," I said.

"Oh, boy. I think we're getting into some astrophysics again." Soo had gotten a D in physics, though I'd tried to tutor her. Too much vodka had made that endeavor challenging.

"It's when an object in space grows by attracting more matter through gravity—it just pulls more stuff toward it."

"And this metaphor fits because?"

"You're all leaving. Just taking it all with you and leaving."

In her silence, I heard reproach and rejection—too needy, too nerdy, too young. Or maybe guilt, or sadness that she was going and leaving me behind. I couldn't tell anymore.

And then Soo changed to her chirping, happy tone. "Hey— I met a neighbor of yours at the record store the other day. Dean something or other. He's staying with your neighbor Mrs. Richmond for the summer—that's his aunt or something."

I stopped playing with my calluses. My hands were starting to feel a little itchy.

"Carrie? You there?"

"Mmm," I said. "I hadn't noticed."

"Well, he's cool," she said. "He has a summer job fixing bikes at Reinventing the Wheel, and he plays the drums."

"Mmm," I said again. Dean: I just loved the sound of it. Sweet and solid and kind of grown-up.

"He has long hair," she said.

I took a deep breath and let it out as slowly as I could, the same way I did when I was smoking. Only there was no joint and no cigarette, just this tidbit of information floating along the wires between us.

"Anyway, I invited him over tomorrow night. Do you think your dad will let you come out? We miss you. And it's Friday!"

I didn't know. I didn't know how to get my father to relent. He had two modes: taciturn or screaming. It had been a long time since I'd seen anything in between.

When my father and Rosie came in the door, I was at the dining room table, writing in my park-issued notebook. I was not chronicling my adventures in nature—at least not the way they wanted me to—but I had taken up three pages with a few of my most cherished Vira memorabilia items, including a black-and-white postcard from 1890 that my mom had found in a flea market down in the Catskills, showing the Meeanee Observatory in New Zealand. In it, Vira was a fiery streak of light in the background, that same exact ball that was coming around now. Vira was trapped, doomed to repeat itself, its journey like that of Sisyphus, for millennia.

I drew another elliptical orbit path. The comet at aphelion was almost four billion miles from the sun, the farthest distance it would go. But it had long passed that point and was now headed back again. Toward us. It was getting closer all the time.

"We got Kentucky Fried Chicken," Rosie said, shoving a cardboard bucket in my face. "Here's yours."

My mother had never, not once, let us have fast food, and my father had told us when we were little that it wasn't actually chicken that they served. He'd called it "Kentucky Fried Rats." But that was before. Now we had it once a week.

I gently moved the greasy bucket off my papers and managed to push the word *Thanks* out of my mouth. Every time my father and I were in the same room, this terrible unease circled us.

"What are you doing?" Rosie asked suspiciously. "Are these plans for a mail bomb?"

I rolled my eyes at her. "Just trying to figure out when the comet will get past Jupiter's orbit."

"It's closer than I thought," my father said, putting one hand down on the table and leaning over me, forgetting for a minute that he normally reacted to me as if I were irradiated.

"Yeah, but there's a giant bummer part of it, which is that it's looking like it's going to be close to the horizon, so not so easy to see."

"Maybe if it's low, it'll be easier for you, since you're so short," Rosie said, looming over me with her extra four inches—she wasn't even done growing yet, as she enjoyed pointing out during our brief periods of social interaction.

My father studied my calculations, losing the veil of disapproval and becoming the man formerly known as Dad, hand curled around the black stubble on his chin in contemplation, finger tracing the figures.

"No, I think the best way to see it would be if we had the old telescope," I said. Maybe I could take advantage of this moment of goodwill and my two weeks of hard work to get the one thing I really wanted back. That is, the one thing I wanted that I could actually have.

But my father's face went dark again, and he retreated back into himself, a switch turning off inside him. "Yes," he said. "That would be great."

How cruel, I thought, to agree with me and still not return the telescope. He turned and walked away. Even Rosie's eyebrows furrowed as she watched him leave, his shoulders now slumped.

"You missed something," Rosie said, pointing to the top left corner of my sketch. "The perihelion is only 0.4 AUs. It's only, like, thirty-nine million miles from the sun. It's way closer to us than this."

"Oh—okay." Usually I blamed my mistakes on too much pot and alcohol, but I'd been too busy pulling poisonous plants from the ground to get wasted. Must have been too much exercise and fresh air. I said something very rarely uttered to Rosie: "Thanks."

She hid the twinge of a smile in indifference. "Whatever," she said, "Rye Bread."

* * *

By Friday my hands were red and swollen and itchy, but I still had to go to work and I still had to wear work gloves—Lynn gave me a temporary pair and told me to wash the other ones with some bleach to get the wild parsnip oil out—and I still had to feed the weeds (minus the parsnip) into the industrial composter, which, contrary to Lynn's prediction, was not one of life's great joys.

It was so hard to concentrate. I vacillated between having imaginary fights with my dad—demanding my telescope, pointing out the ways he'd wronged me—and daydreaming about the boy. His name was Dean. He had long hair. He played drums. He knew how to fix bikes. Had there ever lived a more promising creature?

Our last assignment of the week was to start clearing the path—we had poured wild parsnip killer on it, and those innocent-looking stalks were now withered. We spent the whole day walking along the future trail, mapping out just where it would go, finding the exact spot where it should cross the creek.

"Where do you guys think the best spot is, based on our research?" Lynn asked us.

"Probably just the place where it's narrowest," said Jimmie, the little guy with the unibrow, who for some reason was always standing next to Tonya. Aw, Jimmie. I felt sorry for him.

"The narrowest spot in the creek?" Lynn asked. "I can understand why you'd think that, but there are other considerations, including the height of the crossing, how level the two sides are, and what's in the way—are there really big tree roots, for instance? So, I want you guys to look around and see if you can find some ideal spots. Pair up," he said, instructing Tonya and me to go together. Great.

"Fall out, troops," Tonya called out, and instead of revolting, they fell right in line, toy soldiers all of them. They seemed to have accepted her unofficial role as drill sergeant—maybe boot camp was really working on them.

We plodded around the side of the creek, our ridiculous boots gaining another coat of mud. Tonya crouched every couple of feet, carefully inspecting the ground.

"Hey, Lynn," she called, after finding a large flat and root-free spot. "What about here?"

Lynn hurried over to us, then called for the others to join. "Yes, that's just the spot I was thinking of," he said. Tonya beamed. I wished I had a book about footbridges, anything to read so I could look away from this scene.

After lunch, we wrote in our notebooks. I drew with Lynn's pen the red-winged blackbird that seemed to follow us from site to site, and I wrote down some lyrics—*all this dark matter in the universe that can't be seen, but still its forces pull on me.* But I didn't write about what I'd learned or how the program was changing my sense of self. I ignored Lynn's writing prompts. What was the difference, anyway? It wasn't like anyone was going to read it.

At the end of the day, Lynn handed me a sealed envelope. "Take this home to your parent or guardian," he told us.

"Man, I wish I had a guardian," I said. "That would be so much better."

Tonya's face seemed to cloud over. "That's what you think," she said. I remembered what Tonya's house was like, dim and dirty, the presence of her wheelchair-bound grandmother everywhere, with the faint scent of pee. Even when her father was briefly home from the navy, which was rare, he was fierce and scary, and her mother had died when Tonya was little, before I even knew her. I felt a small pit right in the center of my chest, the size of an olive, but powerful, when I thought about her home.

When Rosie was five, Ginny and I brought her to the front row of our elementary school auditorium so she could see the visiting magician up close. She was smart even then, smarter than us, and she kept yelling out the secrets to his tricks. "It's up his sleeve!" "There's a little space in the bottom of his hat!" Finally the magician turned his gaze on her, transformed from kind to venomous, and said, "Little girl, it's time for you to leave."

Ginny and I took her outside, and she seemed totally unfazed. Back then I used to love having two sisters, one older and one younger. We'd have all these adventures that had nothing to do with my parents; we were a team. They loved Ginny the best and then Rosie. I knew that, and I knew that being alone with my sisters was the only way we'd be even. With Ginny gone, I still came in last for favorite kid.

Ginny had asked Rosie, "What did it feel like when the magician yelled at you?"

She just shrugged her shoulders and said, "It felt like oops." And Ginny just tousled her hair and hugged her and said, "Okay, sweetie," and I knew she was one of the world's great big sisters.

I always thought that should be the title of my autobiography: *It Felt Like Oops.* Subtitle: *One Screwup after Another.*

Now Lynn said, "Bring it to whoever is responsible for you." He said it to the group, but I knew it was addressed to me, Caraway the Insensitive. He already seemed less inclined to regale me with his mini pep talks and more inclined to ignore or correct me. Maybe I had it really good compared to these kids. I could afford new boots. I had two parents who were legally responsible for me, even though I hadn't seen one in three months and the other one hated my guts. I had friends. At least I had friends.

When I got home, I locked my bike against the fence and took off the boots and hardhat and presented the envelope to my father. My hands were still red, a little bit peeling.

"Look how hard I worked," I said, making jazz hands in front of his face.

He said, "Mm." He seemed 10 percent less like my enemy.

He took the manila envelope from me and unlatched the metal clasp, looking at me all the while, his expression deadpan.

He was scary this way. He used to be the happy-go-lucky science teacher, his glasses smudged, his hands callused from playing guitar in the evenings on the porch while my mother cooked her culinary masterpieces of galettes and tartlets and soufflés that she'd learned at cooking school, all the stuff I claimed to hate (Soo's Korean mother made Shake'n Bake and Kraft macaroni and cheese; I just wanted to be normal). I didn't really hate it. In contrast to the TV dinners that now filled our freezer, it seemed amazing.

He handed me my measly minimum-wage paycheck and showed me the paper, a carbon copy that looked suspiciously like the document I'd received on the last day of school. My one saving grace was that I got A's and B's, no matter how many times I skipped out or went to school stoned. I was a good student. Rosie had once knocked on my head and said, *There's someone smart in there. I can hear her calling from the jail you've put her in.*

"They give you report cards?" I asked. Could this job get any lamer? I didn't see any letter grades on the thin paper, but there were handwritten notes. That was almost scarier.

"Sort of." He tucked it back into the envelope, but when he looked at me now, there was less glare in his eye.

"Why do I get a report card?"

"It's more like a progress report. It's a pilot program. They're giving and receiving feedback."

"Well, what a happy, reciprocal relationship. So what's the feedback? What's my grade on footbridge preparation? I can tell you right now, I am not going to get an A in footbridge building. I wasn't any good at shop either, if you recall."

When we made wooden bowls in shop class, mine was the only one that was unsandable—the whole inside scratchy and rough. My teacher, Mr. Feinstein, had tried sanding it for a few minutes and then said, not terribly apologetically, "I have no idea what you've done or how to fix it." Just another variation on my theme. I gave the messed-up bowl to Ginny, who used it for her collection of dangly earrings. "I love it," she said when I handed it to her. She laughed at the still-splintery parts and said, "Don't worry—it's perfect." And then, when she thought I wasn't watching, she slipped her drugs below the dangly earrings.

I had felt in my chest something I couldn't quite identify: maybe some kind of betrayal. Maybe some kind of fear.

"It's so we know how you're doing," my father said.

"How am I doing?" I asked. I put my shitkickers neatly against the wall and set the hardhat on top.

My father adjusted his glasses and made his way toward the screen door, holding it open for me as I slowly followed behind. "Not completely terrible," he said. "At least you're showing up."

Thus I was able to negotiate a furlough, another night of freedom as long as I came home by midnight.

"What happened to your hands?" Soo asked when she saw me. I had covered them with thin cotton gloves that my father kept in his box of dissection tools.

"What? It's a look. Michael Jackson." I twirled my fingers, trying only to look at Soo's face while I talked to her. But I was scanning the basement. Who was here? That jerk Tyler with the Mohawk and studded leather jacket, the one I once went to third base with. And the captain of the football team, Julio Germaine. And one of Greta's cheerleader friends. And of course Tommy and Tiger and Justin. Greta. The whole gang. And me. That was it.

The Ramones' "Pinhead" was on the stereo, and suddenly we were all chanting, *we accept you, one of us,* the whole room erupting in some mixture of anger and joy that felt familiar and comforting and dangerous all at once. The boys were pounding their fists into the air. And then the record skipped and Tommy went, "Screw the Ramones," and replaced it with Flock of Seagulls.

"Tommy, why are we friends with you?" Tiger called, throwing a pillow at his head.

I adjusted the straps of my bra, the little bit of lace that was poking out from beneath the spaghetti straps of my shirt. After a week of crisp canvas pants and flannel shirts and hardhats and work boots, normal clothes almost felt almost indecent: the glittery jelly shoes and the probably way-too-skimpy tank top. I had brought the flannel shirt with me, that worn memory of cloth that had been somehow folded into my daily routine.

Someone handed me a joint and there was a beer ball full of Genesee and, what the hell, I had some of that too, and I sat back in the center seat of the couch and listened to the music because no one was talking to me. Everyone was having fun, and I forced my lips into a smile, and I drank until the familiar ache began to recede. I drowned it. I smoked it out.

And then, a voice. A voice I had heard through the fence. It said, "Hey, man." And then a voice, another male voice, responded, "Hey, man, what's up?"

I looked out of the corner of my eye. There was the boy, the boy named Dean, clasping Tiger's hand and nodding toward Justin, all of them jutting their chins toward one another as if they'd met months, years ago, were already comfortable in some kind of man intimacy — sports and music, blah blah blah, what a bunch of baloney, didn't they talk about anything real, how boring, this guy must be a total a-hole, not a speck of brain tissue in his head, his beautiful head with the beautiful hair and the little wisps of stubble on his chin and, crap, he had green eyes and I really loved green eyes, no, they were hazel and hazel was even better. Hazel was the best. They were hazel.

Then he nodded at me. At me. I sat up a little straighter as he sat down next to me. He was talking to Tiger about the new Neil Young record and he settled back into the couch and his arm touched mine and I wasn't talking to anyone so I closed my eyes because I was so into the music. I pretended I was so into the music. Black Flag. Not my favorite.

"I fucking love this song," he said.

Black Flag: okay, I'd give them a chance. My brain was swimming. Giant gulp of disgusting Genesee.

"Me too," I said, but he didn't seem to hear me. At least, he didn't turn around. He turned his head a degree or two, seemed to see me, or at least a slice of me, the outline of my face — oh, my hair was a mess and I had those gloves on my hands and I was so stoned my eyes must have been totally red and I probably looked terrible. He ignored me. Good. Fine. He should ignore me. I was ignorable. I hated myself. Drink drink drink. I really just hated myself. And then it seemed like I was going to cry and there Greta was, sinking into the couch next to me. I loved Greta, but she was also beautiful as a Barbizon model in her shirt with the giant shoulder pads and the balloon pants with suspenders and the high heels, and all other girls within a fifty-foot radius immediately vaporized in her presence.

"What's happening, Carrie?" she asked, and she reached for my hand, and I said, "Youch!" and then I felt like a jerk for the six-hundredth time since I'd arrived thirty-seven minutes before.

The boy, Dean, turned around now. He nodded toward me. One of the guys. That's right. He'd seen my hardhat and my work boots, and he probably thought I was a lesbian.

"Dean, this is Carrie," Greta said.

And Dean said, so quietly I almost couldn't hear him, looking at his lap when he said it, "I know."

I died a little bit. I drank, huge gulps, to keep myself alive. The music pounded, and I could barely hear Greta and Dean. Soo's mom opened the basement door and called, "Turn it down!" but we ignored her.

"I'd tell you to shake hands," Greta was saying to Dean, "but I don't think she can."

"I'm not contagious," I said, twirling my fingers in front of his face and then hating myself for that, too.

"I didn't think so," he said. "It's national Michael Jackson Day, right?" And he smiled, and the whole world cracked open, and then he seemed to think better of the smile and took it back and sat up a little straighter on the couch and looked at his own, gloveless, hands. He was turning on and off like a variable star, its brightness increasing and fading. And then the smile leaked out again and he put his hand up to his hair, his glorious stringy hair, all a mess and tangled and beautiful, and then he put it down again. He had pale freckles all over his arms and a light dust of soft-looking dark hair and he had a little bit of bike grease wedged under his fingernails, and if he could see beneath the thin cotton of my gloves he would see the same smiles of dirt caked under mine, too. Dirty fingernail twins. We had so much in common. I took another huge gulp of beer. My body was full of beer, so full I could just float away.

"Do you want a drink?" Greta asked him. She was making her exit. She was leaving me alone with him. I loved her and I hated her. Go away. Don't leave.

"Nah," he said. "I don't drink. Anymore."

"Okay," Greta said, unaffected by this announcement. "Carrie, you want another one?" she asked as she stood up.

The beer in my hand suddenly seemed like it was on fire.

He didn't drink. He was hanging out with these people and not drinking. How was such a thing possible? I put the beer on the table and it spilled a little bit. It was on my hands. My hands would smell like beer. I shook my head. Greta left. It was Dean. And me. Alone. Alone-ish, anyway. Tommy was swaying, off-beat, to the rhythm, watching us.

"I have a question," I said, immediately regretting my announcement.

"You're in luck," he said. "I have an answer."

"Oh, well, right. So . . . How come you don't drink?" The music was so loud—the Replacements' "Sixteen Blue"—that I could barely hear myself.

"Um," he said, looking at his hands again. "Stuff. Things."

"Oh." Okay, he wasn't going to tell me. That was fine. Tightlipped. Who was I, anyway? He didn't know me.

He shifted his body toward me now, just a little bit, and I squirmed and adjusted my shirt, I pulled it down a little bit and the lacy top of my bra peeked out and I didn't fix it. I crossed my right leg over my left and bounced it a little on there. No drink, no protection, but my body was leaning toward his, involuntarily.

"I kind of screwed some shit up when I drank."

"Oh." What was wrong with me? Was "Oh" all I could say? What did "screw shit up" mean? What was he talking about? How could he have a good time without drinking? I hated drinking. Why couldn't I not drink?

"Don't worry," he said, and now it was he who put his hands in the air, like I was sticking him up. "I'm not contagious." And he smiled again. And then the shyness overtook him again and he put his hands down and opened his mouth like he was going to say something and then thought better of it, and the same thing was happening to me. We were opening and closing our mouths like fish in water, like fish out of water. It was so uncomfortable and it was so alluring and it was too much. It was almost as bad as the poison, the anger. I felt like I was going to vomit.

"Oh shit," I said, and ran to the bathroom and slammed the door shut and the whole Genesee beer ball came tumbling out of me. I sat by the toilet, defeated, deflated, empty. Soo came in and quickly shut the door behind her.

"Don't say it," I told her. "I know I drink too much." I had that headache I always got from alcohol and I had just ruined my chances and that boy would probably never talk to me again. I laid my whole body down on the cold tile floor and kicked my legs and shook my head back and forth with enough velocity to give me whiplash and I let out some kind of crazy curdled sound that even I could barely hear over the music. I let the fit take over me.

Soo said, "Shhh, it's okay." She took a lock of my hair and put it behind my ear and that was probably the nicest thing that had happened to me in my life since my mom took off. She kept her hands on me until my body calmed down, until I could release the crying.

I stood up and looked in the mirror, cringing at what I saw. Whenever we went around and played the what-movie-star-do-you-look-like game, no one could ever name someone for me. I wanted to be Ally Sheedy, but I wasn't. My eyes were red, drunk-looking, and even with the alcohol out of my system, I felt tipsy and poisoned and poisonous.

I walked out of the bathroom, hanging my head in shame. A familiar beat was pounding. Dean was standing next to the turntable, holding the sleeve of *Thriller*. Dean had put Michael Jackson on. But he didn't look up. Or at least, if he did, I didn't see him, because I walked out without saying goodbye to anyone and went home. I'd be back long before my curfew, riding my bike in the misty night.

My father, perpetually the science teacher even during summer break, was reading a book by the physicist who used to consult on *Star Trek* and *Doctor Who* called *Black Holes and Other Mysteries of the Universe*. I loved that book. He sat in the living room, his glasses perched on the tip of his nose. He'd aged a thousand years since Ginny died.

"This came for you," he said, handing me an envelope that smelled sharply of caraway seeds, as had the others in the last three months. His face bore no reaction.

"Oh," I said. Beside him sat the other envelope, addressed to Rosie and, I knew, filled with rosemary seeds. I could imagine the garden my mother had harvested them from out there on the chilly mountaintop monastery. There was never enough sun here for her to grow her herbs. The wild ginger fared okay in the shade, and her pots of mint sort of limped along, but the rosemary she tried to cultivate failed to prosper, and I supposed she just couldn't look at those wilting, browning needles anymore after Ginny was gone. What was left of her attempts were a few unruly bushes at the front of the house.

"You're not going to open it?" he asked.

That sharp, nutty smell made me recall the whole thing over again: the day Ginny died, the way she died, the subsequent implosion of my family, my mother fleeing to her "temporary meditative retreat" so she could hide among the herbs and vegetables and flowers and cold stone walls instead of people. "I hate people," she'd said to me once, when I found her crying on the floor of her closet. She, like my father, loved stars, the sky, the immutable sun and all its nuclear power. She loved plants and the science of cooking. Since our first family trip to the Hayden Planetarium in New York City when I was five and I had flipped out (in a good way— *We're on a ball hurtling through space and forever circling a ball of fire while a giant rock is forever circling us*), they had plied me with all this information about the universe and its workings. Then they had dumped me here on Earth. I shook my head and started up the stairs.

"Nah," I said. "I know what's in it. And I don't actually like the way they taste. Maybe you guys should have named me cinnamon. Now, there's a spice."

This totally weird and foreign thing called a smile crept onto my father's face. "Thank you," he said.

I scrunched up my nose at him, skeptical. "For what?"

He lifted his book back up, done looking at me, done trying for the night. "For coming home."

Chapter 5

FOR A TREAT, WE WERE HAVING TOOL LESSONS. Lynn, of course, really saw this as a gift as he strewed warped pine boards, screws, drills, screwdrivers, and hammers over the lawn in front of the park offices. He held the items up one by one, asking if we knew what they were. I, unsurprisingly, did not know the name of an unwieldy-looking piece of equipment with a round blade and terrifying-looking curved teeth.

"It's a circular saw," Tonya called out gleefully.

Well, I couldn't judge Tonya for knowing this. My idea of a good time used to be similarly nerdy, involving peering into a telescope for an embarrassingly long time.

Lynn passed out screws to each of us so we could feel them, hold their weight in our hand, he said. "There's not going to be a test, but I'd like you to familiarize yourself with the different sorts of screws." The drywall ones were thin and had flat heads, larger than the others. There was a wood screw, a deck screw, and what he called a self-countersinking screw. Whatever that was, I probably needed it. Or maybe I *was* it.

He explained that he had a particular fondness for drywall screws, not just because they were inexpensive but because, contrary to popular belief, they could be gentle on wood. But if you were screwing two pieces of wood together, he cautioned, you should always go with a wood screw. He said this with all the authority of a parent, as if cautioning us not to take candy from strangers. As if he were preparing us for life.

First we would practice the simplest of tasks: hammering nails into wood. What could be so hard about that?

Almost immediately, I whacked my left index finger with the hammer.

"Jeesh!" I said, lifting my hand up to blow on it.

"First thing to know is to get your hand out of the way," Lynn said.

"I'll be sure to violate the laws of nature next time so the nail can stand on its own."

"Just tap it a tiny bit, applying some pressure," he said, demonstrating. "And then hold it nearer the bottom and give it a couple of solid, but not wild, whacks." His went in with two pounds of the hammer.

"You have arms like the Hulk," I said. "It might take me more than a couple."

"Just keep trying," he said. And I did. After three nails, I sort of kind of did it okay, even though my index finger was throbbing.

Then we worked on drilling the screws into wood, and after

that, we each took turns, under heavy supervision, with the circular saw. Except that Tonya was so good at it that she became the heavy supervision.

"You ready?" she asked Jimmie, who nodded meekly as she fired it up. Poor Jimmie—he was even less likely to have a girlfriend than I was a boyfriend. "Slow and steady," she said, gliding his hands forward.

When it was my turn, I put on my protective eyewear, which was giant on my tiny head, and I had to step on a wood block to get the right height. "I don't need help," I said to Tonya, but it was pretty terrifying when I flipped the switch on this giant monster of a tool that ate its way so quickly through a solid piece of wood. It seemed to be moving without me and then I kind of got the hang of it, gliding it across the wood until I reached the other side. I felt this terrible, embarrassing thrill that I immediately wanted to discard.

"Rye Bread, what are you *doing?*" I heard Tommy's voice calling. He had apparently decided to drive by at this inopportune moment. The benefit of not having to work.

I ignored his fading cackle until he'd driven away. Then I put the saw down and announced, "I'm done."

Later we moved on to what Lynn called "leveling the ground," but I was pretty sure it was ditch digging, whacking at mounds of black soil. We were back on the path between the calcium deposit and the observatory, a path so worn and eroded that it turned into muddy slush anytime it rained.

"The best time to work with the earth is when it's slightly moist," Lynn told us. "Not too dry, not too wet." To demonstrate, he inserted the end of the shovel into a mound of dark dirt and hoisted it up, shushing the dirt off gently toward the tree line. "We are truly blessed today, because even though it hasn't rained, there's enough moisture in the air to loosen the soil."

"Praise the loam!" I said, but only Tonya — ever a fan of earth science — chuckled. What was it about boot camp that made me so unfunny? Tonya resumed her look of superiority. "So, Lynn, why is it better if the soil's moist? Wouldn't it be easier if it was dry?" I said this skeptically, as if I didn't believe Lynn, as if, with my grade-ahead-in-science brain, I understood more about the particles of soil than a psychologist-plus-youth-construction-chain-gang leader.

"It's the same as a blender," Lynn said placidly. "You need some moisture to allow it to move. It gets compacted when dry and too heavy when wet." He paused. "Does that answer your question, Caraway?"

"Completely," I said. I could somehow feel Tonya rolling her eyes.

"Troops, fall out," she called as she assumed her position, hovering over the shovel, raising her right foot to press the shovel's mouth deep into the perfectly moist soil.

Tonya was especially adept at this work and not particularly approving of my tendency to lean on my shovel and watch her. She made mechanical, almost rhythmic movements, the shushing sound of the shovel going in and the maraca-like cascade of the dirt falling off it. But when I took up my own shovel and tried to do the same, barely any dirt graced the end of it. I had to practically jump on it to get it below the surface of the dirt, and then it took all my strength to push it through and get a half shovel's worth of the soil. Apparently this was very entertaining, as several of the other kids had temporarily suspended operations to watch me wrestle a shovel.

"I'm like a foot shorter than the rest of you," I said.

"Nothing to see here, folks," Tonya called out.

"This does not seem legal."

Tonya responded to my observation with a snort. "This is your *job*."

"Not by choice," I replied, to which she just shook her head. Well, add her to the list of people I'd disappointed. She looked over at Kelsey and Jimmie, who were having a contest to see who could shovel the most dirt.

By the time Lynn came over to inspect my work, I'd already given up. I was leaning against my shovel, inhaling the sharp scent of pine needles and the cloudy smell of dirt circulating through the air.

"Caraway," Lynn said, hands on thighs, half crouching to get down to my height, "I know this is hard work, but there are ways to appreciate it. Doesn't it feel good to be actually contributing something to the world?" I managed not to point out that our contribution was digging—in some ways the opposite of a contribution. A subtraction. "Doesn't the weight of the shovel just feel so good in your hands?"

"Not really," I said. "My hands have leprosy." I held them up to show him the still-scarred skin. Two of my calluses had sloughed off, though I had to admit that the occasional application of jewelweed seemed to be helping.

I could see I was wearing him down, that his optimism was eroding much as this path had, and it gave me a rumble of satisfaction inside. I could make anyone hate me. Maybe I sucked at construction work, but my power to alienate was intact.

But for some reason I picked up the shovel and I thrust it into the ground where it filled with that dark, sparkly soil, soil made of elements that had been here since the dawn of Earth, and then I hoisted it out and deposited it onto the growing mound. And, okay. It did feel kind of good. But it wasn't like I was going to say that.

When I called Soo later in the week, her voice sounded faraway and sad. Boy trouble, I figured, and braced myself for listening to the boring details.

"Who died?" I asked. "It's awful quiet over there."

"Nobody died," she said. "We're just sworn to silence like a bunch of monks. We're going to stop being teenagers and become monks."

"I have no idea what you're talking about," I said.

Soo's mother had declared a moratorium on the basement until we swore to be quieter so she could hear the full romantic bass of Ricardo Montalban's accent when she watched reruns of *Fantasy Island*. This had happened earlier in the week, on one of those nights when I was sequestered in my room.

"What are we going to do?" I asked. "Piece of Toast can't live without its practice space."

"Not funny," said Soo. "We're going to soundproof the basement."

"What does that entail?" I picked some dirt from my fingernails and rubbed the spot on my nail that was beginning to turn black.

"We're getting all this foam stuff that we're going to install."

"And who's supposed to actually do that?" I asked. "I don't remember any of us actually having skills other than guitar playing. And even Tommy can't really do that."

In a way I was glad a construction project was going to preempt our normal hangouts. I didn't want to see Dean again after that night. I mean, of course, I wanted to see him again. I just didn't want him to see me. I wanted to see him if I could place a few droplets of some memory-loss serum into his nonalcoholic drink so he'd forget my special hugging session with the toilet.

"You are," Soo said. "Aren't you a construction worker now?"

"I failed the shovel test," I said.

"Just joking. Dean is super handy. He's going to the hardware store to get all this stuff, and he's going to show us what to do."

"Oh," I said. "Well, you guys have fun."

"*Us,*" Soo said. "You're coming too."

And that's how I came to park my bike in front of Soo's on Saturday morning, next to the five cars in the driveway: Soo's mom's Pontiac Firebird convertible (the one we'd taken out and driven around with the top down on several nights after Soo's mom was "asleep," aka passed out), Soo's Le Car, Tommy's BMW, Tiger's Volkswagen Rabbit, and a dusty old green Jeep that I didn't recognize. Well, I almost didn't recognize it. Its form was vaguely familiar — I'd seen it behind our fence.

The gang was gathered in the basement, staring at a giant bucket of something called Noiseproofing Blue Glue and a bunch of big, floppy sheets of foam. I pretended not to notice the presence of the world's most beautiful boy, but then the beautiful boy started explaining the principles of soundproofing, because the world's most beautiful boy was also handy, which made him even more beautiful.

"So, in the ideal world, we'd install additional fiberglass insulation, preferably with a higher R-value" he was saying. Tiger and Tommy nodded as if they were actual men who understood what Dean was saying. "But I don't think Soo's mom wants us to expose to the studs, and we probably can't decouple the drywall, so we're just going with damping the sound."

"So, just pour some Coke on it?" I asked. He was forced

to look at me, a confused smile taking over his face. "You said 'damp' it, right?"

Oh, crap. I was once again in the flat-joke zone. I wanted to hide in the walls with the low-level R-value, or whatever he'd said.

"Mountain Dew would probably work better, but in the meantime I was gonna go with putting this up to absorb the sound," he said, holding up a layer of the charcoal-colored foam. "So, we have to apply this compound over the walls, hold the foam in place with a staple gun. We also have to do the door— we have to put a layer of MDF over it with the blue glue sandwiched in between."

Maybe we needed Tonya to get this done. Or someone who spoke Dean's language?

"So, yeah, we should do it in twos," Dean said. "Um, Greta, why don't you and Tiger do the back wall—you can apply the glue and Tiger can do the stapling."

"That's such a girl's job," said Greta. "I can use a staple gun."

"Okay, you staple, he'll glue. And Justin and Soo can start on the stereo wall."

"It'll probably take half the day just to take the records off the shelf," Soo said.

"It'll be worth it, babe," Justin said. I refrained from the fake vomit sound this time.

"So what should Carrie and I do?" Tommy asked. Shit. Crap. I was not getting picked for the right kickball team.

"Oh, well, Carrie's going to help me with the door," Dean said. We must have suddenly jolted three light years closer to the sun because my whole face turned hot. "You're the floater."

Tommy's face melted into some form of disagreeableness. "That doesn't sound like a good job."

"Oh, it's the most important job," Dean said. "Everybody needs you. Go over and help Greta and Tiger first."

"I've been told you're the only one who knows how to use a hammer," he whispered to me as Tommy walked away. Which only made my face hotter and redder, and then I was embarrassed that my face was red and hot, and it got worse. I was the color of a red supergiant star.

I showed him the expanding splotch of blackness on my fingernail. "If using a hammer means hurting myself with it, then, yes. I'm an expert."

Everyone else moved away to do their jobs, but Dean and I just stood there not looking at each other. It felt like the moment lasted all 31,557,600 seconds that it takes to get around the sun in a year, and for a minute, I didn't know if I was actually there or not. I was so uncomfortable I might have actually evaporated. Then Dean said, "So, um, you want to grab that bucket of glue and I'll take the boards?"

"Yeah," I said. My voice cracked. Wonderful.

I went to grab the glue but I still had my backpack on and it tumbled off me, all its contents spilling out. Dean bent down to help me gather my things as I rushed to get them back, but before I could grab it, he took the opened notebook, with its Vira memorabilia exposed.

"What's this?" he asked.

"Ummmmm," I said. "My notebook?"

"Yeah, it's your notebook," he said. "What's in it?"

"Well," I said. Then—what the hell, I'd already pretty much thrown up in front of him: "These are my calculations. I'm charting the progress of the Vira comet."

"What is that?"

"Oh, um, you know that we're going to see the comet this summer for the first time in ninety-seven years, right?"

"I may have not read the paper the day they announced that," he said.

"So, yeah, the first sighting of it was in the third centry. That same thing has been circling the sun—well, not exactly in a circle but in an ellipse—for hundreds of thousands of years."

Please, would my mouth stop opening and closing?

"You're really into astrophysics, huh?" he asked, putting my wallet and my hairbrush into the backpack.

"Well, I think it's too late for me to pretend to not be." I zipped up the bag and stood up again, hoping we could start soundproofing and stop elaborating on my nerd-dom. We walked up the basement steps to the door. Dean took the hard plastic top of the bucket and gave me a thick paintbrush. The glue was a terrifying shade of electric blue. "Is this going to kill my brain cells?"

"Don't worry about it. You've clearly got plenty," he said. He started taping around the sides of the door so glue wouldn't get on the frame. "So, what do you love about astrophysics?"

"Oh my god, everything." So much for not elaborating. "What's not to love?"

"That's not that helpful an answer for a science-free brain like mine. My brain likes English lit. Ask me anything about Shakespeare and I can tell you, but biology? All I remember is placebo."

"You mean a paramecium. Or an amoeba?"

"See?"

I started slathering the glue on the door. Naturally I got more glue on my shoes than on the door. "Tell me a quote from *Macbeth*," I said.

"What?"

"You said ask you anything about Shakespeare. That's the only play I could think of."

"You couldn't go with something easy like *Hamlet*— 'To be or not to be'?"

"You said anything." I glued up around the corners of the door, too thick and drippy, but Dean didn't seem to mind.

"Oh. Okay. Um, 'Yet do I fear thy nature. It is too full of the milk of human kindness to catch the nearest way.'"

"Very impressive," I said. "What the heck does it mean?"

"Um, it means that Lady Macbeth is worried that her husband is too nice to take hold of the crown. She thinks he needs to be a worse human being." He didn't look at me as he said this, just kept taping as he asked, "Can you answer my question now?"

"Okay," I said. I turned toward him. "Here's the thing that is so totally mind-blowing. Are you ready?" He nodded, looking happily skeptical. "This is kind of just a physics thing in general, but we are all made of the same atoms, the same molecules—"

"What's the difference between an atom and a molecule?"

"Well, an atom has a nucleus with some protons and neutrons and maybe some electrons."

"Right, right," Dean said, joke-pretending to understand, rubbing his chin in a faux-intellectual way and allowing his mouth to curve into a smile.

"And a molecule is kind of when two or more atoms bond together. Right?"

"Right," he said again, still smiling, which made it hard to keep looking him in the eye.

"The coolest thing is that we're all made of atoms from old stars that died or exploded. They've just been recycled over and over again into different shapes."

The skeptical look remained on his face, along with the smile, as he tested the foam to see if it was sticking. "So a cow may once have been a dinosaur?"

"Sort of," I said. "That dinosaur decomposed and went back into the soil and broke down into nitrogen and such and nourished a cow two hundred million years later. We're all just star stuff, packaged over and over again." I swallowed. I hadn't been expecting the threat of tears. "And that's why, sometimes, I feel like someone who died is still kind of here. I almost feel her here."

"Her?" Dean asked.

"Or—anyone. It's weird, I know. It's not like I believe in ghosts or anything."

"It's not weird," Dean said. "Or—it's not *that* weird."

"I just sometimes feel that person's presence because I know her atoms are all around."

"It's not weird," he said again, and I sort of had this feeling that he wanted to put his arm around me, and my shoulder touched his shoulder, and then Tiger came up and inspected what we'd done, and said, "Very nice work, kiddos. But ours is sort of falling apart."

Dean left to help Tiger and Greta, and in came the floater. Tommy walked up the stairs. I'd finished the layer of glue and now was working on affixing the MDF board over the door, but I was way, way too short for that.

"Let me help you with that, little lady," Tommy said.

"Give it a rest, Tommy."

But I did have to let him help me align the top of the board to the door and hold it in place while I grabbed the drill.

"I'll do that," Tommy said.

"That's okay."

"No, really, let me."

"Fine," I said, handing him the blue Makita. Tommy may have had a BMW, but Dean had his own drill. "That's not the right screw, Tommy. That's drywall. You need wood."

"Oh, right," he said, swapping out the screw and trying to drill it into the wood, but it rolled around and eventually dropped to the floor.

"I'll do it," I said. For once in his life, Tommy said nothing. I stood on my tippy toes on the top step to reach the top of the door, and Tommy stood on a step behind me, pressing against the board to hold it in place. I could feel his breath on my neck, and maybe because it was familiar, it activated something in me. I felt stoned by proxy, even though I hadn't had anything since I'd emptied my stomach contents in the bathroom the week before. I felt turned on in some way that also disgusted me, but that was pretty much my relationship with Tommy.

Tommy put his head close to mine. "You know he's crazy, right?" he whispered.

I stopped drilling. "What? Who?"

"You know," he said. "Dean. He's crazy."

I turned around, the drill in my hand. Tommy's face was very close to mine, his almost handsome, stupid face. I literally could have killed him. Or kissed him.

"You guys good up there?" Dean called.

"I think your expertise is needed," I said, still staring at Tommy, hoping to maim him with my non-dilated pupils.

Dean came up the stairs slowly. Tommy didn't turn around or move out of the way or even stop staring at me until Dean said, "I got it, buddy," and slowly, Tommy descended the stairs. He kept looking at me, backing up, until he semi-tripped at the end and pretended he'd meant to do that.

Dean either didn't notice or pretended that he was enthralled with the quality of my drilling, which did seem to have improved since earlier in the week.

"This looks good," he said. "I think we're pretty much done."

"Oh. We're done? Oh. Okay."

"Yeah, we just have to wait for it to dry."

"Oh. Okay. So."

"Yeah."

"I guess we should test it to see if it works," Dean said. "You guys, cue something up loud, and Carrie and I will go upstairs and see if we can hear it." Oh.

Someone put on the Violent Femmes, and Dean and I stood outside the door. "Well, okay, it's not the world's best sound-proofing job," he said. We could still hear the lyrics — *just kiss off into the air*. "But it's a great song."

"This album is just one really good song after another," I said.

"I know, man, I know," Dean said. He'd called me man. Obviously I was too good with a drill.

"So, yeah, I gotta get to work," he said.

What could I say to that? I shrugged and raised my eye-brows, some combination of "Whatever" and "What the hell?" The Violent Femmes sang *Good feeling, won't you stay with me* just as Dean turned to go.

Chapter 6

AND THEN, FOR SOME REASON, I HATED my job 12 percent less. We had now cleared and weeded and leveled the path, so we had to install concrete piers that the wooden slats of our footbridge would rest on.

"This is a three-hundred-foot bridge, so we're talking a pier on each side every three feet. That's around two hundred of these things, laid out perfectly," Lynn said. "It's ambitious, but then again, so are you." Even Tonya seemed a wee bit annoyed by that one.

Lynn had pulled his tan pickup truck full of one-foot concrete piers to the side of the creek and opened the flatbed.

"You guys ready to earn your stripes?" he asked, which was apparently some sort of rallying cry that actually inspired my compatriots in misadventure. "Yes!" the kids said. Perhaps the program had worked, and all of them, save for me, were already reformed.

"Do the stripes come in hundred-dollar-bill form?" I asked.

Lynn said he would push each concrete pillar to the end of

the flatbed and two of us would lower it down to the ground, then roll it to the selected spot along the path. "You and Tonya work together," he said.

I said, "Oh, great," but forced my lips into a smile when she shot me a look.

"The important thing is to use your legs, not your back," Lynn said as he stood above us, the cylinder of concrete poised and ready to come to us.

"I'm trying to think about where else in life I can apply that advice," I said to him.

"This is not a joke," said Tonya. She had one side of her body braced against the truck, ready for her concrete present to descend. "You can really hurt yourself."

"Okay, okay, fine," I said. "Let it rain."

"On three," she said, bending her knees as she placed her hands beneath the concrete block. I did as she did, without bending my knees. She glared at me.

"I'll be fine," I said. "I come from a long line of laborers."

"Huh, that's not what I remember," she mumbled. Then, "One, two, three."

We hoisted the block, and indeed, there was a sharp streak of complaint from my back.

"Ow," I said. "It must have really hurt to build the pyramids."

"Not as much—they all lifted with their legs and not their backs," Tonya said. "Now roll."

We placed the cylinder on its side and rolled it, or tried to roll it, but my back was calling out to me with each move I made.

"Pull your weight, wacko," she said. Did she really mean that, or was it just one of her many nonadorable pet names for her co-workers? Surely she knew. Surely word had gotten to her of the therapist and my dad plotting against me to lock me up, the screaming in the street and cursing, my late-night stumbles home, picked up by the police for curfew, the stomach pumping, and the thing with Rosie. Surely she knew.

We rolled the cylinder over the rough grass as I checked to make sure it was a wild-parsnip-free zone. Finally we made it to the first spot, that shallow black hole of earth.

"Now move the bottom over so we can slide it in."

"What side is the bottom?" I asked.

"The side that says 'bottom.' Some genius."

"I never said I was a genius."

"Yes, you did."

"When?"

"In Mr. Carson's class."

"Wait—Mr. Carson? You mean earth science? First semester freshman year?"

"Yes." Tonya had her arms folded now, and one foot atop the cylinder to keep it from slipping.

"We were in that class together?"

"I hope this is a joke," she said, and then, realizing that it wasn't, "We were lab partners? We did the model of three faults in the earthquake unit?"

I smiled. "Yes, I remember it. Sort of. I was high throughout the entire thing."

Some fuzzy version of a memory returned to me—not so much of Tonya but of the metric ruler and the physiographic map of the world, with its wonderful contours that made me psyched to be on Earth for once instead of staring at it from a billion light years away. It had been a long time since I'd felt that way. First semester freshman year was the beginning of the end.

"And yet you still got an A, am I right?"

I shrugged.

"You seem to be totally unaware that you're leading a blessed life."

I bent down again, my back screeching as I moved Tonya's leg and positioned the concrete cylinder, then slid it into the spot. "Thank you, Reverend, for that inspiring sermon."

Lynn primed us in using bullet levels—adjust the pier until the air bubble rests in the center of the pocket of water—to show us when the concrete piers were perfectly flat on the ground. But since they were in sets, they also had to be the same height as each other.

"You might be doing some digging and tamping, or building

up a bit under another pier," Lynn said. "This is about perfection."

Luckily my partner in perfection was Tonya, who was an absolute whiz with a bullet level and a concrete pier.

"Carrie, that is definitely not straight," she said, looking at the level; the bubble had floated over to the left side.

Magically, Lynn appeared. "She's right, Caraway. You know, none of this will work if you don't do your part. It's up to all of us."

I sighed, but I went ahead and took my concrete pier off and tamped down the dirt below it and placed it back and used all the force of my five-foot frame and my now completely angry back to set it in place. Then I checked the level again.

"See?" asked Tonya. "Was that so bad?"

It was not.

"Now we just have to do a hundred more."

For some reason, I kind of didn't mind.

Riding home in the afternoon down the Avenue of the Pines, my muscles sore, the most unusual feeling came over me, some strange smile that crawled out all on its own. Even in my work boots, my hardhat strapped to the back of my bike with the bungee cord, I sort of felt like the skies over my head were clear, despite the bit of cloud cover that had rolled in.

Then I saw Tommy's BMW coming toward me; he somehow

seemed to be in the park whenever I was. He stuck his hand out the window and called, "Nice hardhat, Rye Bread."

He was gone too fast for me to come up with a witty retort, but I felt enough shame that I forgot to keep my head down, and when I looked up toward the dark canopy of white pine trees that laced together, I saw it. The cross. Tiger had climbed up that tree and nailed it to a low-hanging branch, so it was almost watching over that spot. The white cross.

My front wheel wobbled and twisted in front of me, so fast and so strong that I had no chance to right it, and I just toppled onto the pavement, almost into the road, cars honking. My side scraped, I sat there stunned for a minute as a beige pickup truck pulled over.

"You okay there?" Lynn said, hopping out.

"I'm okay." I stood up and dusted myself off. It stung a little on my right side, but I was more shocked—and embarrassed—than hurt.

"Let me drive you home," he said.

"I can do it." But when I mounted the bike, it wouldn't move. The chain was gnarled, the wheel bent. "Okay," I said. "I can't do it."

Lynn loaded the bike into the back, which was messy with kid toys and gardening equipment, and I told him where I lived. "The steerage-class section of town," I said, and he replied, "There are much worse parts of town than that."

His car smelled a little bit like wood chips. On the dashboard he had a psychology textbook with a bookmark sticking out of it. We bumped along in silence. A photograph of a baby dangled from his rearview mirror.

"Yours?" I asked.

He nodded. "Mine. Though now I have two. I've been too busy with school and work and changing diapers to put a picture of Oscar up there."

"I love that name," I said. I had babysat a kid named Oscar before I was robbed of my career, and I thought about the kid at two, screaming in delight as I pushed him on the swing. I used to love kids. Heck, I used to love Rosie. "Oscar the Grouch was my favorite character on *Sesame Street*," I told Lynn.

"Why does that not surprise me?"

I don't know why that hurt me. My face sort of puckered, and when Lynn glanced at me, he seemed to regret it. What, was I supposed to like Big Bird the best? Who liked Big Bird?

Lynn pulled in front of my house, indifferent, it seemed, to its peeling paint or the sloping front porch. I turned to him and looked for a sec: the strong profile, the big hands, the stoicism —all that my dad was not.

"I'm not an asshole," I said.

He got out of the car and took my bike out. Then he took a deep breath and looked at me, and I hated that look. What was that look? Pity, maybe. Therapist look? I hated therapists. Maybe it was the look of drippy, fake understanding. He nodded and leaned my bike against the porch and raised his hand up and squeezed my shoulder lightly and said, "I know that. It's you who has to learn it."

I took my boots off by the front of the house and stashed the hardhat by the front door before I carried my bike into the yard. I ran upstairs and showered and changed into my cut-up T-shirt and cutoffs, and then I went into the yard barefoot with my guitar and tried to sing that Velvet Underground song—*I'll be the light on your door to show that you're home*—but that last layer of post-wild-parsnip peeling had taken my hard-earned calluses away and it hurt. I sat there holding on to my guitar, waiting, waiting, until I heard the clicking sound of Dean's Jeep arriving at Mrs. Richmond's. Then I forced myself to pluck a few notes despite the pain.

After a few minutes, Dean peered over the fence and said, "Hey," with a nod of his head. Major nonchalance.

"Hey," I said, hoping he couldn't hear my heartbeat from way over there. I twisted my lips up and started nodding for no reason and looked out of the corner of my eyes, and there had to be something to say—something. What could I say?

"Hey, um, Dean?"

"Yeah?"

I screwed up the courage to look at him. "Can you fix my bike?"

* * *

I sat on the steps and played guitar, ignoring the pain, while he worked his magic with a wrench and a chain checker and a tire lever and a bottle of WD-40. I was pretty terrible with a hammer but, man, did this guy know how to use an Allen key — whatever that was. It was a sight to behold.

He'd brought over two cups of coffee from his house. "You want?" he asked.

The truth was that I had never had coffee. I'd had eleven different kinds of alcohol and I'd fooled around with seventeen guys, but I'd never had a cup of coffee.

"Sure," I said.

"It's black — that okay?"

"Perfect," I said. After my first sip, I could only describe it as bitter mud.

"I love coffee," he said. "Especially when it's hot out."

"Yeah," I said, and maybe I did love it because he loved it, even though it was gross. Then what? Every couple of sentences we just seemed to stop, and I wanted it to keep going forever, and I also couldn't take another minute of it. I plucked notes on the guitar as best I could with my decrepit hands.

"So, I have a question," I said.

"You're in luck — I have an answer."

"So, like, what are you doing here?" I played a lick of a Violent Femmes song.

"You mean, besides fixing bikes?"

"Yeah. I mean, you live with Mrs. Richmond now?"

"Just for the summer," he said, spinning the wheel to see where it caught on the brakes. My heart descended into the bottom of my shoes. "My dad sent me to live with his sister while I get my shit together."

"Where do you live the rest of the time?" I didn't ask about what getting his shit together meant, or why he had to come here to do it.

"Oregon," he said. "Eugene. At least, if I go back to college in the fall, that's where I'll live."

If. If was the best word in the entire English language.

"I've only finished one semester," he said. "I'm not sure if they'll let me back in."

He started dismantling the whole rear section of my bike, and he must have seen the panic on my face. "Don't worry—I'm just working on the back rack," he said. As if that was why I was panicking. "So you can get that hardhat on there."

Once again, "Oh" was all I could muster. Die. I needed to die. What could I say? Yeah, I was sixteen, and I had a construction job because I was a screwup, and at some point, he was going to find that out. But what had *he* done?

"Just so you know, I did not want to spend my summer doing construction."

"What did you want to do?"

"Oh, well." He had me there. "Actually, I wanted to go to astronomy camp." Dean laughed. "I know," I said. "That's so nerdy."

"Oh, hell, no," he said. "That's super cool."

He said this casually, tossing off the words, perhaps not realizing that he had almost made me faint.

"So why didn't you go to astronomy camp?" He oiled the chain and pressed the pedals until the wheels started to move with ease. It was hard for me to continue the chitchat. I wanted to rewind, like a VHS tape, go back to that part where the cutest boy in the world, after hearing me say I wanted to go to astronomy camp, said that what I liked was cool. No—super cool.

"Oh, well. It was sort of—my dad wanted me to work instead." I couldn't get into it. There was so much to explain, and so much shame. Without my even realizing it, I'd started playing the guitar really loud, really hard.

"'Gone Daddy Gone,'" Dean said.

"Um, what?"

"'Gone Daddy Gone.' The song you're playing."

"Oh, right, yes. It's the only punk song with a two-minute-long marimba solo."

"Yes!" he said, so emphatically that I felt like I was going to fall off the steps. "Can you show it to me?"

"Wait—me, show you? Aren't you a musician?"

"Just a humble drummer," he said. "I figured since I was exiled here this summer, I'd learn more guitar." Exiled. A drummer. Long-haired. Handy. "Tiger says you're really good."

"*Tiger* said that?" I knew every note, but suddenly I had forgotten them all. I sat there for a minute, shocked, but in a good way, while he stood waiting for my answer. "Um, yeah. I can show you."

He sat down next to me, wiping his hands on his shorts and then taking up my guitar with the care and respect it deserved, which made me ache a little.

"Well, so, um, yeah, it has a funny chord progression." I arranged his fingers on the frets. "It's D suspended second, that's the hard-ish one," I said. One strand of his hair hung in front of his eyes, and I had to force myself not to clear it from his face. "Like this." I adjusted his fingers, nails slightly bitten with a curve of grease beneath them, and he strummed and the notes came tumbling out perfectly. He smelled of sweat and grease and cheap shampoo, and it was all so good. "Then this," I said, showing him the switch to B-flat second, and then the rest of the progression and the tricky fingering in the solo, which he totally couldn't get, so he handed the guitar back to me and watched, and the more he watched me, the more I stared hard at my guitar, unable to break my gaze from it. I got to the end of the song, and I still sat there, eyes frozen in the direction of that delicate curve of wood. The silence was like a presence, delicious and terrifying. I thought maybe he was moving toward me. Maybe that was his head getting closer to mine.

Then my dad's car pulled in, and he and Rosie got out and walked into the yard.

"Hello," my dad said, looking at Dean.

"This is Dean. He's fixing my bike," I said.

"Okay," Dad said.

"He lives over there," I said. "With Mrs. Richmond."

"I know he does." He did? "How are you?"

"I'm fine," Dean said. He was not apparently one of those parent charmers like Tommy, Mr. Suave, who said to my dad, *I'll be sure to keep your daughter safe,* and then two hours later, after plying me with drugs, laid me down on the football field for a night of debauchery. "How are you?"

"Good," my father said. Rosie watched us all, the awkwardness so present we could practically see it.

Dean turned to me. "I'm going to Soo's tomorrow." He paused. "If you want to come or something."

Rosie gaped and gawked and then she just started laughing, and I hated her so much. "She's grounded," she said.

Vomiting was an option for me at that point. So was fainting. Pummeling Rosie—well, but I couldn't even consider such a thing after what I'd done the year before.

"She can go to Soo's," my dad said, much to my shock.

"I can?" I asked just as Rosie said, "She can?"

My dad pulled a paper bag of groceries to his chest. "She can go to Soo's tomorrow if she's back by eleven sharp."

Chapter 7

I CALLED SOO THAT NIGHT, TELLING HER every detail of the afternoon, the way the sun glinted off the hair on his forearms and how strong his forearms were because he fixed bikes. He knew how to fix things. And he knew how to play guitar — mostly — and he knew how to play drums and he was going to be a sophomore in college next year except that he didn't know if he was going back to college. His perfect slightly flat, twangy voice. His smell.

"Good," Soo said. "It sounds good." But she seemed hesitant.

"What?" I asked.

"I just don't want you to freak out again."

I hated it when she referred to that, the one time that I almost sort of went out with a boy, a dark-skinned boy in between my grade and Soo's named BJ, who was, amazingly enough, on the golfing team. I had just turned fifteen, and he came up to me one day and asked if I wanted to go out with him, so I said yes, and then a week later, we still hadn't spoken, on the phone or in person or anything. There was a dance that night and I asked if he was going and he said no and for some reason I said, "I hope you get hit by a car." In fact, as confusion settled into his brows and he turned to walk away from the science lab, where my flour-and-cocoa meteor model stood behind me, I started yelling, "I hope you die a terrible death." Soo held on to me as I screamed, shushing me and then walking with me from school over to the arcade and offering me a cigarette and distracting me with endless games of Ms. Pac-Man. But I wasn't really think- ing about what I'd said to BJ—I was thinking that day how I wouldn't have anyone to go to the dance with. How I would be alone, forever.

Then BJ came into the arcade and said, "I don't want to go out with you anymore," which was one of the only things he ever said to me—we had never even touched for a single second— and he said it right there in the middle of the arcade, the thrust- ing sounds of Space Invaders and Centipede his anti-serenade. I just slumped into a ball and cried. I cried so much that Soo had to pick me up off the floor and drag me to a payphone and call her mom to come pick me up. When she did, her mom let me sit in the front seat and gave me a beer and a cigarette and said, "Men—who needs 'em?" Even though she'd been married to Soo's father for a million years.

And when I couldn't recover, when I went plummeting into sobs, over and over again, saying how I didn't want to be alive anymore, they had to take me to the hospital and they pumped me full of something that made everything fuzzy and dull and they kept me there for a week, keeping me numb numb numb.

All I had to do was promise that I wouldn't hurt myself, that I wouldn't take drugs, that I wouldn't talk to that BJ boy, and they let me go. All I had to do was lie. It had nothing to do with BJ. It could have been anyone.

"I'm the only one who doesn't have a boyfriend," I said now. "When is it going to be my turn?"

"I don't know," Soo said. "Soon."

The next morning, I rode my bike to the enviro-boot camp so fast that I was the first one there. I had stayed up late, adding songs to a mix tape that, I didn't know, maybe I'd give to Dean someday — "September Gurls," the Pretenders, Billy Bragg, the Kinks' "Strangers" — and it was so still and silent when I arrived at the site: crickets and the rustling of the timothy grass. A red-winged blackbird landed on a jewelweed bush. I hooked my hammer into the loop on my pants and sat by the creek, following the muddy path with my eyes, the place where we'd be building the footbridge and saving the day. I had to admit it: I had grown fond of this spot, of the *Star Trek*-ish calcium deposit, its strange sulfuric smell, of being so close to the observatory even though I had not yet dared go in it; I'd only been there once since the night Ginny died.

That night was one of the few times when, instead of tagging along, I'd been leading the expedition, excitedly chattering about the lunar eclipse and selling it without too much nerdiness as "the whole sky's gonna turn dark in the middle of the day, and the moon will be blood-red."

I would have been perfectly happy to view the eclipse in my normal state of mind—not that that was particularly normal, of course—but Tommy had scored some acid, a harmless-looking sheet of purple tabs with white roses on them, smaller than stamps.

Tommy handed out the tabs. "Let it dissolve on your tongue," he said, eyebrows raised and a hint of smile that I guessed was some attempt at wooing me but which only made me stare at my shoes.

I did not want to do it. I tried so hard not to do it. And when I did it, I vowed I would never do it again, and I had kept that vow. But that night I kept saying, "Nothing's happening, nothing's happening," until, slowly, those shoes began to blur. Then the stone walls began to breathe.

Behind me, Greta started having a freak-out, cowering and shaking, and it seemed like every single boy there rushed to her side, one patting her hand and one stroking her hair and one kissing her gently on the cheek until she turned her face to kiss his mouth. That was usually the part where I sank into myself, shrank into a ball of jealousy and self-pity and confusion—where, oh, where was *my* boyfriend?—but that day I didn't. I could feel the shift begin above me, feel the moon pulling around us toward the path of the sun. I looked up, away from the spectacle of Greta and her pawing, gnawing suitors, away from Soo rubbing the breathing wall with her fingers and Tommy dancing with himself. I looked toward the darkening sky. I watched as the moon and sun collided, a black spot in the sky surrounded by a thin band of fire, and in that magical instant I could feel Ginny around me. Matter is always matter. Every cell, every molecule that made up her person was still here on Earth, or at least in Earth's atmosphere, or at least in our galaxy, or in our beautiful and mysterious universe of galaxies, or vanished into the oppositional gravity of a black hole. Nothing mattered here on Earth. Nothing mattered but the stars, my real friends, the source of all life and inspiration. In that moment, that seven minutes and thirty-one seconds of eclipse, my face turned toward the enormous rock in the sky and the source of all light mixed together, I felt completely at peace. There was no life and no death, and Ginny had never existed and always would. All the answers to the questions of life on Earth were in the stars above us, and I loved them as much as I'd ever loved anyone.

"Beautiful morning, isn't it?" asked Lynn, who had wandered up without making a sound. He sat down next to me and offered me a carrot stick.

"I'm good, thanks," I said. "I really overdid it on the carrot sticks yesterday. They're going right to my thighs."

He let out a small laugh as he opened a pint of milk and drank it down like a kindergartner.

"What do you think of that thing?" he asked, nodding toward the crazy-looking calcium deposit.

"Half beautiful, half hideous," I said, sort of describing myself. "Did you know that some supernovae are full of calcium?"

"I hate to say it, but I don't remember what a supernova is." He crunched on his carrots. "They don't talk about that when you're getting a psychology degree."

"An exploding star."

"I thought they were made of gas." He stood up and dusted off his pants.

"Most of them have every single element in the entire universe. That calcium deposit could be billions of years old — it could be made of the stuff that was present when the Earth was born. Is that the coolest, or what?" I figured with Lynn — himself not the embodiment of cool — this side of myself was safe.

He looked at me like he was trying to fit this information in with the person he'd already decided I was.

When the rest of the crew arrived, we started working on laying down the twelve-foot planks. We were supposed to make sure they were parallel and clamp them onto the piers. And then continue for ten thousand years until they were all laid out.

"Are we going to just do this over and over and over and over?" I said to Tonya, my perpetual partner.

"Yes, that's the job." She was chewing gum loudly, with her mouth open.

"This is the most monotonous thing I've ever experienced."

"Believe me, it's a lot less monotonous than your whining."

After we'd set the planks down on the piers, we were supposed to laminate them with an adhesive called Industrial Nail Gel, which Lynn cautioned us was sixteen times stronger than Krazy Glue.

"It's a kind of blue glue, so it washes off with water, but you don't want it to dry on your skin," he cautioned us. Blue glue. Who knew it would be making a repeat appearance in my life?

Tonya and I took turns gluing and clamping and pressing until we got to the edge of the creek. "I need a break," I said, and for once she didn't object. I sat down by the water's edge and I couldn't help it: I had those same poisonous thoughts that I'd had that day that I freaked out at the arcade. I didn't want to kill myself. I just didn't want to be alive.

"Tonya, Caraway," Lynn called, "come get the next one, then we'll have a break."

"Ooh, a break," I said. "Maybe that means we'll get celery sticks and a lecture about the history of concrete."

She tested the two planks to see if they'd set. "The history of concrete is actually pretty interesting," she said. "Don't you remember from chemistry?"

"Were we in chemistry together?" I sat on one of the blocks and lit a cigarette and watched her shift some of the other blocks we'd hauled into the perfect spots.

"Oh my god," she said. "You're incredible. Really."

"What?" I smiled. "I'm joking, Tonya. I remember. Sort of."

"And you're not allowed to smoke. And you are really bad at setting the clamp."

"Yikes," I said to her. "I'm not sure why they would give hammers to kids with anger management problems."

"I don't have anger management problems," she said, though her tone suggested otherwise.

"Then why are you here?" I asked her, sitting on the last bare pier and watching her toil, sweating profusely again from her brow and her armpits, her imitation Izod T-shirt a size too small, her shitkickers worn in as if she'd had them for seasons now. Maybe she had.

"Because it's a *job*." She looked at me as if I were an alien. Though we were in the same grade, we were universes apart. "It's just a summer job. You know that, right? This is voluntary?" She looked at me suspiciously.

I stood up and stamped out my cigarette. "But really it's boot camp for insubordinate youth," I said, trying to make it sort of a question or a joke in case I was wrong.

"But really it's not," she said. "It's a training program for young people to get skills that they can use in the work force later. It's more like vocational school . . ." She squinted as she said this, as if she was trying to gauge whether I was seriously ignorant or pretending. "There just aren't that many summer jobs."

"Right. Of course. Yeah." I remembered Tonya's house

again, the sad little bungalow with a screen door coming off at the hinges. Her grandmother had these milky blue eyes, always kind of faraway even when she trained them on you and smiled and made you feel guilty for being able to walk around and form words and feed yourself. Tonya always wanted to come to my house to play, and I always let her.

I came over and helped Tonya, testing the planks until I knew that all of them had set just right.

At lunch, I preempted Lynn's little lecture by saying, "Yes, Lynn, it's great to feel so hungry—and to have *earned* that hunger—and be nourished by these soap-tasting celery sticks." And this time even Tonya laughed. I sat down next to her and the other kids at the picnic table as I realized that I'd forgotten my sandwich. She shoved her little baggie of potato chips toward me.

"Even a jerk like you should be allowed to eat something that actually tastes good," she said. I took one. It was amazing. "Take another," she said, shoving them toward me. I did.

We crunched away in silence and then she said, "Who do you think you'll have for pre-calc next year?"

"I don't know," I said. "I hadn't thought about it."

"I hope not Mr. Zentz again. We know more about math than he does."

I stopped crunching and looked at her. "You had him for trig? What period?"

Tonya shook her head at me. "Is it possible you have amnesia?" She took the potato chips back.

"I was just joking."

"Something is wrong with you, Carrie." I couldn't tell if she meant it or not.

Somehow I made it through the workday, so grimy by the end that I could barely believe that there was a parallel universe in which I was going to hang out with Dean. I unlocked my bike as Tonya and some of the other kids walked by me, entranced by a discussion of future plans.

Tonya stopped in front of me. "We're going to the disco dance at Civic tomorrow night," she said. "It's basically punk covers of disco songs. Or maybe it's disco covers of punk songs?"

"Good for you," I said.

"You want to come?"

"Disco?" I said. "It sounds like an evening my parents would really enjoy." Well, if I had different parents.

"It's all ages," Jimmie said, all the sweetness of him and his skinny little body standing next to Tonya.

"Well, all my friends are over eighteen anyway," I said, curling my lock around my bike seat.

"Yeah, but you aren't," Tonya said. "You're in our grade."

What could I say to that? Wise beyond my years, but still, rather depressingly, a junior-to-be. I would stay behind in our silly school while my friends scattered across the land without me, fragile comet nuclei coming apart at perihelion, undone by the sun.

"Personally, I like disco," Jimmie said. Tonya was frowning at me.

"Sorry—no can do."

Tonya looked right at me and said, "Oh, well. You'll be missed."

I finished snapping my hardhat into the bike rack. "I will?"

Tonya took her hardhat off and tucked it under her arm, her hair molded into hat-head, and she seemed perfectly content with herself. She said, "No."

Chapter 8

DEAN PICKED ME UP. HE PICKED ME UP. My mind hiccupped over this fact. He drove that battered Jeep around the block from Mrs. Richmond's to the front of my house, parking it next to our total crapbox of a Buick Skylark that I still hadn't learned to drive. Rosie stood at the door and said, "I can't believe this is happening."

"Shut up," I hissed. Hundreds of times she'd seen me pile into the back of Tommy's fake-hippied BMW or Soo's Le Car or Tiger's Rabbit, but never had a young man pulled up to our front door to retrieve me for an actual date. My father sat behind us in that ridiculous flowered armchair. He didn't bother standing up. He just said, "Be home by curfew."

"Okay," I said, involuntarily smiling at him.

The screen door creaked as I pushed it open and walked down the steps as if this were an everyday occurrence. I had made out with strangers at the Holiday Inn, I had taken LSD, I had done disgusting things with boys before I turned fifteen, and by the end of last year, I was smoking two packs of cigarettes a week. But I had never been on a date.

Dean got out of the car and started coming up the stairs as I came down, and he sort of reached out for me but then didn't and I half smiled at him and then raised my eyebrows and I let out a little "ha." He looked straight ahead. This was going great.

Then he, um, he opened the door for me. "That's weird," I said, by which I meant, *Oh my god, he opened the door for me!* but somehow it came out the other way, which I realized was not particularly nice but apparently I had lost control of the sounds I was making. Then Dean got in his side and we sat in the idling car. We both just sat there. A couple of times he turned his head toward me and I thought he was going to say something. But then he didn't.

"I'm just letting the engine warm up," he said finally.

"Okay."

Rosie remained watching us at the door.

Dean smiled before he realized he was smiling and then he took it back and cleared his throat and put the car in reverse and backed out of my driveway. For some reason that act, pulling out of my driveway with the beautiful boy, felt like the most important thing—or at least the most important good thing—that had ever happened to me. Like I was stepping into, or maybe backing into, a new life.

"Will you listen to this song?" Dean asked, pushing a cassette into the tape deck. His face looked so hopeful, his eyebrows raised, waiting for my response. Oh, how I knew that feeling. My whole life, I'd been trying to get people to listen to good songs.

"Who is it?" I'd never heard it before: just the kind of slightly off-key, recorded-in-your-garage sound I loved.

"This band called the Brinks."

"It's really good."

"Thanks."

"It's you?" He nodded. I listened harder to the lyrics — *I did nothing but watch as you fell away* — as our little town passed by, the houses closer together as we headed toward downtown. "It's really good," I said again. "Who's it about?"

"Oh . . ." Maybe I didn't want to know. His Oregon love, waiting for him there on those rocky cliffs, or whatever it was they had out there. I was all twisted up, wanting to hear and yet dreading the story. "Just somebody from back home."

The next song came on, the Velvet Underground's "Jesus."

"One of the greats," I said. "For some reason I love songs about Jesus. Is that weird?"

"It is a little bit weird," he said. "But not Christian rock, right?"

"You don't like Christian rock? What? Let me out of the car this instant!" We both laughed, the turbulence starting to disappear from the air.

"To be honest, I have a little bit of a thing for Judas Priest," he said.

"Grody." I picked up the cassette case to see what else was on his mix tape: A little on the punk side for me — Minutemen and Black Flag, but also Hüsker Dü and Blondie and the Replacements and the Knack and Bob Dylan and Neil Young and the Beatles (of course) and one Grateful Dead song, "Uncle John's Band." A song so familiar from my childhood, the real childhood when my parents were together and my sister was alive. "There's no Judas Priest on here," I said.

"No," he admitted. "AC/DC, though."

"Of course AC/DC. You can't make a mix tape without AC/DC." He pressed the fast-forward button, stopping it occasionally to check until he came to "You Shook Me All Night Long." As he turned onto Broadway, the grumbling Jeep drifting down the wide street, we started singing along, both of us softly at first—kind of sacrilege to sing AC/DC softly—and then louder and louder, until we were screaming the words, the windows open, laughing, both of us staring straight ahead but letting go.

We had listened to Jimmy Cliff and the Modern Lovers and were discussing the merits of Lou Reed solo versus with the Velvet Underground when we saw Tiger walking along the road toward Soo's. To my tremendous disappointment, we pulled over.

"Where's your car?" Dean asked, ducking his head out the window.

"In the shop," he said. "Greta got a ride with Tommy."

"Well, get in," Dean said. I forced a smile. Yeah, get in.

"Hey, Carrie." Tiger climbed into the back. I could barely muster a "Hey" back. Did this make it not a date? It wasn't a date, no, of course, because who would ever date me? Dean probably opened the car door for every girl. "Thanks for the ride."

"Of course," I said, as if it were my car and as if I weren't desperately wishing it had an eject button.

Dean and Tiger talked about electric guitars (I had almost never used an amp and didn't really get the fascination with the Marshall Stack) and cool towns in Oregon (now my least favorite state), and they smoked Marlboros, and Dean handed his to me and I took a puff and handed it back. This, the tiniest act of intimacy, made me warm all over. Or maybe it was just the smoke.

When we walked into Soo's, Tommy called out to me, "Rye Bread, I saw you on your bike with a *hardhat!*" He put on "Le Freak" and started singing *geek out* instead of *freak out*. "I didn't know you were auditioning for the Village People."

I froze, wishing Dean wasn't there to see or hear this.

"Well, yeah, some of us have to work for a living" was my only retort. It was hard to make someone feel bad about driving a BMW, even a vintage one with a tapestry staple-gunned to the ceiling. I knew his parents had spent a bunch of money getting it restored and that the tapestry was just for show.

The truth was, none of them, except for Soo and Greta, had been inside my house, and only Soo really knew me, knew the star-loving nerd I was in, well, in my real life. Somewhere in this world, on the other side of the universe, my real life was taking place.

Dean went over to the stereo and put on the Village People's "YMCA."

* * *

The evening passed by much in the way it had for months, years: records and singing and playing music and drinking and drugs and boyfriends and girlfriends making out, with me occasionally taking my notebook from my worn leather backpack and jotting down lyrics or song ideas or recalculating to find the distance of Vira, now approaching some twenty-six million miles away. I was still in love with the way Lynn's pen felt in my hand —so what if he'd told me to give it back? But this time I didn't do the drinking or the drugs, and I didn't do the making out, even though Tommy made a loose attempt at a proposition in his intoxicated rubbery way— "Rye Bread, come over here," patting the pleather with a droopy, come-hither look.

No, this time I watched. I picked out a couple of records— R.E.M.'s "Don't Go Back to Rockville" and the B-52's— and sat down with a cup of tonic water (the basement had a fully stocked bar with all the accoutrements) and saw how Dean was comfortable, in that awkward way he had, hanging out with a bunch of kids he hadn't known a month ago. They had taken him in the way they had me: the Lost Souls Club.

"You know, I've been thinking about a band name," Dean said, sliding next to me on the couch.

"What, you don't like Piece of Toast?"

He smiled and said, "We should have a band called Supernova."

"Not bad," I said. "What kind of music do we play?"

"Oh, glam rock, I would think. We're going to have to wear glitter and rainbow wigs."

Dean had on that same striped rugby shirt and cutoffs like mine. "I can't imagine you in glitter."

"Oh, I don't know. I might surprise you," he said. He looked right at me and smiled, and I melted into the red pleather. When? When was he going to surprise me?

Chapter 9

I REALLY HADN'T PLANNED IT THAT WAY, but in the morning, Dean pulled out of his driveway in the Jeep just as I hopped on my bike.

"Hey," he said, with the familiar nod of his head. I had known him for a whole month now, 1/192 of my life, and I had memorized the way his cheeks got all mottled when he blushed and how he cleared his throat before he sang and the exact angle of his chin when he jutted it forward to say hey.

"Hey," I said back, as if I were his buddy. I was beginning to lose hope. Or maybe I'd lost it. Nothing was ever going to happen. He just wanted to be friends. Okay, we'd be friends. I would constantly be in pain, it was true, but we could be friends.

He didn't get out of the car. The driver's-side window was open, and he rested his arm on it. "We're going to play at Soo's tonight. Test the soundproofing."

"You are? Cool." It was sort of like he was inviting me and also sort of like he was just telling me for informational purposes.

"No, *we* are. You are too."

"I am?"

"Yes. I was hoping you were too. You are."

I steadied myself on the bike, gripping and releasing the brakes. "Oh, okay."

"I'd drive you, but I'm going straight from work."

"That's okay. I'll ride my bike. It works great, by the way. Thanks for fixing it."

He pretended to tip his hat. "At your service." And then his cheeks got all mottled. "That was dumb," he said, and I wanted to go right up close to him and say, *No, it's not dumb. It's my favorite thing in the world.* But I just said, "Okay, then," and he said, "Okay," and then he put his car in gear and started to drive away.

I stood there like an idiot watching him and then he stopped the car and leaned over toward the passenger-side window and said, "See you tonight." And I was either really happy or I felt sick. Weird that they could feel so much like the same thing.

Tonya was at our section of the bridge-to-be, drilling half-inch holes into the planks. "You're late, nunchucks," she said.

"I don't think you're using that word right," I said. "That's some kind of ancient Japanese weapon."

"Close enough," she said. "You're supposed to be following behind me, filling the holes with silicone." She motioned to a caulk gun, itself somewhat resembling an ancient Japanese weapon.

"I don't really know how to use it."

She let out an exasperated grunt. "Carrie, for crying out loud." She took the thick tube of silicone and inserted it into the gun, pressing the trigger until the white paste came out. "Now all you have to do is press."

"Got it," I said, saluting her, which she seemed to like. I apparently was also not a whiz in siliconing; I kept putting too much in, so it spurted out the top of the hole.

"Just confirming Newton's First Law of Motion," I told her as she peered disapprovingly at my work.

"Right," she said. "An object either remains at rest or continues to move at a constant velocity, unless acted upon by an external force. Hence the comet," she said. "And the silicone explosion."

"Right," I said.

It didn't seem weird to us back in eighth grade that a couple of thirteen-year-old girls would sit around leafing through astronomy textbooks the way other girls flipped through *Tiger Beat* looking for centerfolds of Rick Springfield. Now it was hard to believe that she and I had ever done anything together. But I did remember Tonya sitting a few rows ahead of me in class, her arm shooting up to answer questions about the color of light that a retreating star emits—she knew all about the Doppler shift. Before I started arriving at class stoned every day, I had sat in the front too, my pen furiously scribbling notes.

"Hey, Carrie, off your butt, you idiot."

I had paused for a minute to check my cigarette supply, but

I didn't think that warranted that particular word. I liked *nun-chucks* better.

"Okay, Tonya, that's a little bit much."

"What? My dad was in the navy, you may recall."

As if that explained it, as if that excused her. I went back to my silicone, this time injecting it slower, making sure it didn't burst from the hole.

"What's he up to now, your dad?"

Tonya looked at me, a glaze hardening over her face. "He's in a rehab in Texas," she said.

"Oh god. What happened?"

"Last year. He was on a ship in the Persian Gulf that was struck by missiles," she said. "Apparently there's a civil war over there that he failed to mention when he shipped out last time. One leg, one eye, gone."

"Oh," I said. "Jeez. I didn't know. I'm really sorry, Tonya. I didn't know."

"Luckily he wasn't one of the thirty-seven soldiers who were killed. And in other great news, my grandmother is still alive and in diapers at home."

"Oh."

"She sits in front of the TV all day drinking peppermint schnapps."

"Well, at least it's peppermint," I said. "Maybe she has decent breath?"

"She does not have decent breath," Tonya said. "I assure you."

I wanted to tell her that my parents, too, had turned into

serious disappointments. Not deceased or maimed, but gone or mean. But I knew it was better to have alive and healthy parents than dead or injured ones, no matter how screwed up they were. I took a chance that I'd be called an idiot yet again and sat down on the planks where the glue had already dried, lighting a cigarette.

Tonya came and sat down next to me, waving her hand in front of my face as I smoked.

"I'm sorry about your sister," she said.

"Oh, yeah? I appreciate your sympathy. Rosie really is a pain in the ass."

"No, not Rosie," she said. "You know."

I really wanted to shrug, but my shoulders wouldn't move. Luckily my mouth was also frozen shut. She seemed to be waiting for me to respond, but suddenly I was fascinated with the silicone gun, the amazing machine with a steel trigger that could transverse different-sized cylindrical openings thanks to the beautiful laws of physics.

"I'm sorry," she said again. "I liked Ginny."

I wondered what happened to our old car. Where did it go? It was probably crushed and turned into scrap metal. It might be in this trigger right now.

"We have four more that we're supposed to do by the end of the day," I said, getting up and stubbing my cigarette out.

"Right. Let's do it, soldier."

I started to sand the places where the bubbles of silicone had hardened, whistling the tune to Sam Cooke's "Chain Gang."

"Not funny," Tonya said.

"A little bit funny?"

"Okay, a little bit funny," she said, and softly whistled along, the sounds flat and off-key.

"You suck at whistling," I said to her. "You know this, right?"

"It's not like I was planning to make it my career," she said. And she whistled anyway.

That night, I arrived first at Soo's, as Tommy and Tiger were setting up. Certain other human beings had not yet shown up.

"We are cleared for noise making?" I asked Soo.

"I guess we'll see. I think my mom has already reached the state where she can't make it to the top of the stairs."

We laughed at this, but the corners of her mouth turned quickly down. A drunk mom was becoming less and less funny. "Speaking of altered states—you want a beer?" She went to the bar and pulled out a can of Bud Light.

I shook my head, trying to be nonchalant. "Nah," I said, and I felt strangely powerful. I could, as Nancy Reagan's TV ads had urged, "just say no." Soo tilted her head back and took a huge gulp, just as her mom had done. Her smile, when she was finished, was almost apologetic. Something was off. It had to be me, something I'd done or not done, but before I could descend into a hole of self-doubt and defensiveness, Dean got there, and suddenly my shoes required my full attention. I heard him greet the guys, and I heard him adjust the snare drum and the cymbals and then I heard him say, "Carrie—you with us?" And I heard myself force the word out: "Yes."

And that is how I came to be strumming along to "Knocking on Heaven's Door" and "Fourth of July" and "New Day Rising" and "Oh Sweet Nuthin'." I sang harmony, and Tiger sang lead on everything except a Violent Femmes song that Dean sang because the Violent Femmes did not necessarily require perfect pitch, and Dean made a cute dumb face while he played the drums with his tongue sticking out to one side. I loved the electricity, the beautiful friction of harmony, and I loved when I went low, below Tiger's sturdy voice.

And then Dean called out "My War," and they all went into Black Flag, Justin whaling on his Flying V.

I said, "I'm out," but they didn't hear me, so fast and hard and furious were they playing. It was perfect, really, because I could just stare at Dean, his sinewy triceps pulsing with the thump of the drums.

Dean and I didn't talk much after we were done playing, but occasionally he'd look up from across the room and half nod my way, or half smile my way, baby steps of interaction in the group. He kept talking to Tommy and Greta after Tiger left to get more beer. I waited for some entry, some way to part the Red Sea between me and them. I tried to will his eyes to look my way, his body to stand and retrieve me. Tried to call up the courage from inside me to move toward him, away from the magnetic pull of the records.

Then suddenly he was there before me.

"Um, hey," he said. "I'm gonna have a smoke. You want one?"

"I don't smoke," I said, which was the wrong answer and also not true.

"You want to come inhale my secondhand smoke?"

"Best offer I've had all day," I said.

And then we retreated to the back of the room, alone-ish, though Tommy seemed to be eyeing us with a menacing stare. Dean had Tiger's guitar, and he was strumming it, and I was pretending to be comfortable.

"I saw Billy Bragg in concert last year, and his guitar is totally amazing—this green Burns Steer that's all beat up, but it sounds so good. Like, so bright."

"Yeah, I love the sound of his guitar," I said.

"It's just like Willie Nelson's—you don't need one of these perfect Martins. It can be totally beat up and sound amazing."

"You like Willie Nelson?" I tried not to sound too disapproving, but this was a little outside my musical comfort zone.

"It's impossible not to like Willie Nelson." He started to strum some song I'd never heard before.

"It is?"

"Yes," he said this as if it were obvious.

I started singing "To All the Girls I've Loved Before," which was up there on the Songs with Worst Lyrics list.

"I didn't say you had to love every song." We passed a cigarette back and forth, that satisfying feeling of fiberglass burning in my throat. Why did I like that?

"Hey, do you have any happy secrets?" I asked him, taking a deep drag of the cigarette.

"Like what?"

"Like something that is not some terrible thing about yourself but that you still don't want anyone to know." I handed the cigarette back to him.

"So . . . it's a secret, so you don't want anyone to know it, but it's a good thing?"

"Yes, exactly."

He squinted his eyes. "Can you give me an example of this?"

"Oh, I have to go first?"

"Yes."

"Oh. Okay. Well. Is my obsessively tracking a comet not good enough?"

"Nope. I already know about that one."

"Okay," I sighed. "Here's the happy secret: I'm also working on a bunch of songs inspired by astronomy."

"Play me one."

"No."

"Yes," he said, leaning over so close to me that I could smell his deodorant and the actual smell of human sweat beneath it.

"Hand me the guitar," I said, and he did. "Just so you know: this is going to be really dumb."

"Okay, great. Thanks for the warning."

What could possibly be more saccharine and embarrassing than a song about the stars, but I sang one about white dwarfs because, in my humble opinion, it didn't suck. *I see you, and you're not even here. Long after you're gone, your light appears.*

"No one would think that was dumb," he said when I was done.

"Okay, I never want to talk about that again in my life. What's your happy secret?"

"Man, I don't know if I can top that. Okay, here's one," he said, shifting to face me. "This is much weirder than yours. I really love to brush my teeth."

"Hmm. That's good, I guess. From a dentist's perspective." And from the perspective of whoever might be kissing him.

"Yeah, sometimes I just get super into it and brush my teeth for, like, ten minutes."

"Is that a happy secret? Bleeding gums?"

"Eh, kind of," he said. "It's a lot happier than a lot of other secrets I have."

I smiled at him, just so he'd learn, eventually, that all his secrets were safe with me.

"Also, as you know, I have a weird thing about Shakespeare."

"Not that weird."

He took the guitar back from me and started to sing Shakespeare, apparently: *Though this be madness, yet there is method in it.* Whatever that meant. Then he started to play a song that I instantly recognized: "Carrie." My dad used to play it for me back when he was a nice person. *Carrie, Carrie, maybe we'll meet again.*

"You know that is one of the worst songs in history, right? It's right up there with 'We Built This City.'"

"Yes, thank you, I do know that. What happened to Jefferson Starship, anyway? Or Starship, as they're apparently now called. They were so good when they were Jefferson Airplane."

So then we were just sitting there and it was the worst and best thing in the whole world, but I could see the clock inching toward eleven and everyone was in the room with us anyway and this boy had been put on Earth to torture me. Then the basement door creaked open and Soo's mother appeared above us, silhouetted in the basement doorway, holding the cordless phone in her hand. Soo's mom seemed so wobbly up there.

"Greta," she called down, "it's your dad."

Greta's face crumbled. "On the phone?"

"He needs you to come home."

She reddened as she went up the stairs and grabbed the phone from Soo's mom, turning so we couldn't see or hear what she said. Then, her face cloudy, she handed the phone back and walked back down the stairs to grab her purse.

"I have to go," she said to us. "Shit. Tiger isn't here."

"We'll drive you," Dean said. We? He looked at me. "Right, Carrie?"

Oh. We. "Of course," I said.

"It's okay — I'll walk." I figured she didn't want us to see the grandeur of her palatial house. She lived on North Broadway, in one of those lovely Victorians with the turrets and fifteen complementary colors of paint. I had to admit I was kind of curious. Also: I was going to be in the car with Dean, which was pretty much the most exciting thing in my life besides waiting for the comet.

Greta seemed pretty messed up—drunk and high. I had probably never noticed, since I was usually so drunk and high myself, but it looked kind of awful: makeup smeared, the perfection of her hippie-druggie cheerleader softened and slanted. It summoned something in me I couldn't ever have imagined I'd feel for Greta: pity. Just a little bit.

"No," I said. "Let us drive you."

Even as I felt sad for Greta, or worried—I had no idea what was wrong with her dad—something else skyrocketed through me. *Us.*

Greta was quiet in the back seat. Dean put on the Velvet Underground, and I stared out the window and felt the warm breeze on my face. There it was again: "I'll Be Your Mirror." I looked at Dean, but he stared intently out the window as a mist descended, his windshield wipers doing little more than smearing it across the glass. *Please put down your hands, 'cause I see you.*

The only thing Greta said was, "It's the one on the right," as we neared a big house. Yes, it had a turret. But the paint was peeling—dull brick red, not at all like so many of the other fixed-up houses on the street. And a bunch of fire escapes were grafted onto the side of it, the telltale sign that it had been cut up into apartments.

"Thanks," she said quietly as she let herself out of the car. I'd never seen her like this: dejected, that beautiful smile wiped off her face.

"I'm going in with you," I said, opening the door, placing a hand on my back where it creaked.

"No—don't."

But I didn't listen to her. Dean waited in the car, and I walked with Greta to a scratched-up open door along the bottom of the house, the basement, into a tiny apartment with brown carpeting and a foldout couch on which her father was lying, moaning, clutching his side. He had thrown up, and his breath was short. This was her father? This was where Greta lived? This was how she lived?

She put her hand on his shoulder. "Dad, can you hear me? Dad? Did you take your medication today?" It seemed like his mouth was too dry to speak.

"What's the matter with him?" I asked.

"This is what happens before he goes into a diabetic coma." She opened a kitchen drawer and took out a syringe and a vial. "You should go," she said, loading up the syringe.

"I can stay," I said.

"No. I've got this. I've done it thousands of times." She

inserted the needle into the crook of her dad's arm and he began to quiet down. It seemed like Greta did not want to look me in the eye. "He doesn't take care of himself," she said. "That's probably why my mom left him. He does this sometimes until I have to take care of him."

"I can stay," I said again. I didn't know how to help her, but I so wanted to.

Finally she turned to me and kissed me on the cheek. "I'm happy for you." She squeezed my hand and she gave me the gift of her smile and I could tell it was genuine and she really was happy for me because I liked a boy and maybe, maybe, maybe he liked me too. A really good boy. Not a gross drunken mean boy, not a random boy or a stranger or someone who would never talk to me again. Then she said, "I love you," and all of a sudden, my eyes filled with tears. Tears for her and for me.

Back in the car, Dean asked, "Is everything okay?"

I thought of Greta standing there over her dad, the stink and the sorry sight of him. Greta, poor Greta—she was the last person in the world I'd thought I'd ever feel sorry or sad for, and yet now I did, a streak of it shooting through me. Sad and sorry and then this weird wash of gratitude. My own dad gave up drinking two years ago now, and he didn't have some chronic disease that he made me tend to. No matter what I could say about my dad, at least he wasn't sick or drunk. I'd never thought to describe my parental situation as lucky before.

"Yeah," I said. "Everything is kind of okay." We headed back toward Soo's, and I leaned my head against the window. No sign of the comet, no bright streak of light across the sky, but I did see one small meteor sashay across the night, and it took away the sting of what I'd just seen. Greta's life was so different from what I'd imagined. In many ways, it was more like mine. Maybe worse.

"I have a question," I said.

"You're in luck."

"How come you were up at five in the morning when I came home that day, the first day I saw you?"

"Oh. Well, I have this thing where I like to stay up until dawn. It just makes me feel better." He turned right onto Thames Street, the street where I'd smoked my first joint and found a litter of stray kittens and spent an hour crying and then pretended that I'd had a great time.

"Really? Daylight? I like it better when the stars come out and I'm reminded that we're suctioned to this ball of oxygen and silicon and magnesium because of the strange and amazing force of gravity but that there's a whole universe out there."

He laughed. "Yes, that's good too. But you'd be surprised how good you feel when the stars start to fade and the light comes out." He didn't turn on any music. "So, I have a question," he said.

"You are also in luck." I put my feet up on the dashboard.

"Where is your mom?"

"Oh." I put my feet down again. Not the question I was

expecting. "Well, she's in the Catskills somewhere. At some retreat thing for hippie fuckups or something." Which sort of sounded like my boot camp, but with tofu and yoga.

"Really?"

"Really."

"Doesn't your dad mind?" I watched Dean's hands shift the gears. It just seemed like such a grown-up thing, and it made me feel so young.

I shrugged my shoulders. "I never asked him." It wasn't entirely true. *Where's Mom and when is she coming back?* had been a pretty much endless refrain for the first week, but each week after, Rosie and I had asked less and less. We had lost 40 percent of the residents of our household within two years, and everything was so strange that in some way we got used to the strangeness. The strangeness became normalcy. And we stopped asking.

"That sucks."

"Um, yeah."

"Grownups," he said. "They're the worst."

"Except for Soo's mom."

"She's all right. But I don't think you'd want her for a mom."

"Why not? Soo gets to do whatever she wants."

"I don't know. I think a strict parent who's sober during the daytime is better than a mom who's wasted by noon and lets you do whatever you want."

"Yeah, I guess."

Greta's dad was sick, and Soo's mom was drunk, and my mom was gone, and my dad was mean — it was all some variation on a theme.

We turned onto Soo's street, but I put my hand on Dean's arm as he downshifted. It was so warm and there was that soft hair and a few freckles dotting his skin, and even though I didn't want to do it, I said, "I think I have to go home."

Dean brought me back to my bike, and I rode it home as the mist got thicker, giving way to a gentle rain. I couldn't shake that image of Greta rolling her moaning dad onto his back, or the sight of that dirty brown carpet in their dingy apartment.

I opened the door to my house slowly. He was sitting in his chair in the dark, like some sad figure from a Dickens novel.

"It's midnight," he said. "It's actually twelve-oh-three."

"I know. I'm sorry. I was just —"

"You were not at Soo's. I called her mom."

"No, but I meant to —"

"What is the matter with you, Carrie?" he said, standing up, revealing the full extent of his imposing frame. "You stay out all night. You take drugs. You have tantrums. You sabotage yourself by disobeying me and doing things that get you in trouble. I thought you were starting to do better, but you're making it impossible for me to trust you." His voice was eerily calm.

"Also, she lies and she steals!" Rosie called from upstairs.

"Really. I want to know: what is wrong with you? How can you be so smart and so dumb? Honestly? Honestly, Caraway, I'm getting to the point where I don't even care. If you're going to resist every one of my attempts to help—"

"Oh my god, publicly shaming me is your attempt to help?"

Dean could probably hear me screaming, but it had happened too quickly to stop it. My father had plucked me so violently from that unusual pool of gratitude and calm I'd been swimming in. "Checking me into the hospital? Sending me to juvie boot camp?"

My father talked right over me. "If you're going to drug yourself into oblivion, I just can't help you. I can't help you anymore."

"Drugs? What drugs?"

He took the wooden bowl I'd made in shop class all those years ago off the end table next to his chair of gloom. I had taken it from Ginny's room the night after the funeral, and I hadn't touched it other than to put her flask and her little brown bottle of coke and her still-full minis of Jäger and Bushmills in there, underneath her pile of dangly earrings. I don't know why I kept them. Some kind of proof, or punishment, something so I wouldn't forget what I'd done and what I'd seen.

My mouth hung open. "That's not mine."

"This is going to be good," he said. "You're going to tell me it's Rosie's?"

"It's not mine!" she called down.

I could feel the hatred coming off him in waves. For all

the preciousness, her exalted place at the top of the family food chain, Ginny had been the most corrupt. She was into things — with drugs and with boys and with stealing and with cheating — that would have shocked my parents straight into the mental hospital. Ginger on drugs and having sex? Never. She would never. I remembered the shock, the betrayal in my parents' voices once they found out what she'd been up to that night. Even now, two years later, it was as if he couldn't admit Ginny's failings. He still wanted to believe that night was some one-time kind of thing. The evidence before him still couldn't indict her; it was only proof of what was wrong with me.

The worst part, my most grievous sin, was that I was still here — the bad one, the one who disgusted him. The rage welled up in me — I could beat him at the hate game — and shook through my veins, probably the same way that coke had shaken through Ginny's body that day. It was a supergiant star, swelling to five hundred times its original size, then freezing until it burned bright red.

But my words came out flat. "How could anybody hate his own kid like that?"

"Hate you?" he said, his hands on his temples, pretending to be shocked that I'd say this previously unacknowledged truth. "Why would I be so angry, so confounded, so concerned, if I didn't love you so much? Why do you think I won't let you on the roof? I don't want you to jump off it."

His hands were parted like that painting I'd once written

a paper on, *Mater Dolorosa with Open Hands*. The painter was named Titian, otherwise known in Venice as "the Sun Amidst Small Stars."

All I could say was "Ha."

He sat down, defeated, shaking his head. My father had given up. He'd given up on me. I'd broken him, and he was going to let me descend into the void because there was nothing else he could do to stop me. "What is going to happen to you?"

"How the fuck should I know?" I was going to scream at him more, but when I opened my mouth, some other sound came out, as if I'd channeled a sea lion, a terrible plaintive barking.

Crap. Crying. Crap crap.

It was Ginny's. All that stuff was Ginny's. And even with the evidence neatly settled in the bowl between us, I was the bad guy. I was going to tell him that, but when I started moving my lips, all I said was, "I want my mommy."

Chapter 10

QUIET AS A CAT BURGLAR, I CREPT out my window, onto the porch roof, checking for any sign of my dad or Rosie. None. Then I heard his footsteps and crouched down.

"Carrie?" he called from inside. "Honey, are you there?"

Who you calling honey? I wanted to ask, but I kept my mouth shut. There was no way I could slink back in the window and out of my room, walk past Rosie, and suffer my father's glare, my misdeeds all reflecting in the frame of his tortoiseshell glasses. Finally his footsteps filtered away.

I stood up on the porch roof, ready to slide down to the ground, but as I did, I saw a figure in the yard next door. It was Mrs. Richmond. I froze, hoping that would make me invisible. She was in the middle of taking the garbage out to the curb, and she'd stopped to look at me. Then she nodded, the slightest little movement of her head, and resumed dragging the trash cans.

The streetlights flickered as I rode to Soo's, my shoulders drooped in defeat beneath my backpack, which contained my wallet, my

Walkman, three mix tapes, my notebook, three Fender guitar picks, my flannel shirt, and a change of underwear. My father hadn't kicked me out. He hadn't shouted ferociously for me to leave. But he'd made up his mind about me once and for all. I was a black hole of a human being. I felt as if I were dragging my whole body behind me, reluctant to pedal forward but refusing to go back.

The door creaked as I let myself into the house, where Soo's mom lay, eyes at half-mast, on the couch, her tired but pretty face in the flicker of the TV light. Johnny Carson, interviewing a Tibetan monk.

"Carrie," she said smiling, sleepily, the only adult left in our town who appreciated my presence. On the back of their plaid couch sat an afghan, orange and brown zigzagged, which I spread over her. She sat up a bit, hand to her head as if a fire raged in there. She seemed as rickety as a grandmother. "You know what's going to happen, Carrie?" she asked. I shook my head. She was scaring me. "You're going to get old. Your face is going to droop. There's going to be all sorts of body parts sagging on you that you never thought possible."

"Mrs. Shaughnessy—"

"Sweetie, really. I want you to know something. This is the best. This is the happiest time of your life. So drink it in. Drink it in." She raised her glass to me, which was somehow one of the most sorrowful things I'd ever seen. "Don't forget to be happy." And with that, she gulped her Scotch and soda and laid her head back on the couch.

* * *

The stairs creaked as I went up slowly to Soo's room. I knew what I'd find in there, but still I knocked, lightly, then louder when I had no response.

"What?" Soo called, her voice laced with annoyance.

"It's me," I whispered.

She opened the door, naked but wrapped in her zebra-striped sheets — this month's décor included hot pink and animal print. "Time After Time," saddest song ever, hummed in the background.

"What happened?" she asked. Her eyes and lips were puffy and red — the combination, I assumed, of being wasted and fooling around.

I shook my head. "I don't know. Nothing. It's just — I can't go back there right now. I can't go back." I tried to hold in my tears. "Can I sleep here, please?"

Soo hesitated for a moment, looking behind her and then back to me. "Justin's here," she said, apologetically but firmly. She was good like that — she knew how to be pretend-adult. It was probably why I'd attached myself to her, why, that week after the funeral, I'd ended up at Soo's house night after night, just watching the way she moved, the way she took care of her mother and hosted the gang of shell-shocked teenagers. She'd taken me under her wing, almost literally: wrapped her arm around my shoulders the third night after the funeral and told me, "It's okay, kid. You'll get on the other side of it. We all will."

We were sitting in the basement, which was done up '60s style with macramé and beanbag chairs and beaded curtains back then, and everyone else was out attempting to illegally procure beer from Purdy's Liquor. It was just me and Soo, and she'd said, again, "You're going to be okay."

But I'd shaken my head, back and forth, with such force that she couldn't keep her arm around me, try as she might. I couldn't stop, just shaking and shaking it as if that would ward off the tears, because I was terrified of the tears. If one leaked out, I'd cry forever. Finally, Soo grabbed my head in both her hands to stop me, and she stared hard at me. She wasn't trying to soothe me or calm me. She'd gone into serious mode.

"Everybody misses her," Soo had said. "We're all scarred. We're all going to be a mess together."

Somehow that had stopped the shaking of my voice and my head, and I breathed slower and pulled my head back from Soo's hands and looked at my lap. Then I screwed up enough courage to raise my head and look at Soo. She wasn't like Greta, the red-blond goddess, glossy and model-beautiful. Everything about her was quieter, but stronger somehow, and I knew in that moment that I had an ally. She was scarred like me, but literally—a mean snarl of scab lined her abdomen for two months afterward. Soo and Greta had both been in the car with Ginny. They'd forced themselves into it as Ginny peeled away. They'd walked away from the crash, almost unscathed. Almost.

She liked that scab, Soo had told me. It was, in a way, all she had left of Ginny.

Now I waited, blinking, for her to offer me a sleeping bag on the floor or tell me to go down and sleep in the basement until she could come down to be with me or — hey, better yet — to send Justin home so I could stay. She seemed to be waiting too. For me to leave. She blinked her puffy eyes and licked her chapped lips. What had they been doing in there? Probably something totally amazing that I would never in my life experience. But, okay. I'd be a nun. A runaway nun. Too bad my parents had ditched religion long before I was born.

"I can't," she said. "Not right now. But can I, like, get you anything? Till later?"

I couldn't look at her, couldn't understand whatever she was trying to say to me in some I'm-not-a-virgin-anymore-and-I'm-in-love code. Instead, I looked past her, into the sliver of room that she had deigned worthy of my view. Her hiking boots sat in her open closet, the same waterproof hiking boots I'd borrowed when I'd hiked with my mother in the Catskills two years ago, when my feet were a little bit smaller. Behind them was her rain slicker, hanging on a hook.

Now I screwed up the strength to meet her eyes. "Yes," I said. "There's something you can do."

It was a long ride to Greta's house in Soo's rain slicker and slightly-too-small hiking boots, all the way to the other side of town in the slowly increasing rain. I knew I looked like a vagabond, and I did for a while consider ditching the bike and sticking out my thumb. But for all the recklessness, I was still wary of strangers, of hitchhiking, of getting hurt, or worse. Some part of me really wanted to live, even though I wasn't sure what for.

I passed the cemetery where I'd first drunk whiskey and the playground where I'd taught our old dog Peaches to go down the slide and my old elementary school where I'd first seen Ginny smoking a cigarette while she waited for me. She often used to do that: get off the bus three stops early and stand at the entrance of the elementary school, which got out twenty minutes later than the junior high and high school. She'd lean against the wall in her leather jacket and her torn blue jeans, and smoke, her shiny hair perfectly mussed. She looked like Madonna. She really looked like Madonna. And I would emerge from the school, immersed in my mousiness, the dumb-colored brown hair and the glasses and the braces and the used L. L. Bean backpack slung over my shoulder, and I would be so proud that she was my sister, that I was attached to her.

I stopped in the middle of the street for the short break in the rain. It wasn't the comet, but the Perseids, the pre-Vira meteors, raced overhead, and I shivered. I could see just the faint spark of them in between the thickening clouds. "Ginny, are you there?" A meteor shot across the sky again. It was magical. It really was magical. "Ginny?" I waited. What was I waiting for? Did I really think she'd say something back? "Ginny. I just miss you so damn much." I tried to muster something profound to say to her. "Everything really went to shit when you left." But there were no more meteors. The clouds moved in again, and the whole sky went quiet.

I knocked lightly on the door, and eventually Greta answered.

"Hi, sweetie," she said, and stepped aside to let me in as if she'd been waiting for me. "Come and sit." She patted the couch, that same couch on which her dad had passed out. "It's okay," she said. "He's asleep in the bedroom." Her smile could cure cancer. "Tell me."

I spilled it all out, about waiting incessantly for Dean to like me and about my dad's rage and Soo's rejection. She looked at her own hands, folded in her lap, while I talked. Part of me felt horribly guilty. I knew she'd had a rough time with her dad, and I knew now that she worked hard for the few lovely items of clothing she had that fit her body so perfectly. But I was drowning, and I needed a human life preserver. And Ginny wasn't there to be it. And neither was Soo.

"Carrie," Greta said finally, "she was my friend too, you know. I was there too."

I managed to speak with a shaky voice. "Yeah, but . . ."

"No *but*. I was there too. I was in the car, for god's sake. Soo was too. We saw it—her. You're not the only one who's having a shitty adolescence."

"Okay," I whispered. "Okay."

"I love you, but you have to stop feeling so sorry for yourself.

You're smart and loved and adorable, so just figure out what you have to do to survive and do it."

Greta had never been mad at me before. I had learned to shield myself from my father's anger, since it hardly ever wavered, but in front of Greta, I was shaky and sweating and shamed.

"Okay?" she said. She squeezed my hand. "Okay, Carrie?"

"Okay."

She smiled at me, but I knew I couldn't stay with her, either.

Clearly not ready to be trampled on, the footbridge-in-progress wobbled under my tight hiking boots. The rain plinked around me, seeping into Soo's semi-useless yellow rain slicker as I rolled my bike along with me, my backpack affixed to the rear rack with my father's bungee cord. It had been ages since I'd been in the park at night, and I'd never been here alone (discounting the time I got extra stoned and lost the rest of the group while I wandered in circles for hours, or maybe just minutes, calling for them). What a shame, really, that this was the night to be solo beneath the stars: I couldn't even see them.

The observatory door was locked, but years ago Ginny had shown me how to prop open the window, stained glass that was framed with now-rotting wood. I was eleven, and Ginny was watching out for me while my parents took Rosie to the doctor for her never-ending tests during that period when they thought she had narcolepsy. (It turned out she just had magical powers of sleep.)

Ginny and I had stopped at the bottom of the steps, then pushed our bikes slowly up them. She had her Walkman on and Supertramp was leaking out of it, an alluring and confusing sound, since I was still into Huey Lewis and the News back then.

"It's closed," I said when we got up there. And she laughed and tousled my hair as if I were five, not just two years younger than she was. She was in her hippie phase, her dark hair long and glossy and straight, her earrings enormous gold hoops.

"You're such a rule follower, Car." It was not a dig, and I didn't take it that way. It was an invitation. "C'mere, let me show you." She stood on one stone that jutted out past the others in the wall. She put her hands by the wood-framed window—it wasn't rotted back then—and pushed in a little bit and then up. "It's easy," she said. Everything felt easy when I was with her. Everything felt both wondrous and safe.

Inside, below the glass ceiling, the stars glowed and Ginny pointed out the constellation of Hydra, the water monster.

She wasn't opening the window toward juvenile delinquency, really. She wasn't trying to corrupt me. She was trying to set me free from the parental force of gravity.

Now the observatory had a ghostly quality, its round shape, its dark stones looming over the flat green fields. It was our fault that the observatory was still closed, as if the parks department were still waiting for the cloud of taint to evaporate, even after two years.

I pressed the window open and squeezed inside, scraping my leg on the stone walls as I scaled them. "Crap." My backpack landed with a thud on the hard stone floor. Damp and echoey, the interior was lined with old and faded exhibits about the history of sundials and how craters are formed. I looked up to the domed window atop the observatory, remembering the night it opened when I was little, Orion's belt gleaming and all that hope blinking in the stars. I flicked the light switch and only the palest light washed over the room.

I wanted to go home, but I knew I couldn't. I looked at my own charts in my notebook, the careful pencil drawings I'd done of the elliptical orbit. That was one relief: it wouldn't be tonight. I wouldn't miss it. Not yet.

Two benches stood against the walls, each clad in dark red velvet, worn now and threadbare in spots, but good enough for a bed. I took off the wet boots, rolled up the rain slicker into a makeshift pillow, and lay down. I was so weirdly calm. Not scared to be alone in the park at night. Not scared to be homeless-ish. Not scared to be lying down in the very spot where, two years earlier, Ginny had snorted five lines of cocaine through a one-dollar bill, then washed it down with the contents of her flask, while I watched at the stained-glass window.

After Ginny left home that night, I had sneaked out and ridden my bike, curious to see her glamorous life, the boys and the drugs and the music. I'd ridden up to the observatory and leaned my bike against a white pine tree. The lights of the observatory had glowed warm and orange against the blue-black night sky, and the sounds of the Misfits leaking from the boom box grew louder as I approached.

I'd stood on a bench outside the stained-glass window, and I saw her; I saw what she did, and my feet seemed to slip out from under me and the bench wobbled, and I grabbed on to the windowsill and yelped, and they'd all looked up. Ginny looked up.

I dropped to the ground and heard her say, "Shit. My little sister. I have to go."

She called after me, came after me as I escaped into the woods to get my bike, then crouched down and watched. Watched her friends try to get her to stay, tell her she was too wasted to drive, watched her shrug them off and hurry down the hill to our car, wobbling and yelling and waving people away, angry and sloppy and mean—and she got in the car while Greta and Soo forced themselves in.

I didn't say anything, not then, not later. I wasn't supposed to be there, but I'd been there and I'd watched her do all of that, and I'd never said anything, not even after I rode my bike home and found she wasn't there. Not after the phone rang later that night: the sheriff calling to tell us our lives would never be the same.

The observatory was cold and dank, and it was good enough. Maybe the comet would be here soon. Maybe, like the Paiute Indians used to think, it signified the end of this world and the start of the next.

No, I wasn't scared to be there. But once the tears came, there was no stopping them.

Chapter 11

IN THE MORNING I FELT AS HUNG-OVER as I had a couple of months ago when Tommy and I drank too many wine coolers and ended up in the back of his car, the horribleness of it almost good, confirming for me everything anyone ever said about me. Oh, for a coffee, which apparently I liked now, and a grilled bran muffin at the Woolworth's lunch counter, the beautiful fluff of my own bed, my guitar, my records, my friends.

In last night's clothes and without my shitkickers or hard-hat or flannel shirt, I made my way down to our construction site, Soo's hiking boots still a bit sloshy around my feet. The last time I went hiking with my mom, she led me and Rosie and a grumbling Ginny up Mount Tremper to forage for boletus mushrooms, her careful instruction and the pictures she showed us in her *Encyclopedia of Fungi* guiding us so that we wouldn't accidentally pick something poisonous.

This was when Ginny was changing, though I didn't realize it then. Her wonder was turning into some kind of unwillingness, some reluctance or refusal to embrace us, or at least our parents. She'd worn her Walkman and kicked rocks all the way up, and when we got to the top, she'd sat looking at the view and taken off her headphones, slipping them over my ears.

"Listen to this," she'd said. "It'll make you feel better about everything." I remember wondering why she felt so bad, but, yeah, Leonard Cohen's "Hallelujah" was amazing.

It stung to conjure up those memories, even the bittersweet ones. It was easier to believe that I had never been part of a happy family so I wouldn't have anything to miss. I felt like the planemos we'd learned about at the end of last year: rogue planets that had been kicked out of their own solar system, with no home stars to circle around.

The sheer amount of sobbing I'd done the night before had left my eyes buglike swollen, my shoulders achy. Funny, the footbridge-in-progress felt like a refuge. It was so much cooler there along the creek, and I could see, as Lynn would say, the fruits of several weeks' labor. Yes, indeed, the planks I'd lain atop the concrete piers were less precise than Tonya's, but I loved the way the bright wood looked against the dark soil, the way our creation snaked up toward the observatory. I had to admit it: I was actually looking forward to the day's work, a chance to free my mind from its endless spinning.

The rest of the crew arrived, and I said hi to Tonya. She looked at me and said, "Okay. Hi. What the heck happened to you?"

"Long story," I said, turning away, but I could feel her staring at me.

"Um, you okay?" she asked. "You look like hell."

"Thank you."

"No, I just—"

But thankfully Lynn had arrived and waved us over to him.

"Good news," Lynn said. "This afternoon we're having a little field trip after we screw the planks together and while we wait for the adhesive to dry. We have a guest today, a biologist and arborist who studies trees, and we're going to do some testing on our trees to find out how old they are and if they're still healthy."

My initial reaction was to conjure up a number of snarky remarks, but they were quelled by the dangerous feeling in my gut.

"Caraway? Where's your hardhat?" Lynn asked. "Where are your boots?"

I shrugged.

"And long pants? And your hammer? Where's your fanny pack?"

Everyone was looking at me, a thousand blinking eyes waiting for an explanation or at least my signature retort. I had none. Nothing. I had nothing.

"I hate that fanny pack," I said.

"Do you want me to send you home?" he asked. "Because I can do that."

No, I wanted to say. *I don't want to go home.* I wasn't being defiant. I was being defeated. If he sent me home, my father would surely kick me out or commit me to the nuthouse. I essentially had no home to go to, and by this afternoon, I now realized, the park would cease to be a refuge too. *The arborist.* I couldn't escape myself. Enemies everywhere.

"No," I whispered. "Don't send me home."

Lynn narrowed his eyes at me. "Come with me."

Lynn took me over to the park office and helped me cobble together an outfit from the lost and found: pants two sizes too big, held on with the bungee cord from my bike, and a hardhat for a person three times my size.

"How do I look?" I asked, twirling around so that the hardhat wobbled on my head.

Lynn actually laughed. "You look great. There's a job opening for a scarecrow at the end of the summer."

"Ha," I said, but I was still holding back tears.

The truth was, I wanted to work. I wanted to participate. At least 50 percent of me wanted to ally myself with Tonya, who could stab the end of her six-foot pry bar into the dirt to tamp it down and then carefully lay a track of pine along it, her face set and determined, brow furrowed in concentration, tongue sticking slightly out as she lined up the slats and then—*whack*—slapped that nail expertly into place with her Youth Workforce hammer. An almost imperceptible look of satisfaction passed across her face before she caught me staring at her and narrowed her eyes and said, "Are you getting paid to just stand there and watch me?"

"I don't have a hammer," I said. Every inch of me was

fatigued, too tired to fight. I sat down cross-legged and took my notebook out from my backpack and worked on the standard equation for an eclipse, very pointedly ignoring her.

"You're kidding!" Tonya said. "Carrie, you're being ridiculous." She handed me her hammer. "Here," she said. "Use mine."

Jimmie had looked over at us, and the way he nodded his head and furrowed his brow at her—as if asking, *You okay?*—suddenly I just knew it. I knew all about them. I had nobody, but somehow Tonya had a boyfriend.

"Oh god—you're a couple?" I closed my notebook and put my hand on my belly, faking a hearty laugh.

"Yeah, so what? Ever since disco night at Civic. Which, by the way, is awesome."

I couldn't stop laughing, even though it wasn't a real laugh. "That is too funny."

The look of hurt alarm that rooted in her features—it was fierce. I could feel it like a force whipping from her chest. It nearly knocked me over, but I stayed in place.

"You are the cruelest person I have ever met."

I waved it away. "Me? You're the drill sergeant, ordering everybody around, pretending to be so competent, pretending like you don't care that you're queen—make that king—of the nerds, when you wish you could be cool."

"You just proved my point," she said. She had stopped tamping the dirt temporarily, pausing to take in the pure evil of me. "The worst thing that ever happened to you was when you decided to pretend to be somebody else, when you decided to cloak your inner nerd in some ridiculous thing where you pretend to be cool."

I couldn't remember for a moment how to speak, couldn't identify the liquid of emotion that was now drowning my body. Oh, right. It was regret, all manners and shapes of regret. I regretted everything—I'd made my sister drive when she was wasted and I couldn't get a boyfriend and I'd screwed up all my babysitting gigs and Soo hated me now and I hadn't begged my mom to stay and I had failed my father who'd tried so hard to protect me and I'd been disobedient and rude to Lynn, and I'd been the cruelest person in the world to Tonya. It was me, after all. It wasn't some troll who'd occupied the bridge beneath my heart. It was me.

"*Cloak your inner nerd*," I said. "That's kind of poetic. That should be a lyric."

She rejected my hint of a smile, the tiniest offer of peace, and returned to the planks of wood.

"You think you're so much better than us because you have older friends, but those people are so screwed up. You know how they're going to turn out? Just like their parents."

"They're not." Somehow I was whispering. "They're good people."

"You guys think you're so cool, with your drugs and that stupid band. That band is really terrible. You know that. I know you know that, Carrie." She paused. "You know those people are not your real friends, right? They only have you around because they feel guilty. Everybody knows that."

"What are you talking about? You think you did anything when Ginny died? You think you showed up at the house and took care of me? No, you didn't. Nobody in our whole school did anything except Soo and Greta and Ginny's friends. They were the only ones who cared that she died."

"That's not true," Tonya said quietly, but I could see that she, too, had regret pooling around her. "I'm sorry. I didn't know what to say. And it seemed like from that moment on, you had decided to be just like her. Mini Ginny." I didn't look at her. "We used to be friends," she said.

Was that supposed to be an apology? An explanation?

"Now we're not," I said. It was just a fact, as plain as Ginny's death, as her body burned into ash. Both of us standing, Tonya with a shovel, me with her hammer, staring at each other like Old West fellas in a duel.

"What seems to be the problem here?" asked Lynn.

"There's no problem," I said in my brightest voice, picking up my own park-issued collection of wood screws—which was always far heavier than I expected—and rifling through it in a vague attempt to mimic actual work. I put a few on top of my notebook and pretended to sort through them.

"She hasn't done a single thing all morning," Tonya said.

"Screw you, Tonya. I'm wearing a bungee cord. How hard can I work?"

"Caraway—Caraway." Lynn held his hand out toward my

chest, even though I hadn't moved, hadn't lunged at Tonya the way I'd wanted to. See? I was getting better. "No one is accusing you of anything, but it's true that I have seen you standing here for the last hour while the rest of us—"

"This is bullshit," I said, now collecting the energy to be angry.

"Please don't use that kind of language here, Caraway—"

It was as if I'd made the decision, but also as if I hadn't. Some part of me said, *Screw it. Let's ruin this.* Two paths, and I took the one most traveled, in which I destroyed all that was good.

"I will use whatever language I want to use!" I shouted, throwing my notebook down on the ground, all those weeks of calculations and pages of lyrics subsumed by dirt. "Language has no inherent meaning, and if you think the word *bullshit* is a bad word, that's your problem. It's just four letters strung together to make a sound, okay? You think woolly mammoths got offended when someone made the wrong sound?"

Lynn stopped trying to calm me down or talk to me. Instead, he took a deep breath and dropped his head to his chest and whispered.

"Oh my god, are you praying?"

I wanted to escape so badly, but now all the kids had stopped their toiling and were standing there watching me, watching Lynn with his hand still raised, like Diana Ross in "Stop in the Name of Love," his head bent and his mouth making those delicate wisps of sound.

"I can't take this shit," I said, and a force just started pushing me. It pushed me to throw my hardhat into the ditch below Tonya's footbridge, and it pushed me to pull wildly on my hiking boot and to fall while I was doing it, mud all along the right side of my crappy, enormous Wrangler jeans, and then to finally free my foot from the boot and to give up on the other, grunting all the while, and stomp off with one muddy-socked foot and the other one still imprisoned in the boot, hobbling, the mud making slurpy sucking sounds as it tried to snag my feet, tried to hold me back. But no. Nothing could hold me back. Not the fading sounds of Lynn's protests, the hoots and hollers of the other kids, or Tonya calling, "Yes, I do think woolly mammoths would be offended if one of them made the wrong sound. And *bullshit* has eight letters."

I kept trudging, knowing that all of them were watching my limping, muddy figure disappear, swallowed by the dark canopy of evergreens.

I walked for what seemed like days, though was probably only, like, thirty minutes, muddy and one-shoed and muttering all the things I should have said, all the snappy and sharp-tongued comebacks I should have called forth to defend my honor. Occasionally my internal ranting was interrupted by crying. This was it, the thing where I couldn't calm down, where I could only volley back and forth between rage and despair.

And then, from across the field, I saw them. My compatriots

stood in a circle, gathering around and laughing, and I thought I even saw a Hacky Sack bobbing in the center; nothing like a common enemy—me—to bring the group together. A sea of weeds between us, and nobody wanted me to cross it.

"Caraway?" Lynn called, spying me from beyond. Maybe not nobody. "Come join us, please." For some reason, I came.

I stood outside the circle that had coalesced around one white pine with a few needle-less branches reaching toward the sky. Ginny's tree stood less than fifty feet away, across the street, that white cross staring at me from the bark.

"So, we're trying to find out if this tree is healthy enough to keep standing," the man was saying.

"What are *you* doing here?" I asked.

Pablo smiled. "Carrie. Nice to see you. How are you?"

I stayed on the edge of the circle. "I'm a wreck," I said, blowing my nose on my sleeve. "Why are you here?" I repeated. Every single kid, plus Lynn, was staring at me.

"I helped found the program, to help young people develop an interest in science careers. I'm the one who told your dad about it."

"Caraway," Lynn said, still trying powerfully to smile. I had to give it to the guy—he had a deep reserve of positivity on which to draw. "Caraway?"

"What?" I snapped. "Will you please stop calling me that?"

Lynn nodded and asked me very quietly, "Are you okay?"

I looked at Pablo and the white cross and the dying trees and the smiling supervisor and the nice kids my own age. "Is that a real question? Because if it is, I'm pretty sure you can answer it."

Lynn took me by the shoulder and led me away from the group to sit beneath a tree. To sit beneath that tree. To sit beneath the tree.

"So, Caraway," Lynn said, taking my notebook out of my backpack, which he'd carried with him from the site.

I froze, thinking he'd found the parts where I'd written about his disparagement of gay people or my critique of his John Lennon glasses (no uncool person should ever don such spectacles; it's like playing "Imagine" as elevator music), but he'd opened it to the page where I'd written *I'm so sick of myself, I want to be someone else. I'm so sick of all this sky, I just want to die.*

"I need to talk to you about what you've written in your notebook."

"They're lyrics," I said.

He didn't blink, didn't betray any kind of emotion. "I know there have been incidents."

"Why? How do you know? Did she get to you, too?" The blood rose to my cheeks. "What do you know?"

"A lot," he said.

"You know about my trips to Disney World?"

"Is Disney World the psychiatric emergency room?"

"Yes."

He said, very quietly, "Then, yes, I know."

"How?" I asked. "How do you know?"

He had those big hands pressed together in front of him, a prayer laid down on that patch of grass. "I know because I was looking for a babysitter for my kids that summer, and the Tellers had given me your number, and before I called, they had found out about the struggles you were having. So they told me."

"You don't *have* a struggle," I said. "Maybe you engage in a struggle. Maybe you just struggle."

"Okay. They let me know that you were struggling. Is that better?"

"No," I said. "This is not better. I'm not the one with the problems. My dad has a problem. Tonya has a problem. Friggin' Pablo the arborist has problems!" I was yelling again, a sharp sound that surely could reach the group.

Lynn stayed the picture of calm, his gaze steady upon me, exposing me and comforting me at the same time.

"Listen, I have sworn off anything to do with therapists, so if you're planning to perform any psychology voodoo on me, you can forget about it. You don't know what's wrong with me."

His gaze stayed steady as ever, and there was so much kindness and understanding in it that I couldn't stand it. I grabbed my notebook and made to leave.

"Listen, Caraway. Your mom leaving you like that—that's the kind of thing you just can't do. She can't just do that. I want you to know that—it's against all the laws of nature. It's—it's okay to be devastated by that."

"I'm not devastated."

"Okay. But I want you to know that the amount of loss you've endured—it could knock down even the strongest of individuals. It doesn't mean that it's okay for you to talk to me like that. It doesn't mean that it's okay to not do your work, or to be unkind and ungenerous. It just means that you've been given a truly raw deal, and I'd be mad about it too if that happened to me. I, for one, would be devastated."

I couldn't catch my breath to say anything more. All I could do was leave.

I stood outside Reinventing the Wheel, my bike leaning against me. I had changed back into my cutoffs and put my mother's flannel on, but I was still muddy and one-shoed. When Dean walked out, I waved to him, forgetting for a minute that I looked like a homeless person, and then, when I realized it, not really caring anymore.

He walked over. "Um, wow," he said. "They're really working you hard."

It was the first time I'd really smiled all day.

"Hey, Dean? I have a question."

"You're in luck."

"Can you take me somewhere?

"Um, yeah," he said. "Where do you want to go?"

I swallowed. "To my mom's."

"Yeah, but . . ."

I waited for him to say he couldn't, waited for him to wriggle out of being with me. Instead he pointed to his own bike-grease-stained clothes. "Maybe we should change first?"

I was afraid to go home. He seemed to understand this without me explaining it and pulled into Mrs. Richmond's driveway.

I had never been directly on her property. It was lushly land-scaped, a little fountain gurgling in a rose garden.

"It's nice over here," I said, more ashamed than ever of our low-rent yard, or lack thereof.

"Yeah, right?" he said. "So, make yourself at home. I'm going to take a shower. You can take one after if you want."

"Are you trying to tell me that this is not a good look for me?" I waved my hands before my mud-caked outfit.

"Nah. It's still a good look." My face got hot.

He went upstairs, and I stood for a minute against Mrs. Richmond's cool marble counters. She had art on the walls—abstract paintings with bold colors melting into one another—but few family photos. She and her late husband had never had kids. My mother used to say so with pity in her voice, but now I figured Mrs. Richmond was lucky. She'd been spared the pain of losing them, having them die or go crazy. Spared the pain of having their love transform into hate.

Above the mantel of the huge fireplace in their living room, one gilt-framed photo stood. Dean and his family: a younger sister, two sturdy-looking parents, his mother in a lace-edged shirt and his father in a tie, and his sister in overalls and Dean, on the verge of teenagehood, his mouth full of braces, his hair sculpted into a mullet—dorky and adorable and vulnerable and small. He was holding his sister's hand. Oh, to have a sister like that.

I picked up Mrs. Richmond's phone and dialed.

"Hello?" the voice chirped.

"Rosie."

"Where are you?" she asked. "You're supposed to be home. You are in some serious trouble."

"Keep your voice down," I said. "Can you get me some clothes?"

"Why would I do that?"

"Because you're my sister, and when Dad dies someday, I'll be all you've got."

The silence indicated she was considering my logic.

"And someday, during a solar eclipse when everything stands on its head, you will be in trouble, and I'm going to help you."

"Are you running away again?" she asked quietly. "Or did Dad kick you out?"

"No. I don't know. I just need something to wear, and I don't want to see Dad."

"Okay," she said. "Where are you?"

I took a deep breath, hoping she could keep my secrets. "I'm right next door."

Chapter 12

WHEN DEAN RETURNED FROM THE SHOWER, ROSIE was there with a pile of my clothes.

"Hey," he said. "Rosie, right?"

She saluted. "At your service." Ah, Rosie—possibly even dorkier than I and totally not worried about it.

I took the clothes from her. She'd picked out my best cut-up T-shirt and my favorite jean skirt and my jellies. "Thanks."

"What are you going to do, Carrie? You can't stay away from home forever."

I shrugged. "I was thinking maybe I'd go stay with Mom."

Rosie scrunched up her face in surprise, suspicion, confusion, all of it swirling in her furrowed brows, but before she could say anything, we heard another voice.

"Hello, Carrie. Hello, Rosie." It was Mrs. Richmond. I hadn't heard the screen door open. She had brassy dyed hair set in poodle curls, AKA perm-gone-wrong, and a full preppy uniform of a blue blazer with brass buttons and an elastic belt with little whales. I felt like a monster, muddy and dressed like a bum.

"Oh, hey," I said. I hadn't even known she knew our names.

"Hi, Mrs. Richmond," Rosie said. "Our shower's on the fritz, so Miss Construction Worker over here is cleaning herself up. I hope that's okay." Rosie. She should have been the oldest daughter. She was the only one with any sense or manners.

"It's fine," she said, resting her LeSportsac bag on a table by the door. "I haven't spoken with you since the funeral."

I couldn't think of anything to say in response. I didn't even remember talking to her there. The receiving line, the sea of people greeting us, grieving with us, was still a blur. I only remembered what happened after: Janis Joplin and the wind in my hair and the roller rink and the drugs and the strobe light and the kiss.

"How are you? How's your mother?"

"Um," I said. "I don't know?" Even Rosie had no answer.

Mrs. Richmond must have heard every fight my father and I had ever had, heard every terrible word we'd said to each other, and now I was standing in her kitchen not even knowing how my mother was.

"Well, she has to clean herself up, and I have to get home," Rosie said. She sort of smiled at me, and I sort of smiled back.

"Yeah," I said. "I'm shedding dirt on your rug."

"Upstairs and to the left," Mrs. Richmond said. As I headed out of the room, I heard her say, "Don't worry—I won't tell your dad."

And like that, the world was filled with hidden angles. Rosie. Mrs. Richmond. And Dean.

Their guest bathroom was all white and had a skylight above the shower. I could have stood in there forever, under the hot spray, staring up at the sky, but then there was a polite knock at the door.

"Carrie?" Dean said quietly.

"Um, yeah?" I didn't hear anything, so I turned the water off. "Dean?" Was he going to come in? Was this how it was going to happen, while I was naked and dripping on their white bathmat, soft and plush as rabbit's fur? Well. Okay. Okay. My breath grew shallow and my face reddened, but oh. Okay.

"I have a towel for you." The door opened a crack, and his arm came through, and I took the white towel from him and wrapped it around myself. Then I waited a breath, screwing up the courage to open the door more. But he was gone. I exhaled. Oh.

I changed into my clothes and headed for the stairs, passing what must have been his room. It was mostly bare—he hadn't lived there long, after all—with a blue comforter over a twin bed, a big boom box with a Sam Cooke tape next to it, and his guitar and a mini drum kit of a snare and two toms. And a book, lying face-down on his bed: *How to Forgive . . . Yourself.*

When I got to Dean's car, Rosie was leaning against it, holding her Walkman and her ratty stuffed hippo that she called Beanie.

"What's up? I said thanks for the clothes, right?"

She opened the back door to the car. "I'm going too."

I looked at Dean, but he shrugged. "Up to you," he said.

"Why do you want to go?"

"What do you mean, why?"

"I don't know. I mean, why do you want to go?"

"Why do *you* want to go?"

I shook my head. There were so many reasons, and also none. "I guess I don't know either."

"Please?" Rosie said. "I don't have any friends with cars."

"Do you have any friends?" I asked, smiling. It had been weeks, maybe months, since I'd joked with Rosie.

"Yes," she said. "At least one. Mrs. Richmond and I are tight."

I laughed, and I felt the beginning of a slow release between us. "Okay," I said. "You can come."

I had to send Rosie back to the house to get one of her seed-filled envelopes with the return address of the monastery to which my mom had retreated. I stood by the car with Dean as she went around the fence and tiptoed into the house, closing the screen door oh-so-quietly.

We waited there in a silence I couldn't interpret. I wondered if Dean was turning away from me, slowly, retracting like Vira, the way it hid behind Neptune's orbit for decades at a time.

Rosie came back with Beanie still in tow and an unopened envelope that she handed to me.

"Why didn't you open them?" I asked her.

"Because you never opened yours."

"Why does that matter?"

"Because I'm the little sister," she said, opening the car door. "I learn everything from you."

"Oh, I missed that part," I said. She had already climbed into the car. I bent down to look at her. "Maybe it was all the times you called me a dumbass and said I was stupid and stuff."

"That's part of my job as a little sister too." She stuck out her tongue at me—somehow she did this in a good-natured way—and closed the door.

"Um, you guys ready?" Dean asked. He had assumed an awkwardness that was different from the way he normally was, or at least as normal as I'd known from the last four weeks. Dean took out a map and studied it against the return address on the envelope, running his fingers down the lines of highway from here to there.

"It's south," I said. "About two hours, I think. That okay?"

"Sure. Yes," he said. I couldn't read him. He'd gone a little robotic. Maybe it was due to the fact that I'd shown up at his work looking like a hobo. And I thought the hardhat was bad. "What do you want to listen to?"

I looked through his tapes. Among the Black Flag and Hüsker Dü and Replacements and Michael Jackson in his glove compartment were "Notorious" and "Rio."

"Are you serious? Duran Duran?"

"They're my sister's," he said. "No—really, they're my sister's."

"I like Duran Duran!" Rosie called from the back.

"Sure, sure," I said, pushing the cassette into the car stereo. "Hungry Like the Wolf" came howling out. "It's your sister's."

"It's torture!" he said. "Make it stop!"

"No way." I turned it up, and Rosie and I sang along.

"When you sing it, any song sounds good," he said.

Oh. Oh. I couldn't think of anything but *oh*.

"Keep singing."

Oh.

When the tape ended, I suddenly felt so tired. I leaned my head against the window and listened to the rumble of his sort-of-falling-apart car on the highway. Rosie, the almost-narcoleptic, had already fallen asleep in the back, her head leaning on her stuffed hippo.

"I have a question," he said.

"You're in luck."

"What was your sister's name?"

"Wow, you always have the least-fun questions." I reached down to the console to leaf through the tapes again. "Her name was Ginny. Her real name was Ginger. We're all named after spices," I said, slightly nauseated from embarrassment as I said it.

"I wondered," he said, shifting gears. His hand brushed up against mine, and he held it there for a second, and I forgot everything that sucked in my life. He seemed to be coming in and out of focus, drifting toward me and away.

Before he could ask me anything else about her, I said, "I have a question."

"You're in luck."

"What did you do? What was the freak-out?"

"Oh, yeah, that."

"Yeah," I said. "That."

He took a curve slowly, and for a minute we were the only car on the highway, no oncoming headlights to pierce the darkness.

"It wasn't one freak-out."

"Okay," I said, stretching out the *a* sound, leaving room, I hoped, for him to continue.

"It was, as my father said, 'a cascade of bad decisions that was about to drown me.'"

"Poetic, but could you be a little more detailed, please?"

"Okay, you want to know what happened? I'll tell you." He started driving a little faster. "I skipped school about halfway through last semester and went up to Squire Rock and got really high and drank a lot, because, come on, what else do you do when you're skipping class? And then I challenged this kid Benny to jump off the rock with me into the quarry." He paused. "And then for months after that, I could not stop playing the movie in my head of Benny hitting the rock and landing in the water and going down and down, and me trying to grab him, and the way blood looks underwater, like a feather coming apart, you know, like dandelion seeds or something. And of

Benny in the hospital with his totally useless legs for the rest of his life."

"Oh, god. Oh, that's horrible. That's hard." I wondered if I should talk about the physical properties of blood versus water, its higher viscosity making it flow more slowly, if somehow that would help him feel better—if physics could make him feel better too. "Was Benny a good friend of yours?"

Dean let out one grunt of laughter, but it was a sound full of self-hatred. "Barely at all. He was kind of a fan of the band, which is probably why he agreed to do something so incredibly stupid. I was such an asshole."

It was very hard for me to imagine this. I was pretty sure I was sitting next to the nicest human being in the world.

"So then I stopped going to class and I quit the band and I couldn't sleep and I just couldn't figure out why I should bother with anything. Like, anything. So my dad fired me—he has an auto body shop, and I was fucking up the oil changes—and kicked me out of the house and told me he wasn't going to pay for college until I got my shit together. I still didn't care. I just went from couch to couch and I stayed up all the time—like, every night—and drank until all my friends got sick of me too, and basically I didn't have anywhere else to go and I was out of money, and you know what? I might as well just tell you. I was out there in the middle of town, totally crazy, screaming, and I broke a bunch of car windows and all kinds of ridiculous shit."

"That sounds bad," I said. Understatement of the year.

"They called it a psychotic break." He looked at me from the side of his eyes. "But I'm not broken anymore. Or, at least, I'm less broken."

"Psychotic fix?" I asked.

"Psychotic repair?"

"Should that be the name of our band?"

"It's a terrible name." He hadn't looked at me since his confession.

"Oh, come on," I said. "Is it worse than the Psychedelic Furs?"

"Point taken," he said. "How about the Black Holes?"

"Now, that is a great band name."

His car shook as he sped up a little more, as if trying to zoom past all the information he'd just bestowed upon me. "So now you know."

"Oh my god," I said. "Dean." My hand felt so leaden, too heavy to lift from my lap, but I managed to slip it on top of his, just for a second. "That sucks. I'm so sorry. That sucks." What I didn't say was that I knew exactly how he felt, all those swirls of shame and anger and regret and fear, and I wanted to tell him that, to tell him that I understood and he wasn't alone and he wasn't guilty and he wasn't bad. *Maybe I should tell him now,* I thought, *make him feel better about his own mistakes.* But I still didn't want him to know about me. I was a beast and I didn't want him to know. "Would it be bad if I sang 'Lonely in Your Nightmare' right now?"

He managed a laugh. "I think we both know that Duran Duran is never a cure."

There were a thousand things I should have said to him, but instead I turned on the radio and searched through the few stations that made it through these dense mountains until I found a song I liked.

"Listen — you have to change that. I hate the Smiths," Dean said.

"You hate them?"

"Yes. Sorry. I hate them."

"Really? You had a psychotic break, and you hate the Smiths, the band of all depressed people?"

"I wasn't depressed. I was just temporarily crazy," he reminded me. "I refuse to endorse them."

I sang the lyrics, about a bus crashing into us, about how great it would be to die by his side. What a heavenly way to die.

"Careful," he said. "I'm crazy. Don't give me any ideas."

I couldn't think of any way to tell him that I'd screwed up even worse than he had.

"Listen," he said quietly, slowing down again. "I wound up in the psych ward, if I'm going to be totally honest. And then my aunt called." He paused. "My rich, noncrazy, psychiatrist aunt. So this is the deal: if I can show them that I can keep it together for the whole summer, I can go back to school. I can go back."

"Oh, the psych ward," I said, because I didn't want to tell him that I never wanted him to go back. "You don't have to tell me about the psych ward, Dean. I know it well."

I knew he had another question. And I had an answer. But I didn't want to give it yet, and I didn't have to. We'd arrived.

We pulled onto a dirt road next to a tiny, hand-painted sign that said DHARMA MOUNTAIN MONASTERY. The darkness was a cloak around us, punctuated by stars, brighter and more numerous than I'd ever seen them: sequined disco fabric in the sky.

"Holy shit," Dean said. He peered forward so he could see from the dashboard.

"Right?"

Rosie was still asleep in the back seat. At the top of the hill was an A-shaped stone building, an ancient sort of church with a modern barnlike addition tacked on the side, with a roof that rose from the ground like a ski slope. It had windows all along the side, aglow with yellow light. All around us, tucked into the dense woods, were tiny cabins. The land was covered in gardens and flowers and benches and gazebos, all these places for, apparently, silent meditation. It was somehow both completely quiet and alive in animal sounds: a coyote's howl, an owl's hoot, the croak of crickets, nocturnal creatures scurrying through the woods.

We stopped in the parking lot and just sat there for a minute. Dean stared in front of him and I looked out the window at the buildings, the gold of the windows against the blue of the night. It looked forbidding and inviting at the same time. It was colder up here and I shivered in my short-sleeved shirt.

"Take this," Dean said, handing me his rugby shirt. I slid it over my head. It smelled like him, like his sweat and that lotion he used on his hands to get the grease off and something pine-ish. It just smelled so good.

"So . . ." he said. "What's the plan?"

"Oh, was there a plan? I should have made a plan. Right. A plan."

Rosie came to life in the back seat, rubbing her eyes, then scooching forward to put her hands on the headrests of each of the front seats.

"People," she said, "let's do this thing."

And that's how I found myself at the imposing wooden door of the monastery, knocking lightly. I turned around to look at Dean and Rosie, waiting on the stone path a few feet behind me.

"Again," Rosie said, and I knocked again.

"Oh, for crying out loud, let me do it," she said, moving past me and unleashing three loud raps. When the door creaked open, a guy in an orange sort of toga thing, with wire-framed glasses and a big nose, peered from behind it. He smiled at us in a way that I'm sure was intended to be peaceful and, well, Zen, but it only made me feel disdainful. I wanted to roll my eyes so much that they'd fall right out of my head. He seemed to be waiting for us, so Rosie said, "We're looking for Betty?"

The monk's smile seemed to turn sad, but he didn't move.

"Oh, about yay big," Rosie said, raising her hand to the height somewhere between her tall self and little tiny me. "Grayish hair, long, usually in braids or something?"

"She's our mom," I said to Mr. Can't Stop Smiling. "She's probably never mentioned us."

"She can't talk," Rosie reminded me.

"Technicality," I said.

He motioned for us to come in and installed us on a bench just inside the door. It was a wooden thing that looked like it was chopped out of a tree and crudely fashioned to ensure maximum discomfort. The inside was cold and echoey, all that stone interrupted by the occasional stained-glass window, with pictures of lambs and pastures and rivers and starry nights. The three of us seemed to have agreed to take a vow of silence too. We just sat there, hands on knees, quiet as the night, until we heard footsteps down the hall.

I let that sound grow louder and louder as it neared, but I didn't look until those familiar Birkenstock sandals came into my peripheral vision. I still didn't look up, and Dean and Rosie both stayed next to me. Her smell of patchouli wafted through the air. Then she bent down so we had to look at her, both me and Rosie, we had to. My mother was ex-beautiful; she still had those piercing green eyes and a long, straight nose, her top lip jutting slightly out above the bottom, so it looked as if she was always ready to kiss, but her whole face seemed permanently sad. She wore a flowing robe-looking thing, purple with tassels; the whole scene was *Little House on the Prairie* meets the Grateful Dead. She had always been a hippie type, but well put together, like Ginny. She had worn her hair in long braids, since it was easier to stuff behind a hairnet when she was at the restaurant where she worked; the one thing she hated about cooking was the hairnet. Now, with her hair unleashed, she looked a little bit like a crazy woman who lived in the woods. Well, yeah. That made sense.

If I'd imagined this moment at all, it included my mother's tears, thousands of hysterical tears while she flailed at our feet begging for forgiveness. But instead she had that same annoying half smile as the monk, her eyebrows tipped into the shape of concern, eyes full of questions, but I didn't see penitence anywhere. What kind of lapsed Catholic was she? She put a hand on each of our knees, then turned and smiled and nodded at Dean, as if she'd known him for ages. I didn't look at him. I didn't want to see what he was making of all this madness.

"Hi, Mom," Rosie said, her voice like a bored teenager, disengaged. I felt sad for Rosie. She'd been abandoned too, by her sister when she was ten and now by her mother, at twelve and in the height of her awkward phase and with her too-big, rose-colored plastic glasses — the cheapest frames at the store — sitting hunched in the cool light in the austere monastery to which her mother had retreated without her.

My mom stood up then, and, unwillingly, my eyes followed her. Was she turning to leave? Was that it? Rosie stood too, and my mother pulled her in close. Rosie let herself be pulled but kept her arms by her side, not returning the embrace. Why did she get hugged and I didn't? Not that I wanted to be hugged.

"Mom," I said, "what the hell? Really, what the hell?"

She put a finger to her lips and motioned with her head for us to follow her.

We walked behind her in silence, the longest five minutes of silence in the history of the universe, none of us looking at one another.

"Come inside," my mother said finally, opening the door to the cabin as if she'd been expecting us for weeks or months. She stretched her mouth in an odd shape. "I've barely said anything in thirteen weeks," she said. "It feels kind of funny."

I pressed my lips and nodded, affecting, I hoped, a look of bored indifference.

"I'm so glad you came." She was formal, more like Mr. Roarke welcoming me to Anti-Fantasy Island, or Julie, my truly terrible cruise director from *The Love Boat*.

"This is Dean," I said. I didn't know how to introduce him. My friend? My potential bandmate? The boy most likely to break my heart?

Dean nodded at her and said hi. My mother said "Welcome," to him, that stupid serene smile on her face, her hand gesturing as if she were one of those busty ladies on *The Price Is Right,* revealing to us Showcase #1: the parallel universe of a monkette in the Catskills who had abandoned her kids.

Inside her cabin, the walls were bare wood, undecorated. There was a hot plate and a little refrigerator that hid beneath the sink, a small table and a plain wooden single bed on which sat a needlepointed pillow with the word *Bliss* in white writing on a blue background. In the corner was a portable record player and a few albums. The only thing on the fridge was a picture I'd drawn in eighth grade of a supernova, which was basically just an ice-cream-shaped rainbow, affixed with a Maylor's Funeral Home magnet.

"The funeral home gave you a *magnet?*" I asked.

She shook her head. "The world is a strange place."

"Um, yeah, you're telling me."

Ah, small talk. Not my thing. Apparently not Dean's, either. He decided to closely inspect the wood. I thought he was just trying to cover up his discomfort, but then he said, "This cabin has amazing tongue-in-groove woodwork," after which his face turned red and he went back to burying his face in the carpentry.

"All the residents work on building additional cabins," my mom said. "We learn carpentry skills while we're here." Oh, so she was at boot camp for wayward adults. Perfect.

"So you're a resident here?" asked Rosie. "You live here now?"

"I don't know," my mom said.

Then Rosie asked, "What does *dharma* mean?"

"There's no one translation from the Sanskrit to the English," she said.

"Well, that's helpful," I said.

"It has something to do with living your life right according to the cosmic laws."

"Whatever that means, I don't think you're doing it," I said.

"Probably not," she said to me. "I wish I knew how to."

Rosie sat down on the bed, pressing Beanie against her face, and Dean sat next to her. My mother and I stood. Everyone seemed to be waiting for me, but I was waiting too. I didn't know exactly what for, but I was waiting.

"What are you doing here?" I asked.

"Well, I've been cooking," she said. "A lot of curries, which I know you girls don't like. You prefer cheeseburgers."

Rosie scrunched up her nose. "I'm a vegetarian now," she told my mom.

"Is that right?"

Rosie nodded. "Except for Kentucky Fried Chicken and pepperoni pizza."

"And TV dinners," I said. "And those space ice cream bars you got me for my eleventh birthday, which are probably full of chicken fat or something."

"Really?" my mom asked. She looked horrified. "You still have those?"

I shrugged. "They last for fourteen years."

She looked at her lap and said the only thing she could muster. "I'm sorry. That's no way to eat."

And maybe that was what I had come for. Maybe I'd just wanted her to apologize to me. She had never stuck up for me. Never challenged the therapist, never defended my honor. But here I was, on the edge of being homeless and unemployed and friendless, all before I'd even started my junior year of high school, and I needed something else.

Betty got up and put on a record—Simon and Garfunkel's "America," a song I loved no matter how uncool any of my contemporaries thought Simon and Garfunkel might be. It was a song my mom and dad used to sing together, their voices majestically harmonizing. They'd briefly been a folk-rock duo, thinking they could make a go of it that way before they procreated and had to pay the bills and she got into vegetarian cooking and he became a science teacher: plants and planets. Only one letter of difference, but worlds apart.

I remembered my mom singing to me in my bedroom, her cool hand on my back, the controlled tremor of her voice, clear and raspy at the same time. I could see, all at this moment, each time she'd stepped in to protect me from heartache: my first sleepover when she had to come get me in the middle of the night; the time Dana Palma scratched my left cheek; when our cat Sebastian was run over by a car—an endless litany of moments of actual mothering. And then she was just gone. The craziest part of it, the part that was making my face red and my hands shake, was that she seemed to see absolutely nothing wrong with what she'd done.

Rosie yawned, rubbing Beanie against her face again.

My mother smiled at her. You could almost believe that the smile was genuine, that she cared. "I gave you that, Rosie. Do you remember?"

Rosie nodded, her eyes wide behind her dowdy glasses. She looked so young now—I could see her at five, being presented with the purple hippo and clinging to it so tightly, so thrilled to have this dumb thing she had coveted. She looked five again somehow, only there was a layer of fear in her eyes as my mother spoke.

"I won it at the county fair. Tossing those rings around the old glass Coke bottles. Your father said it was rigged and I could never do it—it was a matter of physics. But you wanted that hippo so badly that I just kept trying, and finally, I remember it was a yellow ring that landed on the bottle and I remember that little ding it made and then the three of you"—here she choked up—"jumped up and down and squealed, and the man took the hippo down from the hook on the ceiling and gave it to Ginger, and she handed it to you, and you were so happy."

By now Rosie's lips were quivering and, dammit, mine were too. How could she tell this story, this story about her moment of being a good mom—no, the best mom—as if she weren't a monster?

"You girls," she said, whispering and crying at the same time. "I miss you so much. I miss you every day."

"Then why the hell don't you come back?" I asked, my voice rising now.

"I wanted to. I want to come back. I thought you didn't want me to."

"I have no idea what you're talking about," I said. "Why wouldn't we want you to?" Rosie had come to stand next to me, arms crossed, suddenly seeming much older and wiser than her years. "What are you doing here? We're falling apart without you."

"I'm not," Rosie said. "I'm fine."

"Fine," I said. "It's me, okay? I am falling apart."

Dean hadn't said a word this whole time. I couldn't even think about him right now, about what he must be making of this whole crazy mess, of me and my self-described falling-apart-ness. But then he was there, standing next to me too.

The song stopped, that beautiful static of the record, and then the next one started, "Kathy's Song," and I knew Rosie was remembering how my mom used to sing that song to us at bedtime too. *The only truth I know is you.*

"What the fuck?" I said. Everyone looked at me but my mom. "What the *fuck?*"

"I was going to come up here for a weekend, maybe a week," she said, leaning her back against the sink. "But then I just couldn't leave, not until I knew you had forgiven me. I just needed to know that I wasn't going to do harm to another daughter of mine."

"So you decided to never talk to us again. That's not harmful." I sort of felt relieved. Okay. That happened. The person formerly known as my mother had fully disappeared from the planet, and I would never get her back. I didn't ask what she meant by harming another daughter — I was just so disgusted by her line of reasoning that I barely registered Dean's hand, holding mine.

"I just, I thought maybe it was more generous to leave than to screw you up, too."

"Jesus," I said. "You think disappearing off the face of the Earth didn't screw me up?"

"I just needed to fix myself up so I could be a decent mother," she said.

"This is your version of decent mothering?" I yelled. "Have you heard of verbal irony? Or maybe self-delusion?"

Rosie started to cry in earnest now, and I put my other arm on her shoulder and squeezed it. I figured Dean would leave. What had he gotten himself into, this ridiculous family drama of someone he'd never even kissed? But he just held my hand tighter.

"Don't make me say it again," my mother said in a whisper-cry.

"Say what?" I asked.

"What's in the letter."

"What are you talking about? You are totally crazy." I turned to Rosie and Dean and said, "Let's go," feeling a strange shell of calm come over me. But then, as we stepped outside the cabin, I noticed it, pointed toward the sky. My father hadn't thrown it out. He hadn't hidden it from me, hadn't punished me by its removal. It was here.

"You took my telescope? You stole my telescope?"

"No—Carrie, I—"

But it was too late. It was starting to happen: the screaming, the shaking. My face went red, my hands trembled. I was ready to shake something, break something, hit something, to lunge and snarl at my mother, a Tasmanian devil of a person now, screaming and screaming, kicking, waving my hands as Rosie and Dean tried to hold on to me. "I can't believe you! That's my *telescope!*" I headed toward my mother but she moved and I hit the wall instead. I hit it and hit it and hit it and hit it, and I was screaming, "What's the matter with you?" but was I saying that to her or to me— *What's the* matter *with you?*—until I felt another hand take hold of mine and pull it back to my side and squeeze it, allowing some anger to leak out. Then a squeeze of my shoulder. I felt my whole body exhale. Rosie. Rosie held on to me until my body stopped flailing.

Many other lost souls had stepped out onto the porches of their cabins now, out of the cool shadows of the monastery, and they were staring at us. I didn't care. I didn't care about anything anymore. I was going to finish ruining my life and then maybe jump off a bridge. Or at least jump off a footbridge.

Our mother said, very quietly, "I just wanted to have a little piece of you."

"Well, you can't," Rosie said. "We'll be taking this with us." She attempted to hoist the telescope, but it was so heavy. I was spent now, plopped cross-legged on the ground, still catching my breath. Dean had crouched next to me but now he stood and lifted the telescope. Or, he tried to. It was too bulky and heavy for him, too, and somehow he started to laugh, and Rosie chuckled, and I almost laughed too. I couldn't believe it. I was actually, sort of, kind of laughing. The only person not laughing was my mother, who sat on the step to her cabin, head in hands, crying.

I would have liked to grab the telescope and throw it over my shoulder, to make a dramatic exit, but my back was still sore from not bending my knees as Tonya had instructed. None of us could lift it, so we had to take it apart: the finderscope and the equatorial mount and the Poncet platform. Dean helped too, not looking at me but attending to the project with his usual handyman skill. It took a ridiculously long time, so long that my mother's community of monks stopped watching us. But my mother stood there, helpless, arms folded across her chest, whimpering, "I'm sorry I'm sorry I'm sorry I love you I'm sorry I love you."

Finally I said, "I get it. I believe you." But I didn't look at her again.

Dean carried the bulk of it, I carried the stand, and Rosie carried the manual. Betty had kept the manual with it—she probably never even really learned out how use it.

My mother ran after us and she grabbed me, wrapped her arms around me, tight as a boa constrictor, but I just stood there, arms affixed to my sides, as if I were her prey, already suffocated. I couldn't have lifted my arms to hug her back even if I'd tried.

Chapter 13

ROSIE SHARED THE BACK SEAT WITH THE *bulky telescope parts.* None of us looked at one another or talked as we pulled away. I didn't care anymore. I knew that was the end of me and Dean. He'd seen it, the true horror that hid inside me. No one could tolerate that, even my own parents. We sat there for a few minutes. I don't think any of us knew exactly where to go or what to do now.

"Here, put this on," Rosie said, taking the tape from her Walkman and handing it to me in the front seat. Dean turned the radio on.

I pressed it into the tape deck. Gloria Gaynor's powerful voice came bursting out. "I Will Survive."

"Rosie—you like disco? I had no idea. You were only three when this song came out. You were still on Raffi."

"'I Will Survive' transcends all musical genres," she said. "It's pure genius."

Rosie. Who knew?

Dean and I looked at each other and smiled, and then I thought maybe, actually, somehow it would be okay.

We drove in the dark night, north, back toward our little town. I realized that I'd been sweating in the cabin and now I had that post-sweat chill, my whole body exhausted and dampening Dean's shirt.

The sky was black now, and cloudless, with a thin sliver of moon and constellations erupting above and around us, Lyra and Hercules and Sagittarius. Rosie stared out the window, her hand around the telescope and her cheek leaning against the side of the car.

"There's a blanket in the back," Dean said to her, and Rosie got the worn plaid wool blanket and snuggled beneath it.

Dean's brow seemed to be permanently furrowed. I could only imagine what thoughts he was lost in, the ways he was trying to conjure up to let me down easy, to remove himself from the path of my wrath. He put a tape in. John Lennon singing "Mother," a song that used to rip right through me even when mine was around. *You had me, but I never had you.*

"So, I have a question," Dean said. My stomach knotted up.

"Do I have to answer it?"

"I'm afraid so," he said. I stared up at the Scorpion constellation's gleaming frame. Was there some way I could sting myself with its tail? Was there some way I could ascend to the heavens and get out of this thing where I screwed up my life on Earth over and over again?

"What is your favorite song?" Dean asked.

Oh. My whole body sighed with relief. I laughed, probably too hard. "Oh, crap—that is a really hard question."

"You have to answer." He was smiling, but he didn't seem all there somehow. This was all filler so he could slip away unnoticed. Still, if we were going to make small talk and pretend nothing had happened, this was probably the best small talk there was.

"Well. Okay. Actually, my favorite song when I was six was 'I Will Survive.'"

"Already demonstrated to be of timeless value," he said. "Go on."

"The first record I bought with my allowance was Elvis Costello, *My Aim Is True.*"

"Marked improvement in your taste."

"I'm really into *Velvet Underground & Nico* right now," I said. "'I'll Be Your Mirror.'"

"Awesome."

"Um, I love X— 'Fourth of July.'"

"A great song."

"I'm not saying it's my favorite, just that I really like it. Maybe this should just be a list of great songs. 'Bohemian Rhapsody'? Queen? Stevie Wonder's 'Superstition'? But then there's Marvin Gaye—anything on *What's Going On.* Anything on Bob Dylan's *Desire.* I feel the need to include a Joni Mitchell song here. 'Blue'? Who has a favorite song? How is that possible? My mind is actually exploding right now."

"It was a trick question," he said. "It's not possible."

"So not fair," I said.

"You guys are total music nerds," Rosie called groggily from the back. "I like Bob Seger."

Dean and I both groaned. "Rosie—watch out. You're going back on my shit list."

"Bon Jovi? Whitney Houston. Madonna?"

"Great-looking, not actual good music," Dean said.

"Kenny G?"

I put my hands up. "Stop it, you're hurting my ears!"

"Cyndi Lauper?"

Dean shook his head, but I said, "I can give you that one."

"Prince?"

"Is that a real question?" I asked her. "Do you dare to suggest that someone doesn't like Prince?"

"Michael Jackson?"

"Everyone in the entire world likes Michael Jackson," I said. I took the tape out from the glove compartment, put it in, and turned the volume way up.

"The Girl Is Mine" blasted from the speakers.

"You do realize this is the worst song on the album, right?" asked Dean. But Rosie sang it anyway, loud and off-key, and I loved her.

When Rosie was asleep in the back again, and the windows were down, the soft night sky on our arms, Dean cleared his throat. "Listen . . ."

I didn't want him to finish. He was going to pre-break up with me. Or say he just wanted to be friends. Or say that he couldn't hang out anymore because he didn't want to get attacked with a shoe.

"No, you don't have to—"

"No, listen, okay? Just listen." He checked in the rearview mirror to make sure Rosie was still asleep. "Listen—it's okay. What happened back there. I totally get it. It's freaky, but I get it. Don't think . . . you know . . . don't think that I won't . . ."

"Oh," I said. "Okay."

"Okay?"

"Okay."

"But, I do have a question," he said. "A real question."

"Well," I said. "You're in luck."

I told him everything.

Pablo the arborist's daughter wasn't at their country house, and I stayed in her room and I did as any fourteen-year-old girl would do, or so I thought—as my friends and I did whenever we were babysitting: I rifled through her things. Then, when my dad and Pablo went out and got stoned on the deck—as if I didn't know what they were doing—I went through Pablo's wife's and daughter's things, and I compiled a stash: an opal and diamond ring, a silver bracelet with carvings of moons and stars (my favorite), an owl pin with tiny rubies. I even took the little framed greeting cards off the wall in the daughter's room and put them in my purple duffel bag with the red handles: one picture of a peace dove, the delicate olive branch balanced in its beak, the other a photograph of a sculpture of two stone bodies wrapped around each other. I was so psyched. I barely had any jewelry, and I loved those pictures.

My dad said I wanted to get caught. He claimed I left my notebook open on the kitchen table to the page where I described the loot in detail—bragged, he said, about the haul. My mom couldn't call up that old-fashioned defense of hers: *She's just a kid, Paul, leave her alone.* She couldn't say anything.

Then it was all four of us in the kitchen, Rosie, just turned ten, and my dad and my mom. He put me in a chair and interrogated me while my mom sat empty-eyed in the corner and Rosie was just sitting there looking astonished and genuinely frightened on my behalf.

You're a thief, he kept saying. I tried to run out of the kitchen, but my dad blocked the door and then it just happened. I grabbed a knife from the kitchen counter, and I held it against Rosie's throat, and I said, *Let me out of here, or I'll kill her.*

The blow from the backside of my father's hand was sudden and strong, and then I was on the ground, my father standing over my crumpled body with his hand pointed at me like a gun, and he said, *Don't you dare touch my daughter.* And the three of them left and locked the door, and I just lay there on that cold and dirty tile screaming and sobbing.

I think I fell asleep. Eventually I heard the click of the door unlocking. I stood up and brushed off my dirty clothes, a colorful tie-dye T-shirt and a jean skirt. I walked out of the kitchen and passed my father, his eyes red from crying or pot I didn't know and didn't care, out of the front door and over to Soo's, and I didn't come home for a week.

Soo's mom didn't mind. She'd always liked me better than she liked her own kid—*Soo, you slob, pick up your room,* to Soo, and *Carrie, honey, how you doing? Come over and tell me what's new,* to me. My mom and dad didn't even call.

And then one day my dad appeared in front of Soo's house in our dented crap-brown Buick, and I came out and got in and he started the car and we didn't talk until I saw that we weren't headed home, when I said, *Where are we going?* He didn't look at me. He just said, *I'm taking you to a shrink.*

I told Dean now what I told the therapist then: the full length of my confession. All the stealing from babysitting gigs and all the gross shit I'd already done with boys and all the cigarettes and pot and drinking I'd already starting doing with Greta and Soo and how I'd put myself in all manner of unseemly situations and how many times I just could not calm down. I unleashed it all.

"I think I thought that some part of me was going to be saved when I told her all that stuff," I said to Dean. "That I would have a real-life ally."

"I get it," he said, his lips still turned down.

"So, then the therapist decided to be the worst human being in the world and told my mom and dad, and they told all the people I babysat for, and I lost all my jobs, and everyone knew, everywhere I went, and then I didn't feel like being alive anymore, and I said so, so they locked me up in the hospital for a week and pumped me full of drugs, and when I got out, each family that I babysat for came to our house and asked me what I'd stolen and if I'd taken drugs or smoked cigarettes around their kids. And I hadn't, but they seemed like they didn't believe me.

"After that I was pretty much banned from babysitting, and the only job I could get was as cashier at my dad's friend's clothing store. So, that was my summer job last year, but this year I got canned and my father sent me to boot camp. Before that, I was mostly sitting around, making a mix tape for my funeral."

Finally, I was done. I exhaled. Dean knew everything, and after that, I'd never see him again and that was fine because nothing was ever going to happen between us anyway. "Everything with my dad and pretty much every other human in this town has just gotten worse and worse."

Dean shifted gears again as we neared the exit. Freckles even on his fingers. I loved freckles so much.

"That's probably the name of our album," he said. *Mix Tape for My Funeral.*"

"Something's wrong with me," I whispered, trying so hard not to cry. "I'm some kind of crazy."

He was silent for a minute, and in that time, the whole world was opening and closing, full of possibility and defeat. "Yeah, something's wrong with me, too," he said finally. "You know what's wrong with me?"

"What?" I screwed up the courage to look at him.

"I like crazy chicks."

I sort of laugh-cried and accidentally spit on myself and said, "Oh, crap," and waved my hand in front of my face as if trying to erase the spitting moment and then I was embarrassed about that, too, and I put my hands over my ears and then on my legs —I just couldn't stop moving them.

"Here," Dean said, grabbing my left hand and putting it on his thigh, the rough jeans, the knee bone beneath it. And he put his hand over it and kept it there. But his mouth was set in a dangerous shape. Maybe that was the look he got when he was retreating, even as he sat there next to me.

Dean pulled up in front of our house. Rosie got out and stood on the porch, waiting for me to follow her.

"Do you want me to go in with you?" he asked, but I got the feeling he didn't want to. I stayed in the front seat, not wanting to leave the perfect retreat of his car.

"No," I said finally, popping the door open. "Listen, if I don't come out alive—"

"Carrie—" He grabbed my wrist. I waited, still, terrified, eager, everything all at once. He leaned into me, his face so close to mine.

"Yeah?"

He looked at me for what felt like a long time. And then he said, "Nothing."

That summed it up. Nothing. I handed him back his rugby shirt. I was calm now, but the whole chemical compound seemed to have shifted between us. The visit with my mother already seemed to have happened days, weeks ago. I may never have gotten my mother back, and I may never have gotten Dean, but at least I had my telescope.

Chapter 14

"WHERE HAVE YOU TWO BEEN?" MY FATHER ASKED. Did he ever leave that chair anymore? He looked as haggard as my mom, though he didn't sound angry—maybe because Rosie was gone too, he was worried instead of pissed.

"We went to see Mom," Rosie said, as if it were an everyday occurrence. Sometimes I liked Rosie. Now was one of those times. She headed toward the stairs with the stand, while I held the heavy metal body of the telescope in my arms. "We took back Carrie's telescope."

All he could muster was "I see that." He stood up and began to walk toward me and I instinctively moved back, toward the stairs.

"Before you ground me, don't bother," I said. "I'm getting my things. I'm leaving." Weirdly, I didn't sound mad, either. It seemed like we had just come to the end of the line. I'd move into Soo's after she left for school in three weeks, then come back for my telescope. Or I'd hide in Mrs. Richmond's basement. Or I'd follow Dean back to Oregon, where someday, after four thousand hours of driving around in his car, we'd kiss. "You don't need to worry about me anymore."

I started up the stairs with parts of my telescope tucked under my arm, heading toward my room. Or at least I tried to, but it was all so heavy and my back still hurt and my fingernail was still bruised and my already-healed hands still had that tender layer of new pink skin. Rosie had already ascended and passed out on her bed, but I was stuck down there at the bottom of the stairs, the victim of gravity.

"Don't," my father said. "Please."

"Don't what?"

"Don't leave."

"Why?" I said from the third stair. "Don't you want to get rid of me?"

My father furrowed his brows and opened his mouth, somehow stunned at my question. "Get rid of you? Is that what you think I want?"

I nodded.

"No, no. Carrie. I love you, and I want you to be okay, and so far you're not."

"I am okay," I whispered. "I am."

"I love you," my dad said again, and I hated him for saying it, because his hating me had been the fuel that kept me running. "I already lost one daughter. I can't bear to lose another."

It was too much for me to hear. I'd always figured that his stinging rejection came from his sense that, if it weren't for me fleeing and Ginny racing after me, he'd still have his pride and joy, her shiny hair and beautiful eyes, her weird genius for remembering the half-lives of every element on the periodic table even though she got C's in chemistry by the very end. But maybe not. Maybe he really didn't know.

I felt like I needed to flee. I needed to be alone in my room with the telescope, me and my old metal friend, and I tried to stand and haul it up, haul it away from my father and his terrible sadness and love, but it was just too heavy. It was all just too heavy.

"Can I help you with that?" he asked me, gesturing toward my telescope.

"Um. I don't know. What are you going to do with it?"

He said, "I'm going to set it up so we can look for the comet."

And that is how, at the end of the longest night I'd ever had that didn't involve tremendous amounts of alcohol and drugs, I came to be sitting on Ginny's old carpet with my father, who, for almost two years now, had been my biggest nemesis. Before Ginny died, Soo had decorated the room in a kind of Hollywood glamour look: coral colored walls and black and white bedding and a fluffy white rug, Christmas lights strung around the window; all of it was perfectly preserved. Her room had windows on three sides and skylights. It had always been the best for stargazing, but none of us ever went in it.

"I need to tell you what happened that night," he said.

"I don't know if you do."

But he pressed on. "Ginger heard us fighting, your mom and I. You must have heard us too."

"I don't know," I said. "I can't remember anything else about that night."

"I mean in general. You must have heard us fighting."

I shook my head, turning the handle of the screwdriver in my fingers. "I thought we were, you know, a happy family. We weren't?"

"Your mom and I weren't happy, no."

I digested this information, tried to fit this piece into the puzzle of our family history.

"What about all those hiking trips to the Catskills? All those trips into the city to the planetarium? You guys weren't happy?"

He put the smaller parts of the telescope in a line on the rug. "Of course we had happy times. Of course. It just kind of . . . it just kind of went sour, past its expiration date."

"Your marriage is not food, Dad."

"No, I know. I just wasn't sure we could resurrect it."

"What does this have to do with Ginny?"

"She heard us that night," he said, his voice catching. "She heard us fighting. It was a bad fight."

"What does that mean—a bad fight?"

"It means . . . it means . . . It's hard for me to say."

"Just say it." I said. "Get it over with."

He couldn't look at me. Instead he screwed the alt-azimuth mount to the base of the lens. "You have to ask your mother," he said. "She has to be the one to tell you."

"This is the world's most unsatisfying conversation," I said, though in some ways, I was relieved. If it was that awful, maybe I didn't want to know.

"We had this terrible fight, and Ginger walked right into the middle of it, and she ran out of the house and took the keys to the car so we couldn't even go after her. That's why Pablo had to drive us to the police station."

I shook my head at this. "You think that's why she died? You think that's why she drove your car seventy-five miles an hour down the Avenue of the Pines and crashed into a tree?"

"I think that had something to do with it, yes," my father said quietly. "Maybe not the fight. Maybe it was because we pretended that we didn't know what Ginny would do after she got in that car."

He was absolving me in that moment—offering me the chance to let myself off the hook, or at least to take my secret with me to the grave. But I couldn't. I couldn't let him walk around thinking it was him when it was me. He had his hands in his lap now, and he was staring at them, his right thumb and index finger stroking the left ring finger, still optimistically encircled in a gold band.

"You didn't know," I said. "But I did."

His hands stopped. He looked up.

"I was there," I said, and I was whispering, but I had never said this before to anyone anywhere—not the therapist and not Dean and not Soo. No one.

Now I told my father about sneaking out and peeking in the window of the observatory and seeing her, bending her head over that rolled-up bill, snorting and drinking and tipping her head back and laughing with her mouth wide open, but maybe crying too. She was a mess, a real live mess.

"I saw Ginny doing that, and I didn't know what it was, but I knew it was bad," I told him. "And right then Ginny looked up and saw me and saw that I'd seen her, and she called out my name, but I just hid in the woods until she got in the car, and then I got on my bike and rode away. I rode home. She came after me, but I just came home and went to sleep. I didn't stop her. And then—" All emotion lifted out of my body, as if it had been carried away by a helium balloon. "She died."

He was quiet for a long moment, that terrible hard quiet of a therapist waiting for the patient to speak. But it was he who broke the silence.

"Where was I?" he asked. It seemed very difficult for him to form actual words. They seemed to come choking out of his mouth.

"You were upstairs, I think."

"And where was Mom?"

I swallowed. "I don't know."

"Right. Because we were here. Because our daughter had stolen our car, and we weren't smart enough to borrow a car and go after her or call the police. Because I listened to your mother, even agreed with her, when she said, *Lay off—she's just a teen-ager. Let's let her be. Let's choose to trust her.* We had never admitted to each other that we knew what Ginny and her friends did. We just pretended that she didn't drink and take drugs and do god knows what with her boyfriends. Sometimes I still pretend that, because if I pretend I didn't know, then it's not my fault. So we pretended. And we did nothing. And she died."

He reached out and squeezed my shoulder for a second, as if he'd temporarily forgotten that I was the worst screwup in our family history. Or, well—maybe not.

"You're no more to blame for her death than any of us," he said. "She was upset, and she was on drugs, and she had the car, and all those parts of the equation added up to that terrible sum," he said. "Elements combine, explosions happen. You of all people know that. You and Isaac Newton and Dmitri Alexandrov."

I shrugged and looked at the floor. I wanted to tell him that he wasn't to blame either, but his temporary kindness was so foreign that I had to keep my eyes down. Then I just said, "Okay," and he said, "Okay," and the telescope was done.

Even though I'd gone to bed at two a.m., I slept better that night than I had in weeks: undrugged, with at least a hint of peace in our household. It rained softly in the early dawn, and I thought as I stirred that Dean was throwing pebbles at my window, but it was just the sound of droplets pecking at the glass. I looked over at Mrs. Richmond's house, willing Dean to make his way out, willing him to be here for his favorite part of the day, the arrival of hope, but the windows over there stayed dark.

In the morning I slipped on my fanny pack and painter's pants and put my hardhat on the bike and tied up my shitkickers, and I didn't even hate them. At least, I didn't hate them as much.

"I'm off," I said to Rosie and my dad, who were reading the newspaper and eating raisin English muffins in the kitchen. I wasn't entirely sure how to speak to them like a normal human being, or if the events of last night meant that we were now on normal human being terms.

"Have a good day," my father said.

"Break a leg," said Rosie.

"I'm not acting in a play," I told her.

"Break a footbridge, then."

"That's also not the intended purpose of my day."

"Build a footbridge," she said again, turning to the science section of the paper.

"Okay," I said. "That I can do."

Everyone stared, slack jawed, as I arrived at work. I tried to pretend that this was a regular day, that the previous day's antics were all figments of their imaginations.

"So, Carrie, to what do we owe this honor?" Lynn asked. Was it possible to ignore him, pretend he wasn't standing there munching on his customary carrots? He seemed neither friendly nor angry, though I couldn't really hear that well behind my headphones. "Carrie?" He tapped on my headphones, and I pushed them back until they were draped around my neck.

"Um, I humbly ask for permission to wear my hardhat and toil for minimum wage," I said. "Completely voluntarily and not because I'm unemployable."

Lynn slanted his eyes and scrunched up his mouth, considering.

"Please," I said. "Can I come back to work? I need some jewelweed." I showed him the scrape I'd gotten from scaling the stone observatory walls.

"Okay," Lynn said, screwing up his lips, furrowing his brows. He was clearly disappointed to see me, but something—fatigue or the soft heart of a therapist type—told him to let me stay. "As long as you've got the right-sized hardhat." He didn't smile at me, just nodded and said, "Give me back my pen." I reached into my bag and gave it to him.

Then there was silent toiling, interrupted by the occasional grunt, and Tonya put on her Walkman, and I put on mine and listened to the Bee Gees sing "To Love Somebody" and I felt kind of okayish. And okayish was strange, but I could handle it.

After work, as I was affixing my hardhat to the back of my bike, Tonya walked by.

"For the record, disco does not suck," she said to me. "You like disco, Carrie."

"How do you know?"

"Because I could hear you listening to it on your Walkman. The Bee Gees do not suck."

"I know."

"No, for real, they don't suck."

"I *know*." She still seemed to be waiting. "I actually like them, okay? Sorry I said that before."

She shrugged. "Okay, then. We're good."

She was still hanging around, so I said, "What?"

"So, we're going to that dance thing at Civic again."

"Oh."

"You coming, or what?"

"What? Me?"

"Yeah, nimrod. You see anybody else here?" Was she joking? Was she plotting her revenge, get me to show up at the dance so she could publicly shame me, à la that movie *Carrie*? If only I had that Carrie's supernatural powers.

I wrapped the bungee cord around the hardhat and took a chance. I said, "Okay. Maybe."

I realized that I hadn't talked to Soo since she wouldn't let me stay with her. Greta, either. They were leaving in less than a month, and clearly they'd already moved on. I tried not to concentrate on the ache that brightened in my chest when I thought about them. Instead I put on a sparkly top and my cutoffs and the sandals with the little bit of high heel, and I brushed my hair out so that, in theory, it was full-bodied (when in actuality it was just frizzy), and I put a sparkly comb on one side and some blush on my cheeks and some blue eye shadow on my eyes. I looked in the mirror and pretended that I looked okay.

Then I took my bike out and stood for a minute in the cool night. No guitar. No sound of his ailing car. No music coming from the house or the whisper of Mrs. Richmond's leather boat shoes on the lawn. Maybe he was so scared of me that he'd left town altogether.

I rode my bike downtown and stood outside the club. I'd been there a thousand times, drunk and swaying to my favorite local band, the Figgs, but never had I attended a wholesome gathering such as this. A gray K-car zoomed past me, Jimmie driving and Tonya in the front seat and Kelsey in the way back, "Funky Town" blaring from the stereo. They parked and walked toward the club, but I rolled my bike into the alley and waited, spying on them. Jimmie was wearing a clay-colored suit with wide lapels and a frilly light blue dress shirt underneath, and Tonya had some sort of pastel spaghetti-strapped getup that sort of worked on her.

After they went in, I locked my bike and went inside. Civic had been transformed into a school-age dance, with patriotic red, white, and blue bunting. It was not necessarily my idea of a cool hangout—it didn't have much compared to Soo's tricked-out basement—and I wasn't sure if it was ironic or not. But the music, I had to admit, was good. "I'm So Excited" and "That's the Way I Like It" and "Love to Love You." I loved Donna Summer. I was ready to admit it. In this drug-free crew of science nerds who had mostly bad taste in music, I was weirdly happy.

I watched from the doorway as Jimmie and Tonya took to the dance floor. Jimmie. He was super happy and nice and a weirdly great dancer. Tonya was even better. It was like a scene from *Saturday Night Fever* with a much more unlikely cast. And it was kind of the best thing ever. I stood at the doorway and watched until Tonya suddenly looked my way. She stopped for a minute in that sea of moving bodies, trained her eyes at me, either to invite me in or shoo me away. I didn't wait to find out which.

Chapter 15

DEAN WASN'T IN THE YARD WHEN I GOT BACK. I stayed home for a couple of nights, reading about Dmitri Alexandrov's discovery of Vira (he had named it after his daughter, whose name meant "faith") and learning all the chords to Bowie's "Life on Mars?" and eating crappy food with my dad and Rosie. I kept sitting out on the roof, playing loud, waiting for the notes to draw Dean out, but he never came. I ignored the slow-growth sickening feeling in my stomach, tried to tamp it down with denial.

Once, when I was sitting out on the roof, fiddling with the telescope, I saw Mrs. Richmond leaving to go to her BMW station wagon.

"Hi," I called out to her—something I had not done before in sixteen years of next-door-neighbordom.

She stopped and smiled. "Carrie. Hi. How are you?" She seemed perfectly friendly and not at all like she knew that her nephew was in the slow and torturous process of breaking my heart.

"I'm kind of good," I said. "How's Dean?"

She hesitated, opening her mouth, taking a breath in, then

exhaling and pausing again. "He's okay," she said. "He's good. Thank you for asking."

Then she got in her car and drove away.

Another time I saw Mrs. Richmond and my dad talking, heads huddled together, and for a flash I thought, *What if those two are getting together?* which led to the delightful fantasy of living in the same house as Dean, not to mention having an actual yard, cable TV, and a dishwasher, and I was happy again before I remembered how sad I was, how much I would miss my friends, and how the boy of my dreams had seen the real me and vanished. They were probably conspiring to keep us apart, Mrs. Richmond asking my dad to keep me on our side of the fence and not infect Dean—healed now, no longer broken—with my particular brand of crazy.

What distracted me from all that misery was the fact that Rosie and I were having actual conversations from time to time, and that apparently—Bob Seger and Madonna aside—she was developing an interest in actual music. She asked me to make her a mix tape, so I put aside the one I'd started for Dean and worked on a starter tape for a budding audiophile. I put a little bit of everything on it, from the Band's "The Night They Drove Old Dixie Down" to Kate Bush to Blondie, to the Specials' "Ghost Town," and Tom Waits and the Silos and the Figgs and NRBQ and Janis Joplin, who knocked Rosie's socks off the way she had mine. Some Neil Young and some R.E.M., too.

One time I had the urge to talk to her about that night, the other worst night of my life, and of hers, but I couldn't bring myself to do it.

A whole week went by, and Earth moved .3 milliseconds away from the sun, the days slightly shorter and a little bit cooler, the full moon winding down to its three-quarter gibbous form. I knew soon Soo would be leaving, and Greta and Tiger and the rest of them. And possibly Dean. But the phone stayed silent, and no rocks at my window and no guitar from the yard and no calls from anyone.

I came home from work that Thursday afternoon, exhausted from actually doing the physical labor that was asked of me. My dad and Rosie were out, but there was a manila envelope on my bed. Maybe it was from Dean? Maybe it was a forty-five of some rare import that would rearrange my world for the three-and-a-half minutes of the song? Maybe it was a breakup letter, even though we were not technically going out. A mix tape? I couldn't open it. Instead, I searched through my records to resume making the mix tape for him, the boy who had disappeared.

I lay down with my headphones on and put on Kate Bush, "Wuthering Heights," a song I'd had to stop listening to after Ginny died because it made me cry too hard. She sang about how it got dark, and lonely, on the other side from the one she loved. Finally I screwed up the courage to open the envelope. It said READ THESE on the front and was filled with smaller envelopes. I poured them out on the bed. My mother's letters. All of them. Apparently my father had rescued them from the trash every time I threw them out. A few had pizza stains on them — he must have dug deep for those. They all reeked of caraway.

In the beginning, they were short and loving and vaguely apologetic.

Dear Carrie,

I'm writing to you from my room in the Dharma Mountain Monastery. It's a truly magical place. The rooms are spare and a bit cold, but outside it's so still and quiet and dark, and the sky lights up like that phosphorescent bay in Puerto Rico that we went to for your dad's 40th birthday. It's absolutely alive with stars. There's no phone here, so this is the only way I can touch base with you.

I'm not planning to stay long, just enough to clear my head so I can come back and do a better job taking care of you and Rosie. It must sound crazy to you, that I'd want to spend a week or two not speaking a word to another human being, but it just seemed like the best way to move forward—by stepping back. I'll be home soon. I love you. I miss you.
Love,
Mom

Dearest Caraway,
Well, as you likely know, the three weeks came and went. It has been amazing. Truly amazing. I've thought about things that had been

absent from my mind for decades, little memories from childhood that had long faded—my mom in her lilac-printed muumuu, digging wild onions from our lawn. The tiniest, most beautiful little moments. It's so strange that Ginny's absence seems to have created an avalanche of these memories, thoughts, and feelings that had been waiting for me to have some crisis so they could swoop in to soothe me.

And they have—I've been soothed. At the very least, I've been made aware of just how much more healing I need. So I've signed up for another three weeks. I can't make phone calls, but if you come here, I will be able to walk down outside the property's boundaries and talk to you. Just write to me and tell me when you'll be here. Or take the bus and walk the half mile up Mulberry Road, and you'll see the gate—you can't miss it, this amazing wrought-iron gate in the shape of those Japanese sloped roofs, and there are these incredible Japanese gardens with cherry blossoms and a koi pond and a whole wave of jewelweed. There's a magnificent herb garden here. It's lovely. I'd love you to see it. So come. Let me know that you're okay and that you're okay with me doing this.
I love you,
Mom

Dearest Caraway,
I haven't heard from you. Is that because you're angry at me? I wouldn't blame you, but I hope that someday you'll understand.

The session ends in two weeks. I'll be home then. I'll hold you and love you, and we'll go to the movies and eat terrible popcorn, and I'll even let you have a soda. I've mostly had brown rice for five weeks anyway.
Love,
Mom

Dearest Caraway,
I love you. How are you? You must be furious with me. You will be angrier when I tell you this: I'm staying for another round. One more month. Well, six weeks in all. Please tell me you'll take me back when I return, that you'll allow me to be your mother again. I am now, and will always be your mother. I just have to get back to the place where I'm not so worried that I'll harm you. I just don't want to harm you. That's why I'm here.
Please, Carrie, please.
Mom

They went on like this, letter after letter of them. They grew increasingly fretful, then angry. Why hadn't I written? Why was I punishing her when she'd already been punished? Had I stopped loving her? The longer my silence, the more she needed to stay away and be silent herself. The letters became more frantic, begging me to write back, to come see her, to tell me she could, should, come home.

And then, the last one.

Okay, Caraway. I'm ready. I'm going to tell you what happened that night.

I told your father that I was leaving him. You may not have known this — I don't know what you knew and what you didn't — but I was having an affair. I was having an affair with Mr. Feinstein — well, Barry. Your old shop teacher. It was a cowardly and shameful thing to do, but sometimes people do terrible things to get out of a relationship. They aren't brave enough to face someone and say, "I don't want to be with you anymore," so they withdraw or fight or cheat — they try to get the other person to be the grownup and end things. So that's what I'd done. I'd bruised and bullied your father until he told me he would leave me — that way he looked like the bad guy. This is what we were in the midst of that night. Your father and I were yelling at each other like children — worse than children. Oh, it was despicable, that I could ever have talked to him that way, your gentle and warm and loving father, who would have done anything for you girls. But the truth is I'd talked to him that way many times. I treated him the way Miss Hannigan treated those orphans in Annie — remember Annie? You loved it so much. I cursed your dad and called him names, and he took it. He didn't fight back. Maybe that's what I wanted: for him to fight back.

But Ginny was the one to fight back. She found us arguing in the living room, and she stood up for your dad. She told me not to talk to him that way. She told me I was a traitor and a liar. She used the word bitch, and worse. She called me as many names in one breath as I'd called your father in a lifetime, and I hit her. I hit her really hard. She fell to the floor. She was gasping for breath, she was so shocked and so hurt, her face red from my hand. There was blood at the corner of her mouth. I hope to god you never make your own child bleed. Oh, it was the worst moment of my life, a moment that I knew then I'd never be able to take back. Your father may have forgiven me for Mr. Feinstein and for all those names I'd called him, but never for that. Your father rushed to her and helped her up, but she seemed to hate him as much as she hated me right then, maybe because he hadn't protected her, or maybe because he hadn't left me when he should have. I don't know. I just know that it felt like she had fled, even when she was in the room with us. She took the keys and left, and I thought, "I'll never see her again." That's what I thought. I thought she'd run away and would be pregnant by 22, like I was, and angry and out of love by 39, just like me. But I let her go. I didn't stop her. I just thought she was already gone.

And we didn't see her again, of course, except in the morgue. And I thought I couldn't submit you to the same fate, the same pain. I had to leave you to save you. I had to leave you to save myself. But I want to be with you. I want to come back. I want you to let me back. I don't know how to work my way back into your heart other than to tell you all this and beg you to forgive me. I beg you to forgive me. And if you don't, I will always love you. Always. Always. Always.

Love,

Mom

I lay on my bed for a long time, staring up at the ceiling, watching the glow-in-the-dark constellations brighten as the sun went down. I felt weirdly empty; all those words swept through me until there was nothing left. They were proof of something, but I didn't even know what. If I didn't talk to someone, I was going to float away like an untethered astronaut.

I picked up the phone and dialed. "Hi, sweetie," Soo's mom said. "We've missed you. Where have you been?"

"Oh, you know—living it up," I said. "Just like you told me to."

"Well, I'm glad to hear that." Her voice was syrupy with drink, even though it was only five thirty on a Thursday night. "Hold on, honey. I'll get Soo."

Then there was the sound of the basement door opening. Music and laughter—a party, which I hadn't heard in the background before then because of our successful soundproofing project. A party, and I wasn't there.

"Soo," she called. "Honey, it's Carrie on the phone."

Then a long, long wait, during which I heard Tommy's unmistakable whine and his terrible selection of the Eagles' "Lyin' Eyes," and for one second, I was glad I wasn't there.

Finally, Soo got on the phone. "Hey, what's up?" she said, her voice cool.

"I don't know," I said. "What's up?"

She sighed. "What is it, Carrie?"

"Are you mad at me?"

"To be honest, yes."

There was no one there to help calm the surprise, maybe the outrage. That person was always Soo. "What did I do?"

"Is that a real question?" she asked. In the background someone hooted.

"It's one hundred percent a real question. What did I do? Can you please just—can you please just tell me what I did?"

"Okay, fine," she said. "You left."

"What? When? When you kicked me out of your house?"

"I didn't kick you out—you're so overdramatic."

"What was I supposed to do? Sleep in your hallway? I was in the middle of a total crisis."

Behind her someone said, "Get off the phone and come drink this beer!" It didn't sound like Justin.

"You're always in the middle of a crisis!" she yelled. It stung, but I knew she was sort of right. "Sometimes other people have crises too."

"Did you have a crisis?"

"Carrie—yes. Couldn't you tell when you were here?"

I wrapped the phone cord around my fingers, feeling smaller all the time. Soo must have moved up from the basement, because I couldn't hear the drunken hollering and the thump of music anymore.

"No," I said. "I couldn't."

"Justin and I broke up," she said.

It felt like oops.

"What? Soo—oh my god. I'm so sorry. What happened? When? Why?"

"Because he doesn't want to live off campus with me when we go to school, and then we had a fight about it, and he maybe doesn't want to have a girlfriend when he goes to college because he wants to 'see what's out there,' and that's what we were in the middle of when you were here," she said, as if that should have been obvious to me.

"But you were naked!" I said. "Do people usually break up naked?"

"We were having breakup sex!" she yelled.

"Well, how was I supposed to know that?" I heard nothing on the other end of the line. "Soo, I'm really sorry. That sucks. You guys were really good together," I said, realizing as I said it that I meant it.

"Yeah, I mean, it's dumb, but I thought we'd be together forever. I thought he was the one. I mean, he was the first person I had sex with, you know?"

"No," I said. "I don't really know. I don't know anything about that. There's that whole I'm-going-to-die-a-virgin thing."

Soo laughed, but I thought about how I'd saved that one thing—I'd loaned out my body for everything else, every drug and every disgusting interlude, but I'd kept one part of me whole, innocent, as if I still believed that there was something good in me to share. And the person I'd saved it for, well, he probably didn't want it anyway.

Then Soo said, "I heard you went to see your mom."

"Yeah."

"How was that?"

I laughed. "Um, horrible? I think that pretty much covers it. Wait—where did you hear that?"

"From Dean," she said.

"Oh. Is he there?"

"Now? No. He hasn't been around for a couple of days. He was here the night after you went up there, but he seemed a little off. Like, sad or something. And extremely annoyed by Tommy, who was being a drunken jerk, as usual. Dean hasn't been around since. What's happening with you two?" she asked.

I shook my head. "Nothing," I said. "I guess nothing."

"Carrie? You want to come over? You want to sleep over?"

"Yes," I said. "But not tonight."

Never before had I actually walked around the block and up the stairs to Mrs. Richmond's home on my own. I'd never even been in the front door, since Dean had let me in the side. But I could see Dean's car in the driveway, and so I just did it. I pressed the doorbell. It rang to the tune of "Yankee Doodle Dandy."

Mrs. Richmond answered. I wondered what it was like for her to live in that big place all alone, after her husband had died.

"Um, hi," I said. "Is Dean home?"

"He's sleeping," she said, in a soothing therapist voice that I hated.

"Oh." It was seven thirty at night. "Really?" If I'd known

which window was his, I could have come back later with a few pebbles to toss at it, to try to rouse him, but I didn't. I thought about making a break for it, knocking past her to run inside and find him, but Mrs. Richmond seemed to be permanently parked there, standing sentry.

"He's had kind of a rough couple of days."

At first I thought, *Oh my god, did he have a bike accident? A car accident? Is he okay?* It seemed like she wouldn't tell me if I asked.

"Okay," I said. I turned to go home, but some broken part of me was emboldened enough to stop. I'd already lost everything. I might as well find out why. I'd find out if the problem was realizing the girl he was into was too crazy to be with. "What happened?" I asked. "To Dean? Why did he have a rough couple of days?"

"Well," she said, hesitating, "I'd rather that he tell you himself."

"He'd have to talk to me to do that," I said, and this seemed to summon some sympathy in her.

"I'm sure he will," she said, her efficient smile making me furious. I turned to go home. "Carrie," Mrs. Richmond said, "I know he does want to see you."

I just waved my hand goodbye, in as polite a way as I could. I tried to hold on to what Greta had said—I was smart and adorable and loved. I didn't feel like any of those things, but I was going to try.

* * *

I'd finished seven weeks of troubled-child boot camp, which I was calling it even though apparently it was just a summer job for budding arborists. As a gift, my father was allowing me to go to Soo's for an official party, as opposed to the secret ones we usually had.

"Don't steal anything, take any drugs, or run away."

"Um, okay," I said. "Thanks?"

"Yes, thank you is an appropriate response," he said. "Don't screw it up, Carrie, okay?"

I looked down at my feet, my toes still a little bruised from their day of being forced into Soo's too-small hiking boots. We had a few more weeks of summer and then everyone I loved—well, everyone but Rosie—would be heading to the black hole of college. At least he was letting me orbit around them one last time.

"Okay?" he asked sternly.

"Yeah," I said. "Okay."

It felt so good and so sad to be at Soo's again, to be in the safe harbor of that basement and all the pleather furniture and the mirror ball and Plastic Ono Band screeching from the stereo, the pumping of the bass in the mostly soundproof-ish walls. There were ways that I'd turned into a different person in these past weeks, as if the calluses that had sloughed off after the wild parsnip incident had let someone new out, someone 6 percent less tortured. And there were other ways that I was still maddeningly the same. For one thing, I still did not seem to have a boyfriend.

Tommy was standing in front of me when the door opened and in walked Dean. He looked a little haggard, but then again, his hair was always mussed and his shorts were always painted with a streak of bike grease. He didn't look over at me, but I kept looking, no matter how much it hurt.

"So you and the bike mechanic, huh?" Tommy said, standing next to me and tugging hard on a bottle of Bud. "Guess that makes sense, since you're a construction worker now."

I shrugged. Me and the bike mechanic? Hardly.

He had a menacing look on his face and he was staring at me harder than he'd ever stared at me before.

"What, Tommy?"

"Just wait there, Hardhat," he said. "Wait right there." And he disappeared into the bathroom.

I watched Dean from across the room, talking to Soo and Tiger, running his hands through his greasy hair, a different kind of nervous from when I'd first met him. Occasionally he shifted his head as if sensing me on the other side of the room, but he didn't turn. I should never have had him take me to my mom's.

Now Tommy came stumbling out of the bathroom. He

pressed a finger against my chest but he was the one who stumbled backwards. Then he smiled and said, "I just brushed my teeth."

"Thank you for that astounding revelation, Thomas."

"Don't you like a guy who brushes his teeth until they bleed? That's what he told you—I heard it. I can't think what else you like about that guy. It can't be what he says about you. Carrie"— and here he stumbled toward me— "I'm the one who really likes you."

I backed up. "What did he say?"

"What do you mean?" Tommy was wobbling slightly.

"What did he say?"

"To me? Nothing."

"Who'd he say something to? About me?"

"Oh, about you. He said you were crazy."

My heart was making a break for it. Or maybe it was the contents of my stomach. I looked over at Dean and now he looked back at me, and he seemed kind of miserable and tortured and not at all like the person who had told me the happy secret of his tooth brushing a few weeks ago, a happy secret that Tommy apparently hoped to emulate.

"Who'd he say that to?"

"To Soo."

I digested this information. Or I tried to, but I couldn't. It was information knocking at my door that I couldn't let in. "When?"

"No, wait. I can't remember. Maybe she said it to him. She said you were crazy. Like, made of broken glass or something."

Very quietly, I said, "Then what did he say back?"

Tommy shrugged. "Just that he agreed." Tommy cleared his throat and righted himself, as if he'd reached back and pulled up the collar of his shirt to make himself taller. "Like I said"—and now he wobbled again, leering toward me—"I'm the only one who really cares about you."

That face had throbbed before me plenty of times, as had others, but I'd never really looked at any of them. I didn't care who they were, only that they'd cast their vote for me, deemed me fool-around-worthy, worth the trouble of trying. I only cared that they plied me with enough booze and drugs and laid me down so I could be excused from my brain for the length of the transaction, whether a half an hour or five minutes. But now I truly looked at Tommy, at the pressed waves of his shiny black hair and the one fleck of black in his otherwise bright brown irises, or the zipper-shaped scar on his left cheek, all the things besides the mysterious makeup of his DNA that made him a unique individual, the current manifestation of those same molecules that fled from collapsing stars billions of years ago. We're all made of atoms that were here in the very first moments of Earth, churned up and spit out in new incarnations every time something or someone was born or died. And I took comfort in this, looking at Tommy's baby-round cheeks and half-closed eyelids and drunken attempt to form his soft lips into a pucker—he had beautiful lips, I'd give him that. I took comfort in knowing I only had to go through this life once.

Tommy's face was still close to mine, his lips puckered into an invitation. I could do it. I could move forward two inches, could fall back into the comfortable pillow of the old, gross routine. I knew Dean was looking at me now, and I parted my lips and moved toward Tommy.

The words to a Paul Simon song coursed through the speakers: how losing love is like a window in your heart, how everybody can see that you're blown apart. I pushed Tommy aside and turned to go, ignoring Dean's voice calling, "Carrie—wait," as I walked out of Soo's basement, got on my bike, and flew away.

I was late, just by a few minutes, but my father was not sitting in the flowered chair.

"Hello?" I called, softly, in case he was asleep and wouldn't note my tardiness.

"Carrie. You came home." My father stood at the top of the stairs. "Come here."

"No." I couldn't bear another fight.

"Please."

"I'm only five minutes late. Please, Dad. Please just leave me alone." The only person I felt like running to besides Soo was Dean. And I'd lost them both.

"No," my father said. "Come up here. Come up. Look." He waved his hands.

"What?"

"Come up here already, you dork," Rosie called. "It's your beloved comet."

I looked up. "What? Now?" Somehow, after all this planning and calculating, I'd forgotten to keep track of Vira.

"It just crossed into the Northern Hemisphere," my father said. "I heard them talking about it on the radio and then I came up here and looked. Come up."

I stayed at the bottom of the stairs, my arms crossed. I couldn't seem to make myself trudge up the stairs; the force of gravity, or the gravity of fear, was too strong. It was a terrible feeling, so uncomfortable, a snake slithering through my intestines, something like nausea welling up inside me and then, crap, tears.

My father waved me over to him. "Look," he said. "Come up here. Please."

I walked up the stairs, sniffling, and then into Ginny's room to my telescope.

"You remember this is the least visible path of the comet in two thousand years, right?" he asked.

"Yes. Just my luck."

"It's low on the horizon. But if you get the telescope in just the right spot, if you make really small adjustments, it'll align. I think you'll get a good view." He tipped the telescope slightly. "See it better now?"

"Yep." My father was staring at me, waiting for my response.

I peered up at the sky, and I saw it, the fiery tail, the white light, *a hand to your darkness, so you won't be afraid.* I stayed there for a long time, my eye pressed against the glass of the telescope until I felt it begin to bruise. Every ninety-seven years, for hundreds of thousands of years, this same rock-on-fire had sailed through our atmosphere, essentially unchanged. Or, actually, it was changing all the time. Just a rock for seventy-five and a half years and then, when it got close to the sun, all that gas and dust burst from it. Just like that, it became something else.

"It's just a ball of rock and gas," I said as I pulled back from the telescope. "Big deal." Then: "Just joking," I said, drying my tears. "It's totally amazing."

And the guy actually smiled at me.

When the phone rang, breaking the magic of the comet, I knew who it was.

"Carrie," my mom said. "I just saw it. Did you see it?"

"Yes. I saw it."

"I just wanted to make sure."

"I saw it," I said again.

"Okay."

"Okay."

"Are you doing astronomy club again this year?"

"That's the plan."

A pause, during which I heard a teakettle boiling.

"Can I come on the field trip to the planetarium this year? Will you let me?"

I really wanted to say no, to deny her access to any part of my life, let alone the almost-the-most-sacred part. Three-quarters of my life was total unbearable shit, but the other quarter had started to seem pretty okay, bordering on good.

And my mouth made the word. "Yes."

I was deep in a flying dream, lost and floating in the sky, part terrified and part awed, with Lynn's pickup truck tracking me below, when a sound made me open my eyes. The glow-in-the-dark stars on my ceiling had lost their light, their outline faint against the thin rivers of cracks up there. My mom had been the handy one, the one to do the home repair. The plinking started slowly at first, and then became more persistent. Finally I crawled out of bed and opened the window, sticking my head out into the cool air. It was descending into the darkest part of the night, that swirly, soothing midnight.

He was just standing there. The cutest boy in the world, who thought I was crazy. Who didn't, apparently, actually like crazy chicks.

"Hi," he said.

"Hi."

"Hi."

"Hi."

He blinked at me. "Hi."

"Um, hi? Is that it? Should we just keep saying hi and then I'll go back to sleep because I don't know what else to say or where you went or if you're okay or if we're, if we're, you know, if we're, I don't know, if we're—"

"Can I come in?"

"In here?"

"Yeah. Can I come up there?"

"Oh. I don't know. Yes, okay."

"Because we are," he said.

"We are?"

He smiled. "Yes," he said. "We are."

I went downstairs and let him in, forgetting that I was wearing a ratty Ramones T-shirt and too-big boxer shorts, my sleep uniform, forgetting that my house was a mess, the banister along our stairs creaky and loose, the hardwood floors worn and scratched, that embarrassing flowered chair clearly sat in for far, far too long. He didn't seem to notice anyway, and what did I care about some guy who thought I was too crazy to date? What did I care?

I cared so much.

He walked behind me as I slowly brought him up the stairs, then he reached for my hand, and it was so warm. It was so warm. But I took my hand away. I led him out my window and onto the roof.

"I didn't say that," he said.

I pretended I didn't know what he was talking about.

"I never said that you were crazy. Especially to that guy. He likes Def Leppard."

"I kind of like Def Leppard," I whispered.

He scrunched up his nose. "You do? Oh, man, I don't know about you, then."

"I know that!" I was too loud. "I realized that you were not particularly fond of me even before you knew that I think 'Photograph' is a catchy tune. I like the Bee Gees, too. And, yeah, I'm crazy."

"This is all that happened. Soo said that you were kind of like fancy crystal—that I had to handle you with care—not because you're fragile but because you're so . . ." He trailed off.

"What? So what? So crazy?"

"I don't know. So special or something. That's all she meant."

"Special like special education?"

He sighed, frustrated or annoyed. "I said just what I said to you. I like crazy chicks. That's all I said. And Soo was just going, you know, 'Yeah, she's pretty crazy,' but not in a mean way, like, in a way that she liked you. Carrie. Carrie, come on. Carrie. Carrie?"

He sang more lyrics to the terrible Carrie song. How when lights went down, he saw no reason for me to cry.

"Stop! Stop, I can't take it," I said, covering my ears. He pulled my hands from them.

"I'm just scared," he said, staring at his lap. "I'm scared, okay?"

"Why?" I could barely hear, that's how hard my heart was beating.

"I just got scared that I wasn't going to be able to handle you with care. That I'd break you. It seems like I break people. I don't know—it was sort of what your mom said. I know what she did sucks so bad, but I worried I'd do the same thing. So I just, I thought I should stay away from you. It's kind of like if I feel too much again, even too much good . . ." He trailed off. "I just . . . I don't want to lose my mind again."

"Well, okay." I said. "You've found your mind, right?"

He smiled and the world was right. "Yes," he said. "My mind and I have been reunited. I'm sorry I was an asshole. I was trying not to be an asshole, and in doing so, I became a total asshole."

"Okay," I said. Then I hugged him, and I loved the feeling of his long hair on my cheek, and I whispered in his ear, "Don't be scared. Please don't be scared."

I told him I wanted him to take me somewhere, and then directed him down the Avenue of the Pines and through the parking lot and up the little dirt road that led to the geyser and its giant pile of calcium, the bright orange flowers of the jewelweed. He left a mix tape in, and we sat by the half-finished construction project.

The comet was still too low and far away for us to see without a telescope up there — it would still be another week or so before we could see it with our naked eyes, but the Scorpius constellation gleamed above us. "What kind of star is that?" he asked, pointing to the constellation's tail.

"Probably a white dwarf," I said. "It's a little star that forms when a bigger star collapses."

"It's the dregs of the big star, you're saying."

"Yes, the astronomical dregs."

"Another band name?"

"I'm thinking no." I had no beer to sip, nothing in my hand to hold on to.

"What kind of star is the sun?" he asked.

"That's easy — yellow dwarf."

"Wait — the sun is a dwarf?"

"Yes, it's only that hot because it has a Napoleon complex."

The music thrummed faintly, the Cure's "Boys Don't Cry," and we were just sitting there looking up at the sky, and time evaporated or it stood still or something, and I was just so uncomfortable. I was waiting and dreading, both.

"All those stars might not even be there anymore," I said finally, trying to fill the silence. "Do you ever think about that? They might have exploded thousands of years ago, but it takes so long for their light to travel here that we'd never know. That's old light we're looking at."

"Yeah," he said. "It's amazing."

And then, I thought it was going to happen. Meteor showers and that warm soft air and his arm lightly brushing mine and the smell of jewelweed and him saying "I love this song" as the Kinks' "Waterloo Sunset" came on. It was too much. I couldn't wait anymore. He was just sitting there, his hands to himself, not even looking at me.

"What's happening?" I asked. I didn't mean to be whining, but I was. "Is something going to happen?"

He said, "Um." That *um* seemed to last for ten minutes. Then, very quietly, "Okay. Can I kiss you?"

No one had ever asked me that before. No one had ever been so solicitous and gentle and kind. His head was moving toward mine, the hair and the tangy smell and the night. He took the lock of my hair that had fallen over my face and tucked it behind my ear and then I couldn't help it, I couldn't take it, my heart was beating so hard that I could feel it in my ears and I jumped up and ran over to his car and got in the front seat and shut the door.

Dean came over and knocked on my window, and I rolled it down.

"Um, I have a question," I said.

"You're in luck." His face was close to mine, even if the car door was in between us, and I could feel him getting closer.

"Why do you like me?" I asked. "And not just because I'm crazy. Or in spite of the fact that I'm crazy."

I was stalling, just trying to find a minute to catch my breath, but he actually paused to consider the question. "Okay," he said. "I'll tell you."

He took my hand in his, my limp little dirty-fingernailed

hand, and he looked at our hands as he talked. "I like your messy rock star hair. I love that one tooth that juts out. I like that you love astrophysics."

It took all my energy not to evaporate from the sheer intensity of feeling; I didn't even know what kind of feeling. Just: it was too much. It was too much good.

"And," he said, "you have good taste in music."

The nicest thing anyone could ever say. Somehow I could exhale.

"But the truth is . . ." He stopped. He was going to tell me that he still loved a girl back in Oregon and too bad for me. "The truth is, I knew I really liked you when I saw you in those work boots with that hardhat on the back of your bike."

Then my lips were on his. I had kissed him without even meaning to, right through the open window. I pressed my lips against his and sort of hurt my lip, and he said, "Ow," but then he kissed me back, and he put his hand against my cheek and our mouths were too open and then too closed and then we hit the rhythm. We kissed and we kissed and we kissed. And then Dean said, "This is a stupid way to do it," and he opened the door and took me out and leaned me against the car, and I was more on fire with desire than I'd ever been in my life. All that heat, all that light, all that white—I felt like it wiped clean the dirty slate of the past two years of my life.

We spent what felt like hours out there by the creek, by my imperfect corner of the unfinished footbridge, kissing until my lips were so red and chapped that I could hardly kiss anymore. I'd never felt any sensation in my life better than that pain.

"I should take you home," he said at some point, pausing to rest his head on my shoulder, to kiss me at the base of my ear. "Your dad." He lifted his head to look at me, and I looked at him, and this was happening. This moment. We were just looking at each other. And then we kissed some more.

We drove home, his hand on mine, moving away only to shift gears. We said nothing, and didn't even put any music on the radio. When we pulled up in front of my house, all the lights were off. I had been out with an upstanding human being, who thought I had good taste in music and liked my hardhat. I kissed him and kissed him again.

Chapter 16

FOR THAT ENTIRE WEEK, THE COMET BLAZED, a fireball making its way across the sky. It watched over us as we put the finishing touches on the footbridge, a glossy coat of polyurethane that had to sit for forty-eight hours before we worked on it again. We built a tent of tarps and dowels to cover the bridge so dirt and bugs wouldn't get stuck to the polyurethane, which had a terrible chemical smell like spray paint that was also kind of a good smell.

"This is it, kiddos," Lynn said, standing before the almost-finished footbridge, all three hundred feet of it snaking up toward the observatory. "We're going to be done by Friday, and I encourage you to invite your family and friends to come celebrate the official opening of the Youth Workforce Footbridge."

"Sounds like a rager," I said. "I assume there'll be a keg."

Lynn started for a minute, then seemed to adjust. "Yes," he said. "It'll be a two-keg party, starting at nine a.m."

"Really?"

Lynn smiled. "No," he said, "but there will be coffee and donuts."

* * *

I rode my bike the long way home, through the park and past the creek and by the racetrack and down along Mansion Row and then out to the wrong side of town, where the houses were far more run-down than mine and closer together, little bungalows squatting next to trailer parks. I hadn't been to Tonya's for a couple of years, but it looked the same: somehow sad and proud at the same time. I peered into the screen door and knocked. She was vacuuming—apparently that was the first thing she did when she got home—and didn't hear me at first, so I had to open the door and call out. "Hey. Can I come in?"

"Enter at your own risk," she said, turning off the vacuum. "My grandmother does not smell any better than when you used to come over."

"Oh, I—"

"It's okay. I heard you saying that to Soo one time. You're right. The smells of pee, perfume, and booze do not mix. But she's in the back with her nurse, so it's actually not bad."

"So, I just came to give this to you," I said, handing back her hammer.

"Right," she said, taking it from me and putting it on top of the TV, the old-fashioned kind with a giant screen in some hideous block of wood.

The screen was filled with animations of the planets. "What's that?"

"Duh, you dipshit. It's *Cosmos.*"

"You didn't used to talk like that, Tonya," I said quietly. I didn't know why *dipshit* made me feel worse than all the other adorable insults she'd uttered over the last two months. But it did.

"Neither did you." She turned the TV off and then it was just me and her and her dank living room, which she started tidying in an aggressive way.

"Yeah, well, I've been through a few things since then," I said.

"Yeah, well, me too."

I sat down, even though she hadn't invited me to. Aging copies of *Reader's Digest* were spread across the coffee table—all the furniture looked like it had been there since 1963.

"Let's see. There was the alien abduction—that whole anal probe thing. A close second in the Miss America contest, which was truly devastating. Oh, wait—that was the Junior Husky Miss America contest, but it still stung. And, um, what else? Still getting over the fact that I missed the episode of *General Hospital* where Luke and Laura got married, which is so devastating that even though it was six years ago I'm still not over it. So, yeah —try to top that."

Even though I hadn't laughed, I said, "I forgot how funny you are."

"Right." She was sorting the mail, not making eye contact with me.

"Really, I did. I love my friends, but none of them are funny."

"I guess it's not cool to be funny." She put the mail in one neat pile on top of the TV.

"Maybe it's not. I don't know. It seems like it would be, right?"

"Yeah. If you were actually cool, you would be into people who were funny. Otherwise you're just a dipshit."

"You don't have to call me that."

"This is a hypothetical dipshit we're talking about. Wait—is that one of your band names?"

"'Hypothetical dipshit?'"

"Yeah."

"No, Tonya. That is not eligible for entry into the contest for great band names."

"Thought I'd try." She collapsed next to me on the couch, leaning over to straighten the magazines on the coffee table but still not really looking at me. "Beats Piece of Toast."

"Everything beats Piece of Toast. They're as good as their name."

"Finally. You are coming to your senses, dipshit." I rolled my eyes at her, but we were managing to almost smile. "You know what the worst part of this whole year of suck was?" she asked.

"Besides your dad's thing and having to take care of your grandmother?"

"Yeah, besides that," she said.

"What?"

"I didn't have anyone to talk to when that Mars rover disappeared. You know? That was something you and I would have talked about forever."

"Yeah, that sucked. That really sucked. I felt like we were going to learn so much about the mysteries of the universe with that guy—really. The real mysteries of the universe."

"Yeah, it was just a giant bummer of a day for astrophysics nerds everywhere," she said.

"Are they everywhere?"

"Yes," Tonya said, with such certainty that I believed her. "They're everywhere. We're everywhere. We just have to find each other."

As I made my way to the door, Tonya said, "So, yeah, looks like we're in the homestretch."

"Yeah, the end of the chain gang," I said. "Three days left."

"No, I meant the comet—it's going to leave the Northern Hemisphere soon."

"Oh, I know," I said. "It'll be back to the humdrum story of the solar system, while it hides behind Neptune for a few decades again. We could totally be alive the next time it comes back," I said. "We'll be a hundred and thirteen. We'll still be digging ditches in the park for minimum wage."

"That is not my vision of my vocational future," she said. "But enjoy that ambitious side of yours. Anyway, Jimmie's dad has one of those Celestron telescopes, if you want to come see it tonight."

"I can't," I said. "Next time."

"You mean in ninety-five years?"

"Yeah," I said. "Ninety-seven."

"Okay, see you then."

I pressed the screen door open but then I stopped and turned around. "What about tomorrow?"

"What about it?"

"You want to do something tomorrow? Something wholesome, involving disco?"

She narrowed her eyes at me, circumspect but curious, I thought. "You know what band is good?"

"I'm looking forward to hearing," I said.

"Jimmie's band. The Disco Balls."

I resisted saying the name was only a marginal improvement over Piece of Toast. "Oh, I thought you were going to say Duran Duran."

"I'm not totally ready to concede that point yet. Jimmie's band is really good. And he's a great drummer."

"This is surprising news, I must say."

"So you want to go see them tomorrow night, or what?"

"Well, I was supposed to go to Soo's." It was not true, but it was what came out of my mouth.

"Yeah, okay," Tonya said, waving her hand at me, a combination of *Goodbye* and *Go screw yourself.*

"But, no—wait. Yes. I want to go. I can totally go. I'm going. Yes." For some reason I was kind of hopping in the doorway, as if she had looked away and I wanted her to see me once again.

"Okay, nimrod, I get it. You're coming. Fine."

"Okay."

"Okay."

"Okay," I said.

When I got home that night, still slightly fumey from the polyurethane, Rosie was sitting in the kitchen, organizing her school supplies. She was the only person I knew who was psyched for school to start. She'd be starting junior high in a week. She held a rainbow pencil between her teeth.

"This came for you," she said, shoving an envelope my way.

I took it but didn't open it. "Did you get one too?"

"Of course."

"What is it? It doesn't smell like caraway."

"Star flowers," Rosie said, not looking up. "They're supposed to bloom well in shade, so says her little card."

"Are we throwing these out, as usual?" I asked. What went on in that twelve-year-old head? I wondered. She hadn't lived with her mom for months, and here she was acting like it was normal to keep getting these seeds from her, but pretty much nothing else, save for — maybe — the chaperoning of a future field trip.

"No," she said. "Don't throw it out."

"No?"

"No. Just grow it. See what blooms. She says they'll come up even in fall. When she'll be back."

"Huh." I opened the barely stocked fridge to see what was inside. Very old peanut butter, very old jelly, and some not-that-old bread. "You hungry?" I asked. "You want me to fix you something?"

Rosie lifted the left side of her mouth in skepticism. "Did you learn how to cook since last time I saw you? Because I don't think you've ever made me anything to eat in my entire life."

"Well . . ." I sat down next to her with the peanut butter, jelly, and bread. "This is true."

It was Ginny who used to make our afternoon snacks, because she was the first one old enough to use the stove, and my mom showed her how to toast these nuts with brown sugar and cook these little grilled cheese sandwiches with basil and tomato, and then she'd sit down with us and look at our homework with us until our parents got home.

But then, by the time she died, she'd stopped all that. She wouldn't be home after school, and Rosie and I either wouldn't eat or we'd shove some crackers in our faces. And then, in my post-Ginny life, I never came home after school either. Rosie— she was all alone.

"Listen," I said. "I have to talk to you about something."

Her face got all cloudy. "You and Dean are moving to Paris."

"We are?"

"Is that what you're going to tell me? You and Dean are eloping."

"As awesome as that sounds, no, that's not what I'm going to tell you."

"Oh, okay," she said, cheerful again. How could two sisters turn out so differently? "Then what?"

I took a deep breath, my hands shaking. "Look—I'm sorry," I said. "I'm sorry I did that to you. That was the worst thing I ever did."

Rosie's eyes widened. "I think you have a lot of competition for the title of worst thing."

"It was worse than the drugs and the stealing and all this shit with Dad. I'm trying to apologize, okay? Could you please forgive me? Please?"

Rosie shook her head. "It's basically a folktale: 'How Carrie Tried to Kill Me'—but not really. I pretty much just blocked it out." She paused. "Just stop screwing everything up, okay? Just stop it. Okay?" She reached out and sort of patted me on the chin in some sort of awkward attempt at intimacy. "Okay?"

I nodded, but no words came until I could puff out a whisper. "Okay."

Chapter 17

DEAN WAS SURPRISINGLY UNFAZED THE NEXT NIGHT when I told him what I wanted to do. He did that thing where he puffed out his bottom lip and nodded in consideration, then he scratched the dark stubble on his chin.

"Hmm, a disco band," he said. "What is this genre you're speaking of? I've never heard of it."

"Come on," I said, tugging at his hand. We were sitting on my front porch, with its sloping, splintery front steps, which he had volunteered to sand if we wanted him to, though we were all pretty used to living this way. "It'll be good," I assured him, though of course I didn't really know if it would.

He smiled at me. God, he had one of those smiles: his lips bloomed, and it seemed like everything would be all right. Forever.

"Oh, and we're taking Rosie," I said.

He nodded again, like he could handle anything I threw his way.

* * *

The gig was somewhat poorly attended: about eighteen high school kids were swaying awkwardly to "Love Train" by the O'Jays and "Dancing Queen" by ABBA, which to me was a band so bad I wouldn't call their offerings music. There were red, white, and blue buntings across the stage again where Jimmie's band was setting up. Jimmie was wearing white sweatbands across his forehead and on his wrists, so he looked more like Björn Borg than Andy Gibb.

"It'll be good, huh?" Dean asked, then he leaned in like he was going to kiss me, right there on the dance floor with Rosie flopping around behind us, but all he did was keep his head close to mine and smile, and I felt like we were in some kind of protective bubble.

"Let's get something to drink," I said, tugging him toward the bar. We outfitted ourselves with Cokes and then sat down on a bench while Rosie went right up to the stage to watch the sound check. She'd hardly ever been to see a band before; maybe she thought that was part of the show.

We sat there on the bench, our shoulders touching, our fingers atop the cans of cold, sweating Coke almost interlocking. I could have stayed like that forever, but then Dean said, "Is it as good as you thought it would be?"

"I don't know," I said. Was he talking about the dance? "I mean, yes?"

"I haven't really seen it yet — it just looks like a giant star."

"Oh, the comet," I said. "Well, I'll show you through the

telescope. I wish Alexandrov could have lived to see that he was right."

"Why? People didn't believe him that it was a comet?"

"They didn't believe him that it was the same comet—that it was perpetually strapped to the sun. Actually, he was treated so horribly—he was thrown out of Oxford and he had to pay to publish his work himself because nobody believed him or cared, and there was all this infighting with Newton—" I stopped. Was Dean listening? "Sometimes I can't stop talking about this stuff once I start," I said. "Which is why I don't talk about it." Jesus, would he stop smiling at me? I turned around, just to make sure he wasn't smiling at somebody else farther down on the bench. Blue Swede's "Hooked on a Feeling" was now blaring from the speakers, as Jimmie rapped on his cymbals to test them.

"I have very little idea of what you're talking about," Dean said. "But I totally want you to keep talking."

"Oh. Okay," I said, and then I told him the whole story of Dmitri Alexandrov and his miraculous, world-changing discoveries and his unfair fade into the background of scientific history and how all that was left of him in the public's mind was this comet, which came around to remind us of its existence every three-quarters of a century. "But then everybody thinks the person who discovered it is named Vira, so then he's forgotten even when he's remembered. I should shut up now, right?"

He shook his head. "It's my goal in life to be able to participate in one of your astronomical rants."

"Are they rants?"

"No," he said, knocking my shoulder lightly. "They're—they're lectures? No—soliloquies."

"Like from Shakespeare?"

"*Doubt thou the stars are fire. Doubt that the sun doth move. Doubt truth to be a liar. But never doubt I*—oh, well, you know," he said. I guess I knew. I guess I knew how that soliloquy ended. He shrugged and smiled and looked at his feet. "Once an English major, always an English major, I guess. Not that I've declared a major or anything, but English was the only class I got an A in. I was pretty much drunk for the rest of them."

"God, yeah, I never asked you what you were majoring in or what you want to be when you grow up."

"I think I'd like to teach, but I'm not sure I'm even going to graduate," he said. "I wasn't even sure if I was going to go back."

He took my hand and pressed his thumb against each one of my nails, and my hand went limp, surrendering to him. He could keep my whole hand if he wanted.

Now the music started up. They were doing a disco cover of Billy Joel, which sounded like the worst idea in the entire world, but somehow they were pulling it off. Jimmie was whaling on the drums, his skinny body now transformed into something lithe and rhythmic, his mouth making crazy shapes that somehow matched the sounds of the drums. He seemed to be on fire with music making, his limbs shaking, his head shaking, everything moving so fast he was a blur of percussion.

"Holy crap," Dean said.

"Right?"

Up near the front, Tonya was shaking and snaking and slithering like a *Solid Gold* dancer. After that first song, she went and got a drink, and then came over to us. She, too, wore a sweatband around her forehead.

"Hey," she said, nodding at me. She had green glitter eye shadow on, though much of it had smudged off from excessive sweating. Her frilly skirt was all wrinkled, and those dark, wet stains had blossomed below her armpits again, and she just looked so happy. *Radiant* was probably the right word, a word that also meant the point in the sky from where the meteor showers begin. The bright light of origin. She seemed to be waiting for information about the young man holding my hand.

"This is Dean," I said.

Tonya stuck out her hand.

"Dean, this is my friend Tonya."

"Sort of," she said. "We're sort of friends."

"This is my sort-of friend Tonya. And that's her sort-of boyfriend, Jimmie, up there on the drums." I said to Tonya, "Dean's a drummer too."

She shook his hand and said, "No, that's my real boyfriend up there," in the singsongy way that meant *You may not believe me because you're an idiot, but it's true.* Rosie came and sat down next to us and grabbed my Coke and started slurping it.

"He's a hell of a drummer," Dean said.

"I know it." She sounded so proud. "So you're Carrie's sort-of boyfriend?"

Oh my god. I was mortified. Was he my boyfriend? When did you get to say that? My shoes were all scuffed at the bottom and the floor was scuffed too, and I was never going to lift my eyes from all the scuffed items below me. I'd just back out toward the door without shifting the position of my head until I'd gotten safely out of the building.

"No," Dean said. The sadness came so fast it almost knocked me off the bench. "I'm her real boyfriend." I looked up. He didn't look at me, but his arm appeared around my shoulder, and that was enough. That was perfect.

"Carrie has a boyfriend!" Rosie cackled, dancing around us.

"I should have left you locked up at home," I said, but she kept dancing and laughing, moving closer to the center of the dance floor and losing herself in the *thump thump* of the music, the music of my life when I was seven years old and everything was good.

Tonya sat next to me and Dean on the bench at the side of the club. I was gulping soda that had no alcohol in it, which I had to get used to—man, it was kind of sickeningly sweet this way.

"You want a sip?" I asked her, offering her the Coke.

She crinkled her eyebrows. "Is it poisoned?"

"Not yet," I said. "I read that if you dry jewelweed and add a little bit of cream of tartar to it, it becomes poisonous."

"Really?"

"No." It was very odd to be laughing with Tonya again after all this time. And also it was not that bad.

She went back to watch Jimmie, and all around us people were dancing. I was a good enough dancer to like it but not good enough to forget I existed while I was doing it, as I did when I buried my nose in an astronomy book or closed one eye to peer into a telescope. But Rosie—she knew all the moves. She'd stayed up so many times watching *Saturday Night Fever* on *The Late, Late Movie* that it must have sunk in. Nobody really disco danced anymore, but Rosie could do it for real.

"The kid can dance," I said, standing up, ready to head to the dance floor now that the band was covering "Stayin' Alive."

"She can," Dean said, but he didn't stand up to join me. I waited for a minute, tapping my feet, and then I grabbed him. "No, no, no," he said, trying to pull away, but I dragged him out to the dance floor. "Okay," he said. He bounced up and down on his feet. It was adorable in an I'm-so-embarrassed-for-you kind of way.

"I'm a terrible dancer."

"I know," I said. "I love it."

"I also hate this music because there's no mosh pit."

"You want to make a disco mosh pit?" I asked, bumping into him, pressing him away, and letting him roll back into me.

"That's it," he said. "That's our band name: Disco Mosh Pit."

"Really?"

"Trust me."

"Come on," I said. "It's bad. You know it's bad."

"It's okay if we're bad," he said. We both stopped dancing, stopped moving. We stood in the middle of the floor, our heads together but our bodies apart, two weaknesses which, leaning against each other, formed a strength.

"It's okay if we're bad," Dean said again, and then he took my right hand in his left, he enmeshed his fingers with mine, and my whole body went slack. I just melted right into him, my head on his chest, the two of us swaying to "Funky Town," which was so not the right song to be swaying to, but we didn't care.

Chapter 18

AT SOO'S, ALL THE MUSIC WAS MELANCHOLY. Greta, who usually steered clear of the stereo, was playing "Leaving on a Jet Plane," even though not a single Peter, Paul, and Mary fan was in the room and no one, as far as I knew, was going to a college outside of driving distance. I was two weeks from starting my junior year, and only Tommy—repeating twelfth grade—would still be here then. Everyone else would be gone. They were all as drunk and high as usual, clumsy and affectionate and reckless and sweet.

"Get away from that stereo!" Justin called out. "You are fired, Greta." She stuck her tongue out at him and smiled, but did as he said, moving over to the Genesee beer ball and pouring herself a cup. Every drink she took now seemed to me full of meaning and backstory, every sip an echo of her father's sick body prostrate on the couch. I accepted her offer of a cigarette, but I just watched as someone else smoked pot and someone else drank and Justin blasted Bill Withers's "Ain't No Sunshine." His house was no home anytime she went away. Great. Cheery. Made for a happy party.

Also: I'd never known that Justin had the least bit of good taste in music, but Nick Lowe came on. He was Soo's favorite. Apparently they had made up. "I think he just didn't want to live with me," she told me. "He says he doesn't want to go out with anyone else, but he's not ready to commit to living together."

"Seems totally reasonable for a seventeen-year-old," I said. "I don't want to live with you either. Although I was sort of thinking about moving in with your mom after you go."

"Not that she'd notice," Soo said. "But sounds like you're not on the verge of getting kicked out right now."

"Yeah," I said. "Weird."

Then Soo and Justin were once again affixed to each other, as if the sides of their bodies were duct taped together. Dean chatted with Greta and Tiger and everyone else. I leaned against the strangely cold red pleather of the couch and looked up at the starry lights of the disco ball. This was the last time, and I knew it. I might be here again, but not with this crowd, under these circumstances. Chances were I'd be with Tonya and other members of the astronomy club, unstoned and earnestly reading *Black Holes and Other Mysteries of the Universe*.

"Hi, kid," Greta said, putting her arm around me and smiling.

I lit my cigarette from hers. "How's your dad?"

"Ah," she said, waving her hand in front of her face as if it were nothing. Or maybe she was just blowing the smoke away. "As bad as always. I can't wait to go to college." She put her arm around me again and then she must have seen my face. "Don't worry, kiddo, you'll come visit me. You'll spend the weekend. We'll hit the keggers running."

I managed a wan smile, but I knew it wasn't true. Keggers no longer held much appeal for me, and beautiful Greta, while she had been kind and loving and inclusive and had welcomed me into her fold—she wasn't my people. Not really. My people were the teetotalers and the nerds. And Dean, with his tainted past and his uncertain future, he was my people.

"Come with," Greta said, pulling me over to where Tiger and Tommy and Dean were talking, depositing me next to Dean. "He's got a whole foot on you," she whispered to me. "You guys are so cute."

"Shhh," I said, but I was disgustingly happy.

Tommy pretended to vomit.

It just felt so different to be there with Dean. *With Dean.* I had to get used to the thing that couples do, where they stand next to each other and talk to people as a single unit. Were we doing that? In public?

He didn't put his arm around me, but he did stand so close to me that his arm touched my arm, which was enough for my arm to feel like it was golden and shiny and special, the whole I'll-never-wash-my-arm-again thing. And then his finger touched my finger and then his finger wrapped around my finger, two index fingers interlocking and then it was our whole hands entwined. And I stood there and smiled-ish as he talked to Tommy and Justin about his Flying V, and it was very hard to stay planted next to Dean, but I did. Because he was mine. Or something like that. We were each other's. I was with Dean.

I tugged on his sleeve.

"What's up?" he asked, turning toward me and raising his eyebrows. "Is tonight the night?"

I was totally unprepared for the question. "Oh. I don't know. Is it?" But then I thought about it for a minute, and I raised my eyebrows and tucked my chin into my chest, taking a deep breath. "Um. I hope so? Okay, yes. Yes."

"Okay," he said. "You want to go now?"

"Now? Okay." Oh. Okay. It was going a little fast, but on the other hand, I'd been waiting my whole life for him. And for it. "Well . . . where are we doing it? I think my dad's home."

"The observatory, right? Isn't that where you're supposed to see it? It's the last night, isn't it?"

"Oh. Yes. Of course," I said. "The comet."

"What did you think I meant?" He narrowed his eyes and smiled. Then he seemed to get it, and he cleared his throat and sort of pretended that he didn't get it, and then he grabbed my hand again for real, for everyone to see. "Well, let's go. You've got me all bent out of shape about astrophysics, which I can honestly report is something I've never said before."

"You've never been excited about astrophysics before?"

"Well, now I'm finally cool. Thank god for astrophysics."

I smiled. "I always do."

* * *

I led him again up the footbridge to the stone steps of the observatory. The pine planks were a little wobbly, making rickety
sounds, and at one point, I almost slipped and Dean caught me
by the elbow. I was just happy to be walking, to not have to look
into his eyes.

I pushed the window open and started to hop up to get
inside.

"Can I help you up?"

"I can do it," I said.

"No, let me help," he said, and he picked me up with those
perfectly sized muscles beneath his soft T-shirt and set me
down on the windowsill. Then I dropped into the building and
unlocked the door, but he wasn't standing by it.

"Dean?" I called. "Dean?"

He was standing in the clearing, staring up at the blaze in
the sky. "It's really amazing from up here," he said.

"Yeah," I said. "I know. Once-in-a-lifetime event. Probably."

"Yeah." I didn't think I could take one more minute of staring up at the sky, even if it was, until this moment, my favorite
activity in the entire world.

"Let's go inside."

I led him into the room and turned on the one faint light
that still worked, and he took it in exactly as I would have wanted
him to: all the decaying beauty and the potential and the muss

and the mist and the mess. We sat down on the floor, facing each other, and I forced myself to look up at him.

"Do you want to do this?" he asked. "Are you sure?"

I nodded, a lot harder and faster than I'd meant to. "I am so incredibly sure."

"Here?"

"Yep. Oh, wait. Why? You don't want to?"

"Oh my god, yes, I want to." He leaned over and kissed me hard, and I felt the fire all the way to my toes. I kissed him back, and I could have stayed like that for somewhere between seventeen and six thousand days, but also the rest of me wanted to be touching the rest of him, just all of my skin and all of his skin. I pulled my mouth away.

"Do you have a condom?" I asked.

Dean swallowed. "Um . . . yes?"

"Take your shirt off," I whispered.

He slipped his Iggy Pop T-shirt off, and he had freckles on his chest, too, and really strong forearms and these beautiful shoulders, and I put my hands on his shoulders, and oh my god. "Oh my god," I said, and he kissed me again and then he kissed my neck, and I wished I would stop saying "oh my god," but oh my god.

"Wait," he said.

"Why?"

"Just one second." He went out to the car and turned the radio on. I recognized "Crimson and Clover." *I don't hardly know her, but I think I can love her.* I sat cross-legged, waiting.

"I don't know this version," I said when he came back.

"Tommy James and the Shondells," he said as he kissed my neck.

"I only know the Joan Jett one," I said as I kissed him back.

"That's good too."

"I think she's underrated." Then more kissing.

"Nah," he said, his mouth on my neck again. "'I Love Rock-n-Roll' is pretty average, considering—"

"Oh my god, shut up!" I said.

Then for a minute, we both sat there, Dean with his shirt off and me with my heart beating and all of my clothes and one shoe, and then he grabbed me and kissed me again and said, "Now is the time when your shirt is going to come off," and he took my flannel shirt off and pulled my tank top over my head and laid me down on the floor, and I said, "Ow, crap," because the floor was stupidly hard and cold because it was a stone floor, and he said, "Hold on," again and went out to his car and got that blanket he'd given to Rosie the night we went to my mom's house and put it on the floor, and there was more kissing. On my neck. My eyebrows. My chest. Everywhere. Ow and wow and oh my god oh my god oh my god.

It was almost dawn, his favorite time of day and the sky a perfect cornflower blue, when I opened my eyes.

"Dean," I said, shaking him awake. "We fell asleep." He sat up and rubbed his eyes and smiled and kissed me and then he kept kissing me, and I was saying, "We have to go. I have work. My dad is going to kill me," but he was still kissing me and I lay back down.

The sun was pretty high in the sky by the time we rose and put our clothes on. I looked away when he stood up to get dressed, and I turned myself toward the wall when I put my bra back on, but then he came over and did the clasp for me and then we had to get to kissing all over again.

"Dean—what time is it?" I asked when I could free myself.

"I don't know," he said.

I looked out the window of the observatory. Down the hill the gang was gathering. Not just the workers but some of their parents—or guardians—and Pablo and, uh-oh, my dad.

"Holy crap," I said. "I think I'm in big trouble." I hurriedly put my shoes on and ran to the door.

"Wait," he said. "I'm coming with you."

And that is how Dean and I came to be walking down the observatory steps together, and onto the footbridge in full view of the entire crowd, and I couldn't help but pretend that this was our wedding because I had in fact already planned out our entire existence together, but first I would have to figure out how to keep my father from grounding me for the rest of my life.

Lynn was standing in front of the crowd, and Dean stood next to me, and we weren't holding hands, and I didn't know when you were supposed to hold hands and when you weren't because I'd never had a boyfriend before. Until now. If I'd taken a cue from Justin and Soo, I'd actually have been humping Dean's leg like a dog right about now.

"Friends," Lynn said, "we are gathered here today"— maybe it *was* a wedding!—"to witness the unveiling of the hard work done by these young people this summer." He then looked earnestly at each one of us, the maybe-not-so-wayward youth.

"They started as novices," he was saying, "and with humility and perseverance, they came to know these tools well." Oh god —he was holding up the hammer and the nail again, and going into the thing about how great the rumbling of hunger in the belly was after a hard day's work. I couldn't help it—I let out a loud yawn.

That made my father turn around. He made an attempt to smile at me—we were still learning how to use those muscles again—and then he stepped back to stand next to me and Dean. He shook Dean's hand, and Dean said, "Hello, sir."

I really had to stop feeling like I was going to faint at everything Dean said and did pretty soon. Suddenly I wanted to be conscious for everything.

After the festivities—Lynn had tied a sorry-looking ribbon between two erect shovels, which Jimmie cut with pruning shears

—there was, as promised, a big tank of Dunkin' Donuts coffee (which Dean happily gulped down) and donuts. My father chatted with Pablo by the food. I was hungry of course, and not finding that rumble of hunger to be particularly satisfying, despite Lynn's constant prattling on about it. But I didn't want to have to talk to Pablo.

"So," Lynn said, "who wants to be the first to walk across the bridge, to the other side of Notch Creek?"

For some reason, my hand shot up. "Me," I said, unable to remove the smile from my face. My feet started walking. The bridge was solid beneath my feet, sturdy. I could imagine it being here for generations. I paused in the middle of the creek and forced myself to look north, toward the observatory, lonely on the hill. Then I turned around and motioned for Dean to come after me.

"Carrie," he said as he stepped off the bridge, "I have to go to work."

"Oh, crap. Okay."

"I'll see you later? After work? I'll come get you?"

"Yes," I said, almost too happy, almost crying with happiness. Did we kiss now? In public? What were the rules? How did anyone have a boyfriend? How could I be separated from this guy for more than seventeen seconds? Of course, the summer was almost over. Our timing was terrible. He might be leaving when everyone went off to start school. He might never come back. We might have only a few nights together, me and the world's best human being/boyfriend. Now I was crying, only a tiny bit but enough that I tucked my head into Dean's shirt for a second to hide.

"Hey—hey," he said, pulling me away from his shirt. Oh. Right. We weren't there yet. No public affection. Right.

I looked at my shoes. Then he leaned down so his face was the same height as mine and kissed me. It was fast, but it was deep, and it was everything.

My father didn't force me to talk to Pablo, and for that I was grateful. I sat along the creek, eating donuts with Tonya and Jimmie until my dad walked up. I stood to meet him.

"You want a ride?" he asked. "Your bike is still at home."

I swallowed. Oh, lord. Here it came. My recent weeks of freedom coming to an end. I would be grounded or, worse, forbidden to see Dean. I couldn't win.

"I could probably take the bus," I said. "Or get a ride with someone."

"Why would you do that?" He looked genuinely confused.

"Um . . . to avoid getting yelled at?"

He offered some sliver of a smile, something vaguely warm but not completely full of forgiveness. "You staying out last night is not my favorite thing you've ever done. But it's definitely not my least favorite thing."

I twisted up my lips for a sec. "I have to admit that this calm reaction is particularly surprising to me, and I'm not totally sure how to respond. Am I grounded? Can I still see Dean?"

"I like him," he said. "I think he's good for you. Mrs. Richmond thinks you're good for him."

"What? Really?" I shook my head. "When did you discuss this?"

"Since before he came," he said.

"Wait—is this, like, an arranged thing? You made us meet?"

"No," my father said. "You found each other on your own."

That night, Dean did the thing where he drove around the block to park in front of my house and he got out of the car and came up the steps to where I was waiting and he leaned in and kissed me so hard that I almost fell over, not from the force of his body but just from the sheer unbelievable goodness of it. It was so good.

"Hey," I said when I recovered. "Can you take me somewhere?"

"Um . . . yes . . . ? Not your mom's, right?"

"No." I smiled. "Much less depressing than that."

We got in the car, me with my work boots on my lap. The days were growing shorter, and by now, at eight o'clock, the sky was softly sketched with darker blue, light that could have been dusk or dawn, Dean's favorite time or mine. I told Dean to drive, fast, down the Avenue of the Pines, and as he did, I opened the window and threw my well-worn shitkickers out the window, not far from the white cross. Yes, true, an act of vandalism, or at least littering, but maybe some young and budding construction worker would find them and discover their inner youth workforce person and live happily ever after among the tent stakes and shovels.

"Aw, man," Dean said, "I loved you in those boots." And then he said, "Oh, no, I just, those boots, I just meant"—I had frozen, my hand on the door—"you looked hot in those boots."

"Well," I said, "sometimes you have to let the things you love —even work boots—go." But neither of us laughed, because neither of us had actually brought up the quickly approaching reality that would involve letting things go.

As we drove farther into the park, we passed Tonya and Jimmie walking. They were holding hands. It made my chest full in some sweet and confusing way.

"Hey," I called out, "see you in physics."

"Yep," she called back. "I may or may not talk to you."

I flipped her off and then waved, and I remembered that first half of the year in seventh grade, when I still wrote notes to my friends in my own grade, bubbly handwriting and *i*'s dotted with hearts, and crushes on boys—crushes, not the thing where you got wasted and lay down and let them do things to you. All that purity, so quickly corrupted. And then I thought that I hadn't lost my innocence by having sex with Dean; I'd gained it.

We parked by the giant calcium deposit, and I reached into my pocket and took out a white paper envelope.

"What's that?" Dean asked. I held it up to his nose. "Hmm. I can't tell."

"It's caraway," I said. "You don't have an advanced degree in Persian spices?"

"I do now," he said.

We went to the side of the creek bed near where we'd had coffee and donuts, and I dug a little hole and pushed the caraway seeds inside.

"That thing is so crazy-looking," Dean said, joining me, nodding toward the calcium deposit. "Is that what things look like on Mars?"

"I don't think so. From what I've read, Mars is red because of all this rusting iron on the surface."

"What's the coolest planet?" He crouched down to spread dirt over the seeds.

"Pluto. Block of ice."

"Not coolest that way."

"Oh, well, hmm." I moved a little farther toward the observatory, scattering the rest of the seeds in the grass. "Jupiter has had constant hurricanes for three hundred years. Planet of psychotic breaks if ever I've heard of one."

He stopped. "I don't think I want to be from that planet," he said quietly.

"I think you're a quasar."

"What's that?"

"A bright object in a very remote corner of the universe."

"Like Oregon?"

I swallowed. "Like Oregon."

He walked over and pulled me up and kissed me and looked me in the eye, and I looked at him, and I knew everything that he was about to say, but I didn't want to hear it.

"I'm going back," he said.

"No no no no no." I shook my head, too hard. It was going to happen. A fit. I could feel my hands starting to shake already. He took hold of them and raised them up to press them against his chest.

"Carrie," he said. "Carrie."

And somehow it slowed, but I couldn't keep it in. "You're leaving and I'm never going to see you again and everybody leaves me, all my friends and my mom and the fucking Vira comet, everybody all shiny and beautiful and then gone."

He kissed my face all over—forehead and eyes and cheeks and earlobes—and then he got to my mouth and just kept his mouth on my mouth until I breathed normally again.

"It's only a six-hour flight," he said.

"It would take me the entire semester to earn enough money for the flight," I said quietly.

"Or a seventy-three-hour train ride. Or, doing the astronomical calculation, three minutes in warp speed."

"That's from *Star Trek,* not Einstein," I said, but somehow a smile had broken through.

"Details, details," he said. He held up the *Black Holes* book —he'd been hiding it in his bag. "I've been studying," he said. It made me almost sick with happiness. "How about a bike?"

"What?" I was still thinking about Dean boning up on black holes and eclipses, all for me.

"It would only take, like, two weeks to ride your bike, assuming you can keep a steady ten miles an hour going over the Rockies and all. But you? You can do it." He pulled me to his chest.

I sure as hell didn't feel like that, but I knew it was the best thing anyone was ever going to say to me. Other than "I love you."

"Okay, I don't have a question."

"You're in luck." I said, smiling and wiping my face on his shirt. Classy, I knew. "I don't have any answers."

"I have a statement. I think you need to be open to the idea that people will surprise you. At any time, someone you're sure will disappoint you may come through. Find a little optimism somewhere."

"Eventually every star will explode," I said. "There's no getting around it."

"Maybe they're not gone, those stars," he said, pushing me away just enough so that he could see my face, which was stubbornly facing the ground. "Maybe they're just lost. Maybe they're just trying to find their way home."

"Is that better? Why is that better?"

"Because they'll be back."

I just shook my head.

"Look, we're all going to die or a black hole will swallow us.

But it might be tens of thousands of years before then. Or millions. Or, as that book you like says, billions."

"Right," I said. "Billions."

"Billions. Nobody knows what's going to happen between now and then. Nobody in the whole universe knows how things will end."

And there it was. I still had a question, but I didn't ask it. I didn't want to know the answer to what would happen to us after he left.

"That should be a song," Dean said. "'Lost Stars.' You should write it." He took the last few caraway seeds and threw them next to the wide blooms of jewelweed.

Chapter 19

AT HOME, MY FATHER AND I ACTUALLY said hello like friendly humans. "You received your final progress report from work," he said, holding up an envelope.

"Did I make any progress?" I asked. I was terrified to see it. If it was bad, would that be the end of my freedom? Would I have failed the test? No astronomy club, no trips to visit Soo at school, no voyages to, hmm, maybe some unnamed state in the Northwest?

He slid his finger across the top of the envelope and opened it slowly, slipping the letter out. He smiled.

"It's good?"

"No, it's not particularly good," he said. "But it's amusing." He handed it to me.

Carrie is lazy and unsupportive and occasionally combative, it read. *But she is also very smart with a great sense of humor. She was able to adequately complete the task of footbridge-building, though her section has some cosmetic imperfections. We do not predict a career in either youth leadership or construction.*

"Yeah, it's not the best report card," I said. "Is it, like, okay? Is it good enough?"

"Yes. For now, considering where we came from, it's good enough."

"Dad," I said, "please can I do something that involves more brains than brawn next summer?"

"It's hard to see that far in the future," he said, "but I'm pretty sure you won't have to do this again."

One by one, I said goodbye to them. Greta, getting a ride to Geneseo in her father's beat-up Datsun. "Don't worry," she whispered to me. "My dad won't go into a diabetic coma until I get back." Tiger, getting set to zoom off in his Rabbit.

I went to hug him, and he said, "I always liked you, Carrie. I always kind of had a crush on you."

"Oh. Wait—you did?"

"Yeah, I did. But, you know, you can't date your ex-girlfriend's friend."

"Right," I said, even though Justin had dated Greta and a whole bunch of her cheerleader friends.

"But, I don't know, I just wanted to tell you that. I never forgot about that night at Diamonds."

"Me neither," I said. It made me feel better about everything. About almost everything.

Tommy, in his hippied-out BMW, wasn't going anywhere

but was still pretending that he hadn't failed his senior year and was heading off for happier adventures. Soo and Justin were getting ready to head to Oneonta in her Le Car.

I stayed in front of Soo's house with Dean. She came and put her arms around me, one of the only other people I knew who was a tiny little five-footer like me. We were evenly matched, head to head.

"I'm coming back for you, don't worry," she said. "I'm coming back all the time."

"I know," I said.

"I love you, Carrie. I really do."

"I know," I said again.

"You're going to be fine. You're going to be great."

"I *know,*" I said. "So are you. Would you get in your car already and go to college? And call me the night before you have a science test so I can help you."

"Always," she said.

"Always," I said back.

And then Soo was gone too.

All summer, ever since the kiss — no, ever since I first heard him playing "English Rose" across the fence, before I even knew who he was or what he'd done or where he lived or how fleeting and life-altering his presence would be — I had been dreading this moment. It had lingered over every pinpoint of happiness, I realized, every shock of tumbling into love. Here it was: me and

Dean, standing together next to his car, in front of my house, the mansion behind us. Thousands of miles would unfold between us, and two more years before I'd be set free. Maybe the second I graduated from high school I'd hitchhike to Oregon. But the thought wavered even as I considered it; I could see it floating downward, a reddening leaf in late fall.

I had no idea what Dean was thinking. He was looking at his shoes again, and then it seemed like he was looking at my shoes, too, my silly jellies — why did I wear those? — the toes of them against the toes of his.

"Um, this is for you," I said, handing him the mix tape I'd made for him. He read the cover, nodded approvingly, and I felt so proud and blessed and cursed.

Then he reached into the car and put a plastic bag down on the top of the car, next to my right shoulder.

"What is it?" I couldn't look at him, the same way he couldn't look at me when I'd first met him. I just wanted too much from him.

"It's a mix tape for my funeral," he said.

"I'm having one of those moments where I don't know if you're serious or not," I said.

"You hate those."

"I know."

He could have been the guy who pressed the bag into my hands and curled my fingers around it and bent his knees slightly so that he was eye level with me, one finger beneath my chin to gently lift my face to meet his gaze and then softly kiss me, his lips parted like petals. But Dean wasn't like that. His hair was a mess, and the bike grease had never come out of his shorts or from under his nails, and he had a stripe of sunburn along his nose, and a few extra freckles where I'd never seen them before, and those freckles would fade, every day as the sun retreated they'd fade further until they disappeared, up there where the sun was watery and pale in middle-of-nowhere Oregon.

Dean pressed me up against the side of the Jeep, sudden and forceful, and the metal of the car was hot on my back and he pressed his mouth against mine and put his hand behind my head and we just stood there together like that: a kiss, melting. And then he got in the car and put my mix tape in the deck —I'd put Michael Jackson's "Beat It" on there—and I thought I could see a hint of a smile on his face, though he had craned his neck to see behind him as he backed up. Or maybe it wasn't a smile. Maybe it was a wince. Trying not to cry. Maybe not.

My hands shook as I opened the bag. The tape was wrapped in his rugby shirt, and two years of my tears waterfalled on top of it. Dean's striped rugby shirt. I was in love with that shirt. I wanted that shirt to be with me always. I felt the sickening and terrifying thud of revelation: I was in love. With this boy. I loved him. For real. And that only made me cry more.

I put the tape in my Walkman and pressed play and heard the first song: Dean singing, with Tiger on drums and Justin on guitar. *Give me a girl who wears flannel shirts. Not the kind from L. L. Bean but the kind you find in gasoline stations.* Was I going to cry or vomit? Was it happiness or despair? Everything. It was just everything.

It was the best mix tape in the world. Bowie's "Life on Mars?" Elton John's "Rocket Man." "Supersonic Rocket Ship" by the Kinks. "Tapestry from an Asteroid" by Sun Ra. Steve Miller Band, "The Joker," which really surprised me until I saw he'd actually written on the sleeve, *This is a joke, but the song is really on here.* It had Kate Bush and Patti Smith and Cyndi Lauper singing "Time After Time." "Across the Universe," which killed me because John Lennon's voice, especially from *Magical Mystery Tour* on and especially "I Am the Walrus," was one of my favorite voices. For a minute, reading the list of songs on there, I felt better. I felt the arrival of the weird, buoyant thing called hope. And then the second song came on.

If you don't know the beauty you are, Nico sang, *let me be your eyes, a hand to your darkness, so you won't be afraid.*

This was a different kind of sobbing, not one that felt like poison but rather a kind of cleansing, something softer and less sharp. Real heartbreak, not the kind made only of loneliness and self-hatred, was almost kind of sweet. Ah, yes, "Hurts So Good." Secretly I liked John Cougar, too. But there would be no secrets anymore. I saw my reflection in the smudged chrome of the Walkman, my own hand white against the darkening sky. This was who I was. I was not afraid. I lifted my hand in one last wave, and I was sure, even as his Jeep disappeared around the corner, that he could see me.

Acknowledgments

One day my friend Aimee Molloy told me she'd done the Moth story slam. "I've always wanted to do that," I said, and looked up the nearest and next one. The theme was "Dirt." *I don't have any stories about dirt,* I thought. And then I remembered that summer, the one with the hardhat, the music, and my first love. So thank you, Aimee, for the initial push to get on that stage and tell the story.

Then I turned that tale into an essay for the *New York Times*'s Modern Love column. So thank you, Daniel Jones, for publishing it.

Then, thanks in part to a suggestion from my friend David Mizner, I (very heavily) fictionalized the story and turned it into a novel. I wrote the ending while on vacation with my in-laws, Marty and Susan Sherwin, who had provided me with the most beautiful writing spot I could have imagined. The indefatigable Hannah Brooks offered the top floor of her home, with Hudson River views, in Newburgh, New York, so I could finish the first draft.

My writing group—Laura Allen, Suzanne Cope, Katherine

Dykstra, Elizabeth Gold, Nancy Rawlinson, and Abby Sher—graciously, generously read that and several other drafts, giving me such great feedback, not to mention so much encouragement.

Then I found a wonderful agent, Faye Bender, who sold the book to a wonderful editor, Elizabeth Bewley, both of whom offered the best edits I could have hoped for. This is the kind of team you dream of when you're imagining the writing life.

Meanwhile, my daughters, Enna and Athena, became obsessed with a song called "Lost Stars," forcing me to listen to it seventeen thousand times. That ended up being a good thing. My kind and hilarious husband, Alex Sherwin, offered me his full support by way of doing extra kitchen and kid duty so I could type. My mother and stepfather, Helaine Selin and Bob Rakoff, stepped in to watch the kiddos while I retreated to the computer.

It was because my father, Peter Davis, and my stepmother, Beverly Lazar Davis, signed me up for that summer construction job that I ended up writing this book. So though I hated every minute of it, and though my teenage years were 72 percent misery, punctuated by 28 percent of music- and friend-filled joy, it all worked out in the end. Thanks to both of you and to my beautiful, wonderful, and, yes, tall sister, Adrienne Davis, for forgiving all my older-sister-failings, especially the really big one. (For the record, none of my parents are anything like the parents in this book, except that one's a really good musician and one's a really good cook.)

A few astrophysics types weighed in on the science. Thank you to Dr. Federico Bianco at the NYC Center for Cosmology and Particle Physics; A. I. Malz; and Richard and Sidney Wolff.

The people to whom I'm forever indebted are my friends from those years: Amy Knippenberg, Guy Lyons, Julie Natale, Katie Capelli, Kristin Brenner, Mike Migliozzi, Rachel Kieserman, Pete Donnelly, and Reid Lyons. Thank you for all that adventure, love, companionship, and music, that soundtrack of our teenage years.